THE DEAD OF WINTER

Shortlisted for the Arthur Ellis Award for Best First Book

"A powerful ride through the dark and raw of Montreal."

– Kathy Reichs

"Taut. Claustrophobic. Compelling. A chilling tale – in every sense of the word. Peter Kirby's story of murder and its machinations tightens around the reader like a noose."

– Will Ferguson,
winner of the Scotiabank Giller Prize for *419*

"Saints, villains, the homeless and the powerful are held in winter's suspenseful grip. In a riveting new series, Peter Kirby reveals Montreal at the worst of times, its underbelly exposed and dire forces at play."

– John Farrow, author of *River City*

"Gripping. Compelling."

– *Montreal Gazette*

"Vanier reveals himself as a worthy series detective."

– *National Post*

With comparisons to Michael Connelly's Harry Bosch, Ian Rankin's John Rebus, and John Brady's Matt Minogue, "Irishman Kirby joins John Brady and Peter Robinson in the ranks of the best English and Irish expat crime novelists living in Canada."

— Nuacht

"Colourful and gritty. Kirby puts Vanier through his paces chasing a killer in a book that's fast-paced and enjoyable."

— Maclean's

"Luc Vanier is likely to join the ranks of Canada's enduring sleuth figures."

— The Toronto Star

"A writer to watch"

— The Globe and Mail

VIGILANTE SEASON

One of 5 Best Crime and Mystery Books of 2013
— Quill & Quire

"This novel is one for our times. I suggest you pour a glass of Jameson, as would Luc Vanier, then sit back and enjoy a good read. Peter, you've done it again!"

— Nuacht

"More than a simple tale of the worthy few against the corrupt many. The author, himself a lawyer, provides bold heroes, but he also explores how corruption can be self-sabotaging... A promising follow-up to 2012's lauded *The Dead of Winter*."

— *Publishers Weekly*

"*Vigilante Season* is a fine tale that can hold its own with the best of what's out there. Kirby's writing has become even more assured ... An ability to capture the atmosphere of various districts of Montreal in all their glory or squalor, coupled with a believable storyline drawn from the headlines, lends Kirby's books an immediacy that will keep the reader enthralled."

— *Montreal Review of Books*

OPEN SEASON

OPEN SEASON

A LUC VANIER NOVEL

PETER KIRBY

.ıl.

Prepared for the press by Katia Grubisic
Cover design by Debbie Geltner
Cover image by Julien Roumagnac
Book design by WildElement.ca

Library and Archives Canada Cataloguing in Publication

Kirby, Peter, 1953-, author
        Open season / Peter Kirby.
(A Luc Vanier novel)
Issued in print and electronic formats.

ISBN 978-1-927535-78-3 (pbk.).--ISBN 978-1-927535-79-0 (epub).--
ISBN 978-1-927535-80-6 (mobi).--ISBN 978-1-927535-81-3 (pdf)
        I. Title. II. Series: Kirby, Peter, 1953- Luc Vanier novel.
PS8621.I725O64 2015   C813'.6   C2015-9018595
                                                            C2015-901860-9

Printed and bound in Canada.

The publisher gratefully acknowledges the support of the Canada Council for the Arts and of SODEC.

Linda Leith Publishing Inc.
P.O. Box 322, Victoria Station,
Westmount Quebec H3Z 2V8 Canada
www.lindaleith.com

To my brother Jim and my almost-brother Frank.
And to my sisters Esme, Carol, and Lisa.
I love you all.

ONE

Katya Babyak was lying on a steel bed in a dilapidated three-storey public housing unit in Rotterdam. The room was small and unheated, furnished with only the bed and a small dresser. Her battered suitcase lay open on the linoleum floor. She spent all her time on the bed, shivering under a threadbare blanket that made no difference in the damp cold. Three days so far, three days inside a locked room, waiting.

She had waited in Kiev too, waited until they told her it was time to go, and put her and four others in the back of a truck, hidden behind cardboard boxes piled to the roof. The drive from Kiev to Rotterdam had taken two days, with stops every now and then to allow her and the others to go to the toilet in desolate service centres just off the highway. At each stop they gave her water. Once, they gave her a sandwich and a coffee.

Now, in the room in Rotterdam, a daily routine had already been established. Just after sunrise the same small man unlocked the door and let her out to use the bathroom. He never said anything, just leered and gestured to where she had to go, as if he hadn't given the same instructions the previous day, and the one before. If she took too long, the small man pounded on the door to hurry her along. Afterwards, he watched her walk back to her room. He locked the door, and then she could hear the same routine repeated in three other rooms. When everyone had finished with the bathroom, the man would start a second round, opening Katya's door to hand her a plastic-wrapped sandwich, the kind you get from vending machines in bus terminals, and a bottle of water. Sometimes there was a bag of potato chips. That would be the end of any contact until the man came back, about two hours after it got dark.

Nobody told her what was happening. She knew she just had to wait. They had promised to take her to Canada and they had taken her this far. However long it took, she would wait. She had tried to shout to the people in the other rooms. The small man came running. He opened the door and slapped her across the face. "Quiet. No noise. You understand?"

She nodded at him, her cheek burning from the slap.

She spent the time lying under the thin blanket, flipping through an English phrasebook. When the intricacies of *I would like to have breakfast, please*, and *How much does this cost?* became too difficult, she did what everyone with nothing but time and no distractions would do. She retreated into her thoughts, reliving memories, the only things of value she had.

Katya began to catalogue her life, putting everything she could remember into chronological order. The early memories were nothing but fragments, like broken pieces of coloured glass that hint at what they once were, or snapshots that force you to imagine what was happening before and after the moment they were taken.

Her earliest memory was the colour and taste of a glass of lemonade that someone, probably her mother, had poured from a large bottle. She knew this had happened at the seaside. The lemonade was a shade of yellow she had never seen since, a yellow that even now made her mouth water, a yellow as clear as sunlight. The lemonade tasted of summer fruit, tart and sweet at the same time. She tried to build on the fragment of memory, inventing more than remembering the before and after that might have surrounded the taste. She reconstructed a family outing to the coast when she and Stephan were still very young, when their parents were still alive. She knew her father would have been there. Her mother had kept a photograph of a visit to the coast. Katya was a baby, sitting on his knees as he beamed into the camera. That wasn't the lemonade day. She was too young in the photo to drink lemonade, and Stephan was not yet born, and on the lemonade day, the whole family had been there, her mother and father and Stephan, she was sure of it.

She remembered sitting with Stephan on the brown couch in the living room of their first apartment, her mother crying in the armchair while two large policemen yelled. They wore dark uniforms that made creaking noises when they moved. Katya couldn't remember the words, just shouting and rumbling growls from the men, and the sobbing from her mother. After that, her father's absence had become just another fact, like a crack in a window that had always been cracked, that had always let in the cold.

She probed the memory the way you probe a cracked tooth with your tongue. The policemen's voices had been accusatory, delivering bad news, as though whatever had happened was Katya's mother's fault. Her mother accepted everything, not arguing with the policemen, nodding her head as she cried.

After that, they had lived with her grandmother, an angry, dried-out husk of a woman who spread misery thick enough to eat, and in all those years, there wasn't a single good memory.

Her mother's death was another blur. From one day to the next her mother had simply disappeared. Now, Katya realized there must have been an illness, and it must have lasted weeks or even months. But she remembered no hospital visits, nothing, just a void where their mother had been. One morning, sometime after their mother disappeared, their grandmother dressed Katya and Stephan in formal clothes and led them across Poltava to the crematorium.

They were sitting in a huge room, just the three of them. At the front of the room a cheap wooden casket was mounted on what looked like a ladder lying flat. Her grandmother pointed at the casket. "That's your mother. She had bad blood."

Then, the sound of machinery, and the casket was drawn along the steel rails towards the curtains. The curtains opened to receive the casket, and then closed.

That was the last Katya had seen of her mother.

TWO

There's something special about walking down the street with a woman who looks like she's three leagues out of your own. She gets the looks from passers-by, then they look at you, and you've just scored a point. For Roger Bélair, this was one of those walks—a warm June evening when everything seems right with the world. The woman walking beside him was good-looking by any standards. Bélair wasn't going to be having supper alone for the first night in weeks, and he was beaming.

It wasn't a date. She was a client who had turned up late for a meeting. Bélair was hungry, so he suggested a working supper. She accepted, probably felt sorry for keeping him waiting.

The sun had just set, but it wasn't yet dark. Bélair could see the light from the large bay windows of the restaurant illuminating the street, beckoning to them. When they reached the doorway, he stopped on the narrow sidewalk and gestured like a hotel doorman.

If he hadn't been so distracted he might have seen the huge SUV speeding towards them, its wheels half up on the narrow sidewalk. He noticed nothing until the driver's door opened directly into him and sent him flying forward to the ground. He lay on the pavement for a few seconds before rolling slowly onto his back, struggling to sit up. The woman was being manhandled into the back of the vehicle by two men. Only when the doors slammed shut did he register her screaming. She had been screaming the whole time, but now it was quiet.

Bélair struggled to get up, but only managed to make it to his knees. The SUV was already speeding away on Saint-Paul. The licence plate was covered by a rag or paper, he wasn't sure. Turning to see whether anyone else had been watching, he felt the searing pain from his arm. It was bent back at an unnatural angle and blood was seeping from his sleeve.

Immediately, people converged on him.

"Call the police. Somebody call the police," he shouted to no one in particular. Several people raised cellphones to their ears.

The owner of Les Pyrénées stepped out of the doorway. "Maître Bélair," he said. He took Bélair's good arm and placed it over his own shoulder to help him off his knees. "Come inside. The police will be here soon. And an ambulance. We called an ambulance."

"These people," Bélair said, gesturing to the crowd, "they saw it. They're witnesses. We need to get their names."

The owner turned slowly, with Bélair's arm still

7

draped over his shoulder, and said in a loud voice, "Please wait for the police to get here. It's important. And I will serve a cone of pistachio sorbet for everyone who waits. I'll send someone out now."

In Montreal, there aren't many things that convince people to wait around for the police, but on a warm June evening, a pistachio sorbet will do it.

Anjili Segal was sitting across from Luc Vanier, absent-mindedly scanning the menu. She closed it and looked across the table. "Does the thought of moving in with me scare you that much, Luc?"

As a conversation opener it was a showstopper, one that promised a difficult supper.

Vanier liked to say they that he and Anjili had met over a dead body. It was true. One of Montreal's busiest coroners, Segal made dead bodies give up their secrets. The first time they met, the victim had been stabbed and shot, but Segal ruled that he had drowned; he had been alive when he was thrown in the river. Vanier was impressed. After crossing paths professionally a few more times, Vanier had asked her out. Now, three years later, they both agreed that moving in together was the next step.

"I don't know why you say that, Anjili. We just need to find the right place."

She leaned down and pulled glossy folders out of her bag. Six in all. One for each of the condominiums they had visited. But after two months of looking, a pattern was developing. Vanier would point out the obvious drawbacks, while she focused on the good, increasingly ready to settle for anything. Now they were sitting on a pizzeria terrace on Phillips Square, two blocks from their last visit.

"I know you're nervous, Luc. But that's all it is." She paused. "I hope. We're good together, and we'd be better living together."

"I know. And I'm looking forward to it. It's going to be great. But we need the right place."

She managed a tired smile. "So we keep at it. Until we find the perfect place?"

He reached for her hand. He couldn't tell her that he was nervous. The more places he looked at, the more he realized that it might actually happen. He had been on his own for years. Even when Alex was living with him, it had been Vanier's place and Vanier's rules, and none of the rules applied to Vanier. He wasn't sure if he could make the inevitable compromises that living with Anjili would mean. But he couldn't voice his doubts. They were his problem, not Anjili's.

"Don't look so glum," she said.

"I'm not glum. We'll find the right place. Soon, I promise. And if we don't, we'll settle for almost right."

The waiter appeared and she looked up at him, ready to order. Vanier continued reading the menu, rubbing the muscles in the back of his neck.

The waiter left.

She tapped the pile of folders. "So which was your favourite?"

Vanier closed the menu. "That's the problem. They all

looked great."

Wrong answer. The smile was gone.

"I can't work with that. Here," she tapped the pile again. "I've put them in order. My order. What do you think?"

Vanier gulped a mouthful of the house wine and puckered. It tasted homemade. He reached for the first folder, a high-rise on McGill College. Their condo would be on the thirty-sixth floor, looking north.

"This one had great views. I liked it. And the furniture was good."

"Luc, it was a showpiece. We'd put our own furniture in there."

"I know. But I liked it. I mean with the furniture and all, it looked good. I liked it."

"That's it? It looked good? *I liked it*?"

"It's great. No, it's not great. It's good. Lots of space, great views. The balcony was a bit small, though, barely room for two chairs and a table."

"Okay. What else didn't you like about it?"

"You sure you want to know?"

"I'm sure. You're going to be living there too."

"It was sterile. Like living in an office building. No character."

"Okay. I know what you mean. Like living in a hotel." She reached over and took the folder out of his hands. "Right, number two." She placed another folder before him.

He opened the folder and tried to remember which

10

one it was. Six places in one day had blurred in his memory. Beautiful kitchens, small bedrooms, living rooms that looked like they came out of some German decorating magazine, and all the time he was wondering where he'd put his stuff, or even if he would be allowed to bring his stuff. Bad thoughts, he knew. But he didn't know how to stop them.

"Good. No, better. This one was better. It seemed to have more space."

"You guys ready to order?" The waiter picked up the carafe of wine and refilled Vanier's glass. Anjili's was still full.

Vanier ordered a seafood pizza. Anjili, goat cheese and prosciutto.

"Luc, if this is too hard on you, you'd better tell me now."

"It's not that, Anjili. I want to live with you. I also want you to be happy, more than anything. But I have yet to see a place where we wouldn't be rubbing shoulders all the time. You and I both need to have space."

"Rubbing shoulders?"

"You know what I mean."

"I'm trying to find out. What is it that you're looking for?"

"A place with lots of room. It could be an old place, doesn't have to be modern. But lots of room."

"You said that."

"Space for us to be together, but space to be alone too. Maybe a terrace, but a big one. Not a birdcage balcony."

"You know that nothing we've seen today fits that

description. Damn, nothing we've seen in the last two months fits that description."

"I know."

The silence hung there. Vanier reached for the wine. Homemade or not, it was taking the edge off the condominium day. Finally, he asked, "What do you think of renting?"

"Like giving it a try before we buy? And when I say 'it', I mean us, you and me. Is that what you're saying, Luc?"

"Maybe. We've both lived on our own for years, and living together is going to take some getting used to."

"I think you mean it's going to take compromise."

"Well, compromise, if you want. But maybe if we rent for a year we'll get a better sense of what we really want."

"Luc, just so we understand each other, there is no way on God's earth that I'm moving into your place."

"I figured that out a long time ago."

"So we need to find neutral ground and rent for a while. Is that what you're suggesting?"

"Maybe we should think about it. As a first step."

She straightened up in the chair, backing away from the table, as though she was backing away from him.

Vanier's phone rang and he was tempted to heave it into the street, but Anjili nodded, giving permission.

He put the phone to his ear. "Vanier."

It was Detective Sergeant Saint Jacques. He listened for a few minutes. "Okay. Maybe twenty minutes." He clicked *End*. He opened his mouth to say something, but

Anjili beat him to it.

"Don't tell me, Luc. You've got to go."

"It was Saint Jacques. There's been a kidnapping. I …"

"Go. Call me when you're through."

Vanier bent down to kiss her on the lips and she returned the kiss, barely. Then raised her hand to hold his arm.

"Luc. It's been a long day. It's your job, I understand. Call me, okay?"

"I'll call."

The cobblestone streets in the old town were picturesque, but hell to drive on, and Vanier's Volvo shuddered from the punishment. He was crawling along slower than a horse and cart. He turned right on Saint-Paul and continued along the cobblestones until Saint-Laurent, back on tarmac. Up ahead, the street was closed off by a wooden barrier. He waved his badge out the window and a uniform lifted one end of the barrier to let him through. Farther up the street, he could see a knot of people and an arc light, as though they were shooting a movie.

He drove on and parked up on the sidewalk, scanning the crowd for Saint Jacques. She looked up from her conversation with a woman and waved him over. She was finishing when he got there. "Thank you very much, madame. We'll be in touch if we need anything else."

Saint Jacques turned to Vanier and led him away from the crowd.

"Kidnapping, sir. A woman. Two hours ago."

"Domestic?" asked Vanier. It was the obvious possibility. When a woman was grabbed off the street it was almost always an angry lover, father, or brother.

"Could be. But witnesses say two men grabbed her and pushed her into the back of an SUV. So there were at least three people involved, including the driver. Probably rules out the jealous boyfriend."

"Could be a family dispute."

"Like an honour thing?"

"It's all the rage these days."

"A couple of the witnesses said she looked foreign."

"Foreign? Everyone looks foreign to Quebecers."

"One says Arab, the other Mexican."

"Any ID?"

"Not yet. Our best chance is a guy she may or may not have been walking with. He was hit by the car door as it passed. He's been taken to the Montreal General."

"Serious?"

"He'll survive. Apparently he was standing up and talking before the ambulance took him. We should be able to talk to him as soon as someone gets to the hospital."

"Any other witnesses? Besides the ethnologists?"

"A bunch, but nothing strong. A big black SUV. It comes speeding along Saint-Paul. The driver's door opens and smacks the guy to the ground. The woman starts screaming and is dragged into the car and they take off. Nobody got the licence plates. Depending on who you talk to, the SUV turned first left on Saint-Pierre or kept going along Saint-Paul and then north on McGill."

Vanier scanned the street as she talked. Rue Saint-Paul was one of the oldest streets in Montreal, dating back to the sixteen hundreds. It was narrow, with businesses, restaurants, and art galleries at street level, and lofts or businesses above. There were no CCTV cameras. Montreal was still far behind on tracking its citizens in public.

"The owner of the restaurant identified the guy who was hit."

Vanier looked back to Saint Jacques.

"He's a lawyer. Roger Bélair. He's a regular at Les Pyrénées. Bélair didn't have a reservation but the owner says it's common for him to just show up. Apparently, he always eats alone. So the owner couldn't help with the woman."

Vanier had a flash of Anjili finishing her pizza without him. He'd have to make up for that if he didn't want to be eating the rest of his meals alone.

"We need to talk to Bélair. We're going nowhere without the name of the victim. Are you about finished here?"

"I was first on the scene, so I need to close it up."

"Okay. Have someone canvass all the residents of the lofts up there," he said, gesturing to the upper floors of the surrounding buildings. "And anything on the street that was still open."

Vanier looked around and saw Detective Sergeant Laurent's bald head towering over a group of people further up the street.

"I'll take Laurent to the hospital. I'll let you know how it goes."

THREE

They came for Katya at two in the morning. A man pounded on her door, told her to collect her things, she was leaving. In minutes she had put on an extra sweater and her coat, tossed her few belongings back into the suitcase. She followed the others down the staircase.

A van was waiting, with two men inside. Katya and two other women climbed into the back through a haze of cigarette smoke. The van took off, and they drove through the deserted city, street after street of darkened factories, homes, and stores. The man in the passenger seat was talking quietly on a cellphone, pointing out directions to the driver. After fifteen minutes, he said something Katya couldn't understand, and the driver killed the headlights, driving by the light of street lamps. Both men smoked non-stop, lighting each new cigarette from the last one.

The van slowed at a steel gate; it slid open and they drove into a vast open yard filled with containers stacked three or four high. The driver navigated slowly through the tight lanes between the stacked containers waiting to be loaded onto ships. When he pulled up next to a darkened freighter, the man in the passenger seat turned to the women. "Quick. You hurry. And no talking."

The driver was already opening the side door, gesturing the women out. Katya was the first out. She stood on a dock clutching her suitcase, staring up at the looming structure resting in the water like a sleeping giant. Even in the darkness she could see the ship was rusting, its paint dull and peeling.

The driver hustled them up the gangplank where two men waited. The younger of the two gestured them along the deck. As she followed him through a doorway into the ship, Katya looked back towards the gangplank and watched the driver pass a large envelope to the man on the gangplank. She hadn't seen her passport since she had handed it over in Poltava. She hoped it was in the envelope.

The younger man led the three women down a metal staircase and along a corridor to a cramped cabin. It had a single bed, a dirty sofa and a table with four chairs. There was hardly room for the four of them. "In the day you stay here," the man said. "At night you stay in here. I show you."

He pulled the sofa away from the wall and knelt down. After struggling for a few minutes pushing a penknife into a crack in the wall, he pulled a flap up and away to reveal a rectangular hole.

"In here," he said, pointing to the woman who was standing closest to the hole. "You first. There is a string for light inside. You pull."

The woman went down on her knees and crawled through. She disappeared. Then her head reappeared. "My bag. I need my bag."

"After I push the bags in." He turned to Katya. "You next."

Katya went over to the hole, got down on her hands and knees and crawled through. It was pitch-black inside. She could sense the first woman waving her hands in the air to find the light string. The light clicked on as Katya was standing up. The room was tiny, perhaps six feet by four, with narrow bunk beds on either side. A windowless hole. The third woman crawled in and Katya sat on one of the lower bunks to make room for her. They watched the three suitcases being pushed in through the hole. The flap dropped into place and they heard he sofa being shoved back against the wall.

One of the women reached out her hand to Katya. "Hi. I'm Alyona."

Before Katya could respond, a fist pounded the wall. "Silence. No speaking. Silence."

It sounded like he was standing in the hole with them. The wall was paper thin.

Katya smiled back, mouthed *Katya* in an almost silent whisper. They turned to the other woman.

"Natalka," she whispered.

The man pounded on the wall again. "Silence, I said. No talk."

Within an hour the ship began to move. Katya lay on the

bed and calculated how far she had come, and how much farther she had to go. But this was the last stage. The next stop would be Canada. What would her family be like, she wondered, and how many children would she have to look after? She knew the family would be rich. Only rich people could afford a nanny to look after their children. And she was sure they would be kind; kind people, living with wonderful children in a large house in Canada.

For the first two days, Katya was sick. On the third day she managed to keep down a thin chicken broth without vomiting, then she graduated to the stew that was the only other food on offer. The women spent their days in the small cabin, playing cards and talking. Their nights were spent in the box. They all agreed that calling it the hole was too depressing.

"I have family," Katya said. As soon as she had said it, she regretted it, like boasting of good health in a cancer ward. They had been playing cards for hours, using a mix of barely remembered rules and others made up on the fly. The other two stared at her, waiting for her to continue.

"Not a family, exactly. A brother. Stephan. He's younger than me. I promised to send for him when I get settled."

"It must be wonderful to have family," said Alyona. "Even one person counts. It's a gift."

Alyona had grown up in an orphanage. It was all she had ever known. They gave her everything: food, shelter, uniforms. And rules, more rules than she could ever need.

No love, though. Love was not necessary.

"A brother? So what kind of brother?" said Natalka.

"He's smart. I mean, he's book-smart. He just has to read about a subject and he understands it. He wants to be an engineer. And he's handsome."

Natalka shrugged. "And one day he will marry and forget all about his sister."

"Maybe not. Who can forget family?" Alyona said, putting a card down on the pile and picking up another.

Natalka looked at her. "I have family too. If they were all in the same house together, I would burn it down. Forget family."

Katya wished she hadn't started the conversation, but she couldn't let it go. "Everyone's different. There are good people and bad people. It's the same everywhere. When you find a good person you should be happy. That's all."

"Good luck finding a good person," said Natalka.

"And us? We're not good?" Alyona teased her.

"How do I know? Sure, you seem good now. But who knows? When things get tough everyone looks after themselves." Natalka placed a card on the pile and picked up another one. She laid all her cards face up on the table. "I win."

There was nothing to win.

Katya pulled the cards together and began shuffling them. "Again?"

"No," said Alyona. "I've had enough of cards."

Katya began playing solitaire. The others watched.

"Okay," said Natalka. "What's the craziest thing you know about Canada?"

They looked at her. "I heard that polar bears walk down the main streets. I saw a picture once, a polar bear wandering down the middle of the street."

Alyona scoffed. "That can't be. There wouldn't be any Canadians. They would all be eaten."

Katya let out a shriek, laughing. "Not necessarily. Maybe after a bear eats someone he rests for a few days. So to be safe, you only need to avoid the hungry bears."

"And how do you tell which ones are hungry?" Alyona said.

"They look like men." Natalka stood up and did an impression of a hulking bear-man walking down the street trying to grab a victim. When they had stopped laughing, Katya said, "I heard it's so cold that dogs get stuck to fire hydrants when their pee freezes."

More shrieks. "Their owners have to snap them off!"

They turned to Alyona. "I heard there are no orphanages. Every baby gets adopted. It's crazy."

Finally, Katya broke the silence. "That's not crazy. It should be normal."

FOUR

Vanier pulled into a reserved space opposite the emergency-room entrance and put a cardboard card with "Police" written on it on the dashboard. It wasn't official, just something he'd made himself. Vanier still thought of it as an experiment: sometimes it worked, other times it only seemed to encourage the tow-truck drivers. Laurent followed. "Where did you get the sign?"

"Made it myself. Pretty good, no?"

"It works?"

"More often that you'd think."

They had to navigate the usual sad clot of smokers in front of the doorway. A guy in a wheelchair was sucking on a cigarette while his free hand steadied a drip stand. Two bags of liquid were attached to his arm with needles and tape. His bony white legs stuck out from the blue humiliation gown that hospitals force on patients.

The emergency room was hot and crowded, like every emergency room in the province. When health care is a public service, you control costs by restricting access, and the cheapest way to do that is to make people wait. Even so, the system was buckling under the assault of baby boomers descending into decrepit old age. The people working in the hospitals had become survivors in lifeboats, beating off anyone trying to climb aboard. Whether you needed a knee operation, a new lung, or a consultation with a psychiatrist to deal with the voices in your head, you waited, and if you died while you were waiting, or ended up in jail because you did what the voices told you, there was always someone else to take your place.

Emergency rooms were the entryway into the system, an earthly purgatory clogged with lost souls waiting for salvation, and the gatekeepers to salvation were the triage nurses. It used to be that you just walked up to a desk and talked to them. Now they huddled behind locked doors and thick glass windows with small holes to speak through.

Vanier held his badge up to the window and bent down to speak through the hole.

"Roger Bélair. He was admitted this evening. Where can we find him?"

The nurse looked up without smiling, her face strained with fatigue. She looked down and began slowly looking through papers as though she had lost something. Finally she gestured to the hallway to her left, half-standing to speak through the hole.

"He should be on a bed in the hallway. He's waiting for a room. But he'll probably be discharged before one comes up."

Six beds were lined up end to end in the hallway, all of them occupied. Most of those bedridden were in various stages of unconsciousness, definitely the best way to spend time in an emergency room. One guy, was sitting up with his head leaned back against the iron rail, staring at the ceiling.

"Let's start with the guy who's awake," said Vanier. They walked up to the bed. "Mr. Bélair?"

Bélair turned his head and winced. "Police?" It was less a question than a statement to himself. "I was hoping for a doctor. Can you get me some water?"

Vanier looked back at Laurent.

"Sure." Laurent turned to walk away.

"I'm Detective Inspector Vanier." He pointed up the hallway at Laurent. "That's Detective Sergeant Laurent. Quite the night you had. Can you tell me what happened? Start to finish?"

Nobody looks good in a hospital bed. Bélair's eyes were dark and puffy with blood, and he had a strip bandage over his nose. A drip tube was taped to one thin arm and his other arm was bandaged to his chest. Wisps of grey hair stuck to his head in disarray. He caught the look in Vanier's eye.

"I always wondered what being hit by a truck would feel like."

"It was an SUV, from what I heard. Don't suppose there's much difference."

"Yeah. It was an SUV. It hurts. It hurts everywhere."

24

"I can imagine. What happened?"

"Where do you want me to start?"

"Anywhere."

"I had a meeting with a new client for six o'clock. She called to say she was going to be late. She didn't arrive till seven-thirty."

"What was her name?"

"Sophia Luna. I did the checks."

"Checks?"

"Yes. It's a new rule of the Bar. It's called the know-your-clients rule. You have to be certain who your client is. I think it has to do with money laundering or anti-terrorism, some bullshit like that. So every time I open a new file, I need to photocopy some ID. You know, to make sure they are who they say they are. So I got her name and address. I got a photocopy of her passport."

Laurent came back with two bottles of water and handed one to Bélair. Bélair grabbed it with his good hand. "I'm supposed to unscrew it with my teeth?"

Laurent took it back, unscrewed the top and handed it back to him. He broke the seal on the other one and propped it by the wall where Bélair could reach it.

"Thanks." Bélair pulled himself up and winced. He put the bottle to his mouth and finished the water in a single go. He wiped his mouth with the back of his hand. "You could die of thirst in here and nobody would notice."

"But you knew her. You were going to dinner with her."

"It's the first time I had met her. She was late, I was

hungry. So I suggested that we grab dinner and discuss whatever she wanted to talk about over dinner."

"Did she tell you why she needed a lawyer?"

"Not really. We didn't get a chance. Look, I was starving and she looked like she would be a good dinner companion. She said she was looking for a trustworthy lawyer, and Sarah Delaney had recommended me. I did some work for the Delaney woman a few years ago. I got lucky. I got a great result. Anyway, Madame Luna said she was looking for somebody trustworthy because she was trying to arrange an important trade and wanted someone to organize it."

"A trade?"

"Yes, a trade, like an exchange. She didn't say what kind of trade. I didn't ask questions, I wanted to get something to eat. So I suggested we continue the meeting over dinner and she accepted. We left, and that was it until the truck hit me."

"So you don't know her?"

"Never met her before. I didn't even get a chance to find out what the mandate was."

"What address did she give?"

"I don't remember. I remember her name, but that's it. The address is on my desk, with a photograph of her passport. She's Guatemalan."

"Can you give us the keys to the office? We need to move fast on this."

"I can't. I would love to. But there are rules. I'm a lawyer and I can't just hand over the keys to my office to the police. There's lots of confidential stuff in there and I have to protect my clients' interests."

"Maître Bélair, Sophia Luna was kidnapped. Every minute counts. Why don't we call the Barreau and have someone there when we go in. I need her address."

Bélair thought for a moment. "Okay. The number's on my membership card. It's in my wallet. Give me that bag." Bélair pointed at a stuffed plastic Abercrombie and Fitch bag lying at his feet at the end of the bed. Laurent handed it to him, and Bélair struggled with one hand to pull out a crumpled jacket. Then he reached into the inside pocket.

"Shit. They took my wallet."

"Last night?"

"No. I had it when I came in. I had to show my health-care card. Somebody stole it while I was lying here."

He was still checking the pockets. "And my phone's gone too. Bastards."

Vanier knew it was all part of the hospital experience.

Laurent pulled his own phone from his pocket and went online to get the number of the Barreau du Québec. He punched in the number and handed the phone to Bélair. "Can you leave a message to say to expect us in the morning, and that we can have access to your office?"

Bélair pressed the phone to his ear, and then pulled it away to punch numbers. He listened to instructions and took the phone away from his ear to punch in more numbers. He did it three times before handing the phone back to Laurent. "I can't understand this phone system. Anyway, they probably wouldn't accept a phone message to authorize you to go into my office. They'd want to talk to me. You'll have to wait till tomorrow."

Vanier grabbed Laurent's phone and handed it back to Bélair. "We'll go to the Barreau first thing in the morning and have them call you on Laurent's phone. Is that okay?"

"Sure." Bélair pulled his keys from the plastic bag and pointed out two keys on the ring. Laurent separated them from the ring.

"You bring back the keys and I'll give back the phone," Bélair said.

"Promise." Vanier reached into his pocket and pulled out a notepad and pen. He handed them to Bélair. "Just in case, can you write something authorizing us to go in and look for the address of Madame Luna? In case we can't get you on the phone. You never know, you may be getting tests or X-rays."

"Sure." Bélair started writing on the pad, signing his name with a flourish. He handed the pad back to Vanier. "Sorry I can't be more help."

"That's okay," Vanier said. "We'll find her. You got a business card?"

"You need a lawyer?" A light flickered in Bélair's eyes.

"For the address."

"Oh, yeah." Bélair reached into the top pocket of the crumpled jacket, pulled out a business card.

"Thanks. And if ever I do need a lawyer, I'll think of you. Now get some rest, Maître."

Vanier dropped Laurent in the police headquarters parking lot and watched as he climbed into his car and drove off. Home to his wife and kids.

It was half past midnight. Vanier knew if he went home it would be hours before he fell asleep. He pulled Bélair's business card out of his pocket and checked the address. It wouldn't hurt to figure out where the place was.

Bélair's office was on Saint-Jean just north of Saint-Sacrement, in a nineteenth-century building of ashlar-cut limestone. It looked solid enough to outlast any modern building. Vanier climbed the steps and peered through the glass pane in the wooden door. The inside hallway was deserted. He fingered the keys in his pocket for a few seconds, and pulled them out. As he reached to push a key into the lock, the door slid open. He grabbed it to stop it swinging back against the wall, and stepped into the dark hallway.

He stood for a few moments, pulled out his gun and strained to listen for any sound. The building was silent; the only noise came from the occasional car passing in the street. Bélair's office was on the second floor. Vanier moved slowly along the carpeted hallway towards the staircase, waiting for his eyes to adjust to the gloom. He put his foot on the first step of the staircase. It didn't creak under his weight and seemed solid enough for him to risk walking up on the carpet runner rather than sticking to the edges. He hesitated for a second at each step, but heard nothing except the faint sounds of the street.

On the second floor, the darkness was cut by a slice of light from under one of the doors. Vanier moved towards it, transferring his gun from one hand to the other, wiping sweat from his palms. He stopped short of the door and checked the number. It was Bélair's office. He listened again until he had almost convinced himself that the office was deserted. He spun across the doorway, launching a kick at the lock as he went, and ending with his back against the wall on the other side. The door swung open and he listened again. Nothing. He leaned forward, holding his gun in both hands, and could see at least half of the office through the open door. There was no one there. He swung back across the doorway, and could see the rest of the office, except the corner next to the hallway. He went in quickly, aiming for the corner, and breathed a sigh of relief when it was empty. He holstered his gun and looked around.

The office was a mess. The desk drawers had been pulled out and emptied onto the floor. Two filing cabinets stood against one wall, their drawers open, but the files apparently still in place. Vanier took a quick look through the papers scattered on top of the desk, but he couldn't find anything with Sophia Luna's name on it. He sat in Bélair's chair and leaned down to rifle through the papers on the floor. Bélair had said he'd left the photocopy with Luna's passport details in plain view on top of the desk. Whoever had searched the office must have taken it. He thought of Bélair lying on his metal bed in the hospital hallway.

Vanier pulled out his phone, dialled central dispatch, and asked to be put through to the supervisor on duty at

Station 20. Station 20 handled most of downtown. Its jurisdiction stretched halfway up the mountain and included the Montreal General. He had to argue, but eventually the supervisor promised to send a car to the emergency room to check on Bélair. Vanier went over to the filing cabinets and flicked through the folders until he found a file marked Delaney, the name of the woman Bélair said had recommended him to Luna. He copied down the address and phone number. He looked around one last time and backed out of the office, using his shirttail to pull the door closed.

It took him fifteen minutes to drive back up to the hospital. No sign of a patrol car. Vanier cursed under his breath. He parked his car quickly in an empty taxi spot and made for the door. He was still swearing to himself as he ran through the emergency room and up the hallway to Bélair's bed.

"You came back?" Bélair looked up at him with a half-smile. He looked groggy and exhausted.

"I had second thoughts. You should have some security. You're an important witness."

"I'll be okay."

Vanier was already on the phone with the supervisor of Station 20.

"I didn't promise. I said I'll try."

"It sounded like a promise to me. Anyway, I need someone up here for the night. I have a witness in a bed and he needs security."

"For the night? You must be kidding. Do you know

31

how busy we are? A beautiful night like this, every stoner in town is out walking the streets, or getting fuelled up for trouble in the bars. We're going to be busy all night, and I need everyone."

"Maybe someone needs overtime."

There were a couple of seconds of silence at the other end. "Maybe. Can you wait until two? I've got a shift change at two. I know someone who wants the hours."

"It's a promise this time? You can have someone here by two-thirty?"

"Yeah. I promise. Might even be earlier."

Vanier had an hour and a half to kill. He turned back to the bed. "You want a coffee?"

Bélair was asleep, snoring. Vanier pulled out his phone and punched Anjili's number. It rang, four times, went to voice mail. "It's me. Sorry. It's late. I got distracted. Talk tomorrow."

He dialled Laurent. A cellphone started ringing under Bélair's sheet, and he remembered Laurent had loaned him the phone. He cancelled the call and punched in Laurent's home number, got a groggy *oui*?"

"Change of plans for tomorrow morning. You go to the Barreau and get someone to go with you to Bélair's office. I'll leave his keys on your desk in the morning. I'm going to take Saint Jacques up to the hospital. Maybe in the morning Bélair's memory will be better."

Laurent didn't sound like he was in any shape to ask questions. "Sure, sir."

"Call me when you get to Bélair's office, okay?"

"Okay."

The uniform turned up at two-fifteen. Roberge, the name badge said. He was already yawning as Vanier briefed him.

"You stay with him, and nobody goes near him except doctors and nurses. Got it?"

"Yeah, sure." Roberge was looking around. "Is there anywhere to sit?"

Vanier had been standing, leaning against the wall. "I'll ask. Maybe someone can find a chair."

Vanier turned and left. Near the door he grabbed an unused chair and walked it back up the hallway.

Roberge smiled. "That's what I call service."

"Don't push it." Vanier dumped the chair seat next to Bélair's bed. "And don't fall asleep."

Roberge sat down. "Good night, Inspector."

Back at his apartment, Vanier poured himself a Jameson and let the water from the tap run, testing the temperature with his fingertips. Hoping for cold, he settled for lukewarm, held the glass against the flow and added a splash to the whiskey. Then he sat down heavily on the sofa, listening to the sound of traffic floating up from the street below.

He was thinking of Anjili, and his fears. Was this what he wanted, what he didn't want to give up? The right to come home whenever he wanted and sit alone in the dark, to sleep on the couch if he chose to, not to have to explain anything to anyone, not to have to talk if he didn't feel like it, to listen to whatever the hell music he wanted to hear at whatever the hell time he wanted to?

Vanier poured himself another drink, pulled *Beyond the Missouri Sky* out of its place and loaded Pat Metheny and Charlie Haden onto the player. A long, slow walk through pastoral landscapes was just what he needed. He sat back on the couch and thought about the message he had left Anjili. He had apologized for not calling her, apologized for doing his job. Whoever said love means never having to say you're sorry knows shit about love, Vanier thought. Love means saying sorry as often as necessary, even when you're not. It was pretty much necessary all the time. Vanier sipped the Jameson and listened to the pristine guitar and Haden's double bass fill a space as wide as the prairies. He pulled his feet up onto the sofa and closed his eyes, picturing himself walking alone across the grasslands. Only solitude means never having to say you're sorry.

FIVE

Saint Jacques was sitting at her desk reading emails when Vanier arrived. It was seven o'clock.

"Couldn't sleep?" Vanier asked.

"Slept like a baby. You?" She looked up at him.

He didn't answer, didn't need to. "Change of plans. Laurent is going to the Barreau. We're going back up to see Bélair. He was groggy last night. Maybe there's something else he remembers. You spoke to the witnesses, so maybe you can jog his memory."

"Sure." Saint Jacques got up, reaching for her protein shake.

Vanier was writing a note to Laurent. "I told him last night to go to the Barreau and then over to Bélair's office. Did anything else turn up last night?"

"Nothing. Black SUV. Three men. Vague descriptions from the witnesses. One of the guys that got out of the SUV was in a dark suit. The other was wearing an Adidas tracksuit. Nobody got a look at the driver. That's about it."

"If it had been a cop beating some citizen, somebody would have taken a video, it would be all over YouTube by now."

"True. But this happened fast. Cops take longer to give the beating. It gives people a chance to focus."

Laurent was pacing the carpet at the Quebec bar association. He was waiting to see Cyril Plante, who was apparently the guy to talk to if you wanted access to a lawyer's office. After a few minutes, the receptionist led him down a hallway and stopped outside an open door, waving him in. Laurent hesitated for a second. The office looked more like a showcase, like its only purpose was to show delinquent lawyers what a well-organized office should look like. There was hardly anything in it, a filing cabinet with a printer-scanner sitting on top, two small glass-fronted bookcases holding books meant only for display, and two straight-backed chairs facing the desk.

The desk and chairs sat on a dark red Persian carpet as if it were a raft. Plante stared at his visitor from behind his desk, sitting as stiff as a military judge. The glass-topped desk was empty except for a yellow legal pad, a pen, and a closed laptop. The lawyer didn't get up, just gestured Laurent to one of the chairs. He winced slightly when the detective moved it out of position.

Plante was a small man, lost in his black faux-leather chair like a prematurely aged twelve-year-old. His shiny black hair was plastered to his scalp. He might have been the last man on earth to use Brylcreem. He skipped the usual pleasantries and got straight to business, asking Laurent for identification. Laurent fished in his wallet. Plante made a show of studying the card before transcribing the information onto the yellow notepad. He stood up and walked to a scanner and made a copy. He handed the card back to Laurent and sat down.

"If I understand correctly, you are looking for someone to accompany you while you search the offices of Maître Roger Bélair, a member of the Barreau du Québec. Am I right?"

"It's not exactly a search, sir," said Laurent. "I'm looking for two specific pieces of paper that Maître Bélair told us were lying on top of his desk. That's all."

"And you have a warrant, I presume?"

"Permission. I have his permission. He's in the hospital."

"How can I ascertain that?"

"That he's in the hospital? I was with him last night. You want to call him?"

"And how would I know he was who he said he was. You said you had permission."

Laurent put Bélair's note on the table and pushed it forward. Plante leaned forward and read it without touching it.

"Why is he in the hospital?"

"This is urgent, Mr. Plante. You can call him if you like, but he's suffering. A woman has been abducted and one of your lawyers was seriously hurt. Are you going to help us or not?"

Plante looked up. "It is precisely in times of crisis that rules are broken and mistakes are made."

Laurent leaned forward. "Let's put it this way, sir. If I'm not out of here in five minutes with someone to accompany me to Maître Bélair's office, you may be charged with obstruction of justice."

"That's preposterous." Plante said, placing the palms of his hands on the glass desktop. When he lifted them, Laurent saw sweat marks. He leaned forward and read Bélair's note again, then stood up, all five foot two of him.

"All right, let's go. You have the keys I suppose?"

It took them ten minutes to walk to Bélair's office building. The front door was open, and they went up to the second floor. Laurent took out the keys before seeing the damage to the lock. He reached out and turned the handle. The door swung open.

Plante was disappointed. "Very careless. And against the rules."

Laurent grabbed Plante by the shoulders and moved him back from the door, pulled his gun. With his back against the wall, he gently nudged the door open with his foot. He took a quick look into the office and then walked in, holding the gun in front of him. He saw what Vanier had seen the night before: a mess of file folders, papers, and books on the floor, every drawer open. He did what Vanier had done, hoping to find the two pages with Luna's personal details. Then he got Vanier on the phone.

"Vanier."

"Hey, boss. There's nothing here. The place has been turned over. Looks like they went through everything."

"Get an SOC team over there. Maybe they can get prints."

"You don't sound surprised."

"Surprised?"

"About the search."

Laurent knew. He also knew that Vanier would never admit it.

"We're just turning into the hospital now. Maybe there's something else Bélair can tell us. I also tracked down the Delaney woman. Saint Jacques and I will go see her as soon as we're finished with Bélair."

"Okay. Let me know."

Laurent clicked disconnect and turned to see Plante sitting, shaking in a chair.

"Mr. Plante. You need to get some air."

"I've never seen anything like this," he mumbled.

"I know, sir. It's traumatic. Come on, I think I noticed a coffee shop downstairs."

The choice parking spots in front of the entrance were full, so Vanier again parked in an empty taxi space. Two taxi drivers came rushing over to protest and he waved his cardboard *Police* sign. They stopped running. He dropped the sign on the dash.

"You're kidding me, right?" said Saint Jacques.

"What?"

"The sign. You just made that yourself, didn't you?"

"The Lord helps those who help themselves."

At ten o'clock in the morning the emergency room was as hot and crowded as it had been the night before, and Vanier recognized some of the same people still waiting for their turn, forever being bumped to the bottom of the list by someone sicker, someone closer to death. The same family members hovered over the same beds as Vanier led the way up the hallway to Bélair's bed. He was asleep. The cop, Roberge, was asleep too, sitting on a folding metal chair with his head resting against the wall.

"Mr. Bélair," Vanier said as he approached the bed. Something was wrong. "Shit."

The cop opened his eyes and immediately stood up, looking sheepish.

Vanier reached out two fingers and felt for a pulse on Bélair's neck. "Shit."

The sole of his shoe was sticking to the vinyl floor. He looked down. A dark pool beneath the bed was slowly spreading outwards. As he looked down to get a better look, another drop fell and splashed into the pool, viscous, like oil. Vanier pulled back the blanket. A folded towel lay over Bélair's chest. He pulled it back to reveal a small stab wound over the lawyer's heart. The towel had been keeping the blood away from the top blanket. It would have taken some time before anyone noticed Bélair had been stabbed.

Vanier looked for the bag that Bélair had had on the bed. It was gone. So were Bélair's clothes. Vanier turned

40

to the cop, trying to decide whether to lash out at him, or just tell him to get the hell out.

"You. Write down every fucking minute you were gone from the bedside. Taking a piss, having a smoke, looking for a coffee. Every minute. When you were sleeping too. Write that down too."

Roberge stood with his mouth open at the head of the bed, staring down at Bélair's blood-soaked chest. He looked like he was about to say something, but nothing came out. There was nothing to say.

Vanier turned to Saint Jacques.

"Sylvie. Get a team in here. Right away. We need witnesses."

"Right." She pulled her cellphone out.

Vanier was gone, running towards the triage station, where a woman was holding a screaming baby up to the glass and shouting questions into the hole. The nurse looked like she was at the tail end of a shift in hell and was mumbling back the same words she had probably said a hundred times already.

"I said, go over there and wait. Someone will call your name."

The woman backed off. The baby kept screaming. Vanier leaned into the hole. "Who's in charge?"

"Of what?"

"This place. The emergency room. I want to see whoever runs this place, right now. There's a man dead in the bed over here."

She looked up at him with tired eyes, as though it were

just another ploy to jump the queue. Vanier held up his police badge before she could ask any more questions. "A man's been killed and I need someone in authority, right now."

The nurse lifted herself out of the chair with both arms and leaned forward, trying to look up the hallway. Then she leaned in towards the hole. "It's Dr Cohen. I'll page him. But it could be a while. Everybody's busy."

"Then get his deputy. Keep going down the list until you get someone."

"I'll page him."

"Say it's important."

"He's dead, you said?"

Vanier wondered what would qualify as important. Maybe dead meant there was no rush. He turned and saw a guy in his late twenties leaning against a wall, wearing an oversized white coat, a stethoscope draped around his neck. He was breaking the first rule of emergency medicine: never stand still in an emergency room, the sick will start forming a line to talk to you. Vanier walked over to him. "Doctor?"

The young man looked up without answering, breaking the second rule. Don't acknowledge someone calling you doctor.

"You're a doctor, right?" Vanier asked again.

"Yes. Well, a resident, actually. But look, you need to wait until your name's called. Somebody will see you in a few minutes."

Vanier flashed his card again. "There's a dead man in

one of the beds over here. He's been murdered. I need someone to take charge."

The doctor looked in the direction of Vanier's finger, but didn't move. Vanier put his hand on his shoulder and motioned him over to Bélair's bed. Saint Jacques was still on the phone. Roberge had disappeared. The resident pulled the blanket back and lifted the bloody towel out of the way. He put the stethoscope to his ears and listened to Bélair's heart. "He's dead."

"Genius. He wasn't when he came in here."

"Wait here. I'll get someone."

This time the resident didn't need encouragement. He turned and ran down the hallway, disappearing through a set of swinging doors. He was back seconds later with two more doctors, not the white-coated kind who don't want to get body fluids on their suits, but trauma specialists dressed for action in short-sleeved green surgical suits. Without a word to Vanier, they grabbed Bélair's bed and wheeled it back down the hallway and through the swinging doors. Vanier tried to follow but was stopped by a beefy nurse. "They'll try to revive him."

"Some hope," Vanier replied, turning back to the doorway. "I suppose that's one way to jump the line in this place though."

"What?"

"Die."

The atmosphere in the emergency room had changed. Two uniformed cops had arrived and were listening to Saint Jacques. Vanier approached. She was telling them what to do. She wanted names, addresses and phone numbers of everyone in the place. Had anyone seen someone approaching Bélair's bed? Vanier scanned the room looking for Roberge, but all he saw was a room full of people, numbed by hours of waiting, now alert, watching the show.

Saint Jacques turned to Vanier. "The uniform left. Didn't think he'd be welcome."

"Damn right."

"He left the list of times he left Bélair alone." Saint Jacques pulled a sheet of paper from her pocket. Vanier reached for it and read the scribbled notes. "He took a fifteen-minute break every goddamn hour." Saint Jacques said nothing. Vanier pocketed the paper. "Okay. Let's start getting names and addresses. Someone must have noticed something." Vanier scanned the room again and noticed a security guard standing off to the back, uncomfortable with real cops invading his space. "I'm going to talk to him."

The guard was in his early twenties, with a pencil-thin goatee and short clipped hair. He had accessorized the security guard uniform to make it more intimidating, with a black canvas vest that looked like bullet-proof Kevlar from a distance, but close up seemed more like a fishing vest, all pockets and flaps, filled with pens, a notebook, a pocket flashlight. He had tucked his trousers into his shiny black Doc Martens boots, and an assortment of black leather accessories hung from his belt. He wasn't wearing a name tag.

"Your name?"

"Gaston Hade, sir."

"So, did you see anything?"

"No sir. But maybe it didn't happen on my shift. I saw him. He's been lying in that bed since I got on duty. That's eight o'clock this morning. He didn't move all the shift."

"And you didn't see anyone approach the bed?"

"No, sir. Nobody that I saw."

Hade had nothing to offer, so Vanier asked him where the cameras were monitored.

"In the Central Security Office. I can take you there."

Vanier gestured to Saint Jacques to follow. Hade led them through a labyrinth of hallways, walking with the swagger that uniforms give some people. Finally, he led them through an unmarked door, and they were in a windowless room with banks of screens on the wall and a large control console on a raised deck. Hade pointed to a portly guy sitting at a desk. "The sergeant's in charge." Hade turned to the sergeant. "Sarge, there's two police officers to see you."

The sergeant turned in his swivel chair and gave Vanier and Saint Jacques the once-over. Then he turned to Hade. "Okay, Gaston, back to your post. I'll take things from here."

"But Sarge, maybe I can help. It could be important."

Before the sergeant could respond, Vanier said, "Let him stay. I need him."

Hade grinned, but dropped the grin when nobody responded.

45

Vanier walked across the room. "A patient was killed in the emergency room sometime between two-fifteen this morning and half an hour ago. He was in a bed in the hallway and I want to see the videos."

"I would have heard. If someone got killed. I would have heard," the sergeant said.

"You've just heard. I'm in a hurry. I need to see the footage."

The sergeant slowly raised himself out of the chair and led them over to the control desk, where a bored, middle-aged man was monitoring thirty screens.

"This is Ken."

Ken grunted to acknowledge the two cops and pointed to the screens.

"Look at screens eighteen and nineteen."

Ken typed some commands, and each screen showed a different view of the emergency room. The first was from a camera mounted over the main door, showing face shots of people leaving and the backs of those arriving. The second was a camera mounted in a corner of the waiting room, with a good view of most of what was going on in emergency.

"Those are the only two angles we have for emergency."

Vanier pulled out the list of times Bélair's guard had been missing. There were five time slots. "Okay," Vanier said. "Start with the room. Go back to two-fifteen and go forward from there."

The controller typed, and the date and time appeared

at the bottom of the screen. They watched the video unfold in real time for a few minutes. "Ken, can you speed it up?" Saint Jacques said.

"A little." Ken looked around to make eye contact with Saint Jacques.

The image sped up. At first it was hard to follow, but once you got used to following what was going on, patterns emerged from the chaos.

They went through two of the time slots without noticing anything except Roberge walking outside to have a smoke. Two minutes into the third time slot, Saint Jacques stopped the controller.

"Go back."

Ken put the image in reverse.

"Stop. This guy."

Ken punched a key and the screen froze. Saint Jacques pointed to a figure on the screen. "Watch him."

Saint Jacques was looking at a guy in an Adidas tracksuit, with a cap pulled down low on his head. He was sitting, like all the others. In the background, Roberge was frozen on his way to the exit, his hand pulling a pack of cigarettes from his pocket.

"Ken, go back thirty seconds and then go forward slowly." She turned to Vanier. "Watch."

On the screen, the roomful of people looked like they had been anaesthetized. Then Bélair's protector appeared, walking towards the door. Nobody seemed to care, except the guy in the Adidas suit, who sat up and followed the cop with his eyes. When the cop had disappeared,

Adidas got up and walked in the direction of the hallway.

"Fast forward for a few minutes," Vanier said. The time on the screen sped up, until this time it was Vanier's turn to interrupt. "Stop."

The Adidas man reappeared around the corner of the hallway, walking slowly towards the exit. He was carrying what looked like a bundle of clothes and Bélair's plastic bag. His cap hid his face as he turned for the door. The two cops stared at the screen, knowing they were watching the man who had just killed Bélair walk calmly through the emergency room, carefully avoiding the camera. Vanier turned to Saint Jacques. "Good catch, Sylvie." Saint Jacques almost broke a smile.

Vanier asked Ken to switch to the camera covering the entrance. It wasn't hard to find the man walking to the door, but still no headshot. The baseball cap was low over his eyes. All they had was a guy in a blue Adidas suit, maybe in his thirties.

Vanier was already on his feet. "We need these images, both cameras from two-fifteen to five a.m." Then he realized that any half-assed defence lawyer could sell reasonable doubt to a jury with hours of missing tape. "On second thought, everything from eleven last night to right now."

"We'll get them on DVDs for you," Ken said. "I can email them too. Hour by hour. Okay?"

"Soon as you can." Vanier handed him a business card.

Vanier knew that if they made the image of the Adidas man public, they might get something. You could pick people out of crowds just by the way they carried themselves, a distinctive gait or a piece of clothing. It might be worth a try. They didn't have much else.

"What next?" Saint Jacques asked as they were walking to the car.

"Sarah Delaney. Bélair told me that Luna got his name from one of his clients, Sarah Delaney."

Sarah Delaney's address was on Oxford Street in Notre-Dame-de-Grâce, a leafy enclave of family homes on postage-stamp lots that barely had room for front gardens. The neighbourhood had once been the starting point for upwardly-mobile anglophones searching for the middle-class dream, professors from the nearby campus of Concordia University, young professionals, and media types. Even today, it remained anglo at its core, but too many kids had left for Toronto, where speaking English was considered normal. A new middle class was moving in, bilingual francophones, circling the aging population of abandoned parents, waiting for them to die or get pushed into retirement homes.

Delaney's house had four separate doors lined up on the front porch. The house would have started out as a single-family home with only one door; now it was four apartments. Two old maple trees crowded the house for control of the lot, and the trees were winning. Saint Jacques took the porch steps two at a time and pushed the buzzer marked Delaney. A door opened just as Vanier walked up, and a woman in her late forties looked out at them. Vanier did a double take. Her long hair was black as a raven, and piled in a mound at the top of her head, the fierce blackness clashing with a bloodless white face. Pure Irish. She looked at them guardedly. "Yes?"

"Police," said Vanier. "Sarah Delaney?"

"Yes." She stepped out onto the porch.

"We're here about your friend Madame Luna."

"Sophia? I can't help you. I have no idea where she is."

"We believe she's been kidnapped."

"Just because you can't find her doesn't mean she's been kidnapped. Look, I can't help you. Go find her yourself." Her gaze left them as she looked across the street. Vanier turned and saw two neighbours staring back at them.

"Ms. Delaney, Sophia Luna was snatched off the street last night, kidnapped. She had been meeting with Roger Bélair on your recommendation. So we either question you here or bring you in for questioning."

Startled, the woman stepped back into the hallway. "You'd better come in."

They followed her into a large living room. Even though the sun was blazing outside, the room was dark, the light blocked by the trees outside. Delaney looked like she belonged in the dark.

"I'm sorry. I misunderstood," she mumbled. "I thought you were from immigration. They're looking for her, you know."

She offered them coffee, and Saint Jacques declined for both of them. Vanier sat in a high-backed chair and said nothing, leaving the questions to Saint Jacques. Delaney

50

sat on the sofa, and Saint Jacques pulled an ottoman over and sat on it facing her.

"Can you tell us why Ms. Luna was meeting with Maître Bélair?"

Delaney was only half listening, distracted, obviously shaken by the notion of a kidnapping. She looked up at Saint Jacques. "What? I'm sorry. What were you asking?"

"Why was she was meeting Maître Bélair? She asked you to recommend a lawyer. Did she tell you what it was about?"

Vanier had all but disappeared into the background as the two women spoke face to face.

"No. Well, not really. Sophia was very careful with information. I suppose you get that way if you're trying to avoid deportation. She just asked if I knew a trustworthy lawyer, and I gave her Maître Bélair's name. She was having bad luck with lawyers. Who doesn't? I went through three lawyers before I found him. What is it about lawyers? Anyway, I used him when a contractor sued me, and I was happy with him."

"How so?"

"I won my case."

"No, I mean, when you say she had bad luck with her previous lawyers. How so?"

"She told me bits and pieces of her story over the last two years. I don't understand how someone with a good refugee claim like hers can get rejected. She paid a fortune to two different lawyers. They were supposed to be experts, but they got nothing. They didn't even answer her calls most of the time." Delaney was picking at the fabric of the sofa with a broken fingernail.

"How did you know Sophia?" Saint Jacques asked.

"She was my tenant."

"Here?"

"Yes. It's my house. My parents left it to me."

"Which apartment did she have?"

"She didn't have an apartment. She had a small room in the basement. It doesn't have its own address, but there's a private entrance on the side. She said it was all she could afford."

"If she didn't have a mailing address, do you know if she kept a post office box?"

"No. At least I don't think so. All her mail came to me, and I'd give it to her."

"So, just to be certain. And this is very important. She didn't give you any idea why she was looking for a lawyer?"

"No. We didn't discuss it. I just assumed it was for her refugee claim. I told her that I didn't think Maître Bélair did refugee claims. I don't suppose that matters too much." She stopped picking at the fabric, looked at Saint Jacques. "It's better to find someone you trust than an expert who just wants to take your money, isn't it? Anyway, I figured if he didn't do immigration, he could probably recommend someone who could."

"And?"

Delaney thought for a moment. "Now that we're talking about it, maybe it is odd. I remember she wasn't fazed when I told her that Maître Bélair didn't do immigration. She said it didn't matter, she was just looking for an honest lawyer. We both laughed at that, like it was the hardest thing in the world. When I think back on it, it might have had nothing at all to do with the immigration. It could have been anything, maybe something to do with her work. Not immigration at all."

"Her work?"

"Yes. She was a journalist. You knew that, didn't you?"

"We barely know anything about her. Anything you can tell us would help."

"I don't want to get her in any trouble. But she used to do some small jobs, freelance assignments."

"Did she tell you what she was working on?"

"The last time I saw her was about a month ago. She didn't say anything about work."

"A month ago? But I thought you had recommended Maître Bélair recently."

"No. I mean, yes. I gave her his name over the phone. She called to ask if I knew someone and I gave her his name. Since she left here, we used to meet for coffee every once in a while. At first it was just so I could give her whatever mail had come in. Sometimes cash a cheque for her. Then we seemed to just get into the habit. We'd have coffee and chat about all kinds of things. She's a good person."

"Did she ever mention what she was working on?"

"She said mostly things were quiet. But she had some good leads on a story about human trafficking and prostitution. She just talked about it in general, nothing specific."

"Did she mention any names, places?"

"No. Like I said, it was all very general." Delaney looked down at the carpet, then lifted her head quickly. "Girls from Eastern Europe. I remember she said that. Boys too, sometimes. Apparently they are brought here and forced into prostitution. But you must know more about that than me."

She looked at Saint Jacques for confirmation. Saint Jacques nodded noncommittally. "Anything else?"

"Not really." Delaney was remembering the conversation. "She mentioned movies too. Apparently, these people were forced to do things on camera."

Saint Jacques turned around and looked at Vanier. She raised her eyebrows as if to ask, *You have any questions?*

Vanier sat up and leaned forward. "Did she ever mention anyone she was working with?"

Delaney thought for a moment. "No. In fact, I don't think she knew that many people in Montreal."

"You said you were cashing cheques for her. Who were the cheques from?"

"The cheques? Oh, right. She didn't have a bank account, I guess because of her status, so everything had to be cash. Since I've known her, she probably gave me ten cheques from *The Gazette*. Always $250. I remember that it was the always exact amount. I would give her the cash and she would sign the cheque over to me so that I could deposit it."

"Anyone else?"

"I remember *The Gazette* because that's easy. I was impressed she was working for them. And there was also a translation company. I guess she did work for them too, but I have no idea what the name was."

"When she called to ask about a lawyer, did she sound worried?"

"Honestly, she didn't sound any different. This refugee business had her scared all the time, like she could be picked up and deported at any moment. She was really afraid of going back to Guatemala. She said she would be killed if she was sent back."

"So she did sound scared?" Saint Jacques said.

"Yes. But that's the way she always was. In the café, she was always looking around her. Every time the door opened she would look up to see who was coming in. So I can't say that she was any more scared when she called than she had been in the previous six months."

Back at headquarters, the images from the hospital had arrived as promised, and Saint Jacques set about going through them carefully. She was staring at her computer screen, isolating every moment when the Adidas man was in the frame, or when Roberge was taking a break. Vanier sat down opposite Laurent's desk.

"So you went there last night?" Laurent asked.

"I don't know what you're talking about. I dropped you at the parking lot and went straight home to bed."

Laurent rolled his eyes. "Anyway, we've got some

leads," Vanier continued.

"Shoot."

"First, Sophia Luna was a failed refugee claimant. So that means there's a trail. Immigration is going to have a file on her, and she appealed her case as far as she could, so there's going to be court records. We need copies of everything. She was getting occasional cheques from *The Gazette*, so they would have a record. See who she was working for and what she was doing. That might lead us somewhere."

Laurent was scribbling notes.

"I'm going up to see the chief. I want to get the pictures from the hospital out to the press. Have you seen this man, that sort of thing. I need his sign-off."

SIX

Katya was still waiting. But this was a different kind of waiting. Every night she waited, lying on her bed, waited for hell to begin.

Pavlov never knocked. He just unlocked the door and stood in the entrance with a man. Waving the man into the room, he'd say the same thing every night.

"She's all yours. One hour. Have fun."

Then it was her and the man. Some were shy, and she let them take their time undressing. Most were in a hurry, not wanting to waste a second, pulling themselves out of their pants as they crossed the room to the bed, holding themselves out to her mouth for immediate attention. She had become numb. Shutting down her mind and simply being present physically, doing what she was told.

Most of the men didn't care. She was a soft body. Smiling, or looking like she was enjoying herself, didn't matter. A few craved reaction, and could only get it by being rough, by hurting her until fear showed in her eyes.

They choked her until she stopped breathing, and bent her arms almost to the breaking point. The fear brought her back, forcing her to be there. But she would never smile.

That night, the door opened and Pavlov stood there alone. "Get up. It's tattoo time."

The other girls had one. All the same design, and always on the forearm, a double-headed Russian eagle. Katya had watched hers grow over two sessions. Now it was almost finished, except a blank scroll held in the eagle's talons. Katya hated it. Not just because it was crudely drawn, but because it was a symbol. She was being marked, against her will, and she would have to wear it forever.

She rose from the bed and followed Pavlov down the hallway to a large room that was set up as a movie studio. The man with the needles looked worse than ever, the sweat on his face glistening in the bright light he used to illuminate his work. She figured Pavlov was paying him in drugs, and he would only be paid when he was done. He was always rushing to finish, not caring what his work looked like.

She took a seat at the table and rested her arm on an ink-stained towel under the lamp. He didn't acknowledge her, just leaned forward to inspect the half-finished tattoo, like he was trying to remember where he had left off. He grunted and picked up the needle. The machine kicked into action with a low hum, and he started to work. It was black ink this time. He was filling in the empty scroll. He picked up a dirty rag, splattered with blood and ink from previous customers. Katya looked away, trying to get her mind to drift.

More and more she was living in the past, digging up memories. The present was too painful, and she had no dreams left for the future. She closed her eyes, tried to ignore the drone of the machine and the stabbing of the needle. She had an image in her mind, no more than a flash. She tried to hold onto it, to go back to the beginning.

A heavy thump of boots announced their father was at the door. Her mother's eyes lit up at the sound, and Katya rushed to be the first to greet him.

She smiled up at the giant bulk of her father. He had a basket slung over his shoulder with a leather strap. In his right hand he held a fishing rod. He bent down and scooped her up with his free hand. "Anna, see what I've got!"

His wife came out of the kitchen and kissed him on the lips. "That's all you've caught? A little girl?"

"Just wait."

He pulled the chair away from the table and placed Katya standing on it. Then he looked around, pretending he couldn't see the boy clutching at his leg. "Stephan, Stephan. Where's my boy?"

"I'm here, Papa. Down here."

He reached down and hoisted the boy up and onto another chair. Putting the basket down in the centre of the table, he reached out for the clasp and slowly raised the lid. "Tah-dah!"

"Oh, they're beautiful." Anna put her hands up to her mouth.

He reached into the bag and pulled out a fish, its scales glistening in the light. He laid the fish on the table and reached into the bag for another one, six in all.

"Can I touch, Papa? Please!" Stephan yelled.

"Here. Hold your hand out." Katya's father picked up one of the fish and laid it in the boy's outstretched hands.

"Me too. Me too," Katya begged, holding her hands out, palms up.

Stephan's fish fell to the floor, then Katya's.

"Quick. They're trying to escape." The father got down on his hands and knees and the two children jumped to the floor. He stood up with a fish in each hand. "Kids, into the kitchen with them. Into the sink!"

The children watched him place the fish gently into the sink and turn the tap on.

"Go get their friends." Anna said, "before they escape."

Katya and Stephan ran back into the living room and each returned with a fish. They dropped them into the cold water and ran back for the others. When the six fish were safely under water in the sink, the father lifted the children up to look into the water.

"Aren't they beautiful?" said Anna.

"But they're dead," said Stephan.

"Of course they're dead. They're for supper. We're going to eat them," said Anna.

Both children were silent, looking down into the water.

Their mother broke the silence. "Why don't you go into the living room. If you're lucky, Papa will tell you how to catch fish one day. Go. I'll clean the fish, and we'll have our best supper in months."

In the living room of their father sank down in his armchair and the two children climbed up onto his enormous thighs.

"Catching fish is not easy," he said. "You have to be strong and brave, like a great hunter, but most of all you must be able to sing the fish song."

"Teach me. Teach me the fish song," said Katya.

The song had only three verses. In the first, you let the fish know you have a basket. In the second, that you have placed it close to the water, and in the third, if they jump into the basket, all their worries will be over.

Katya could still smell the aroma that had filled the apartment. She could hear the laughter. She could still taste the fish.

"Done."

She was shaken back to the present. The scroll on her arm contained one word: the name Kedrov.

Pavlov looked at her. "Nice, isn't it? Now there's no question who owns you."

SEVEN

Most of us still believe Canada is open to the world and full of caring individuals. We believe our governments are pretty much like us, and we let politicians get on with government, waking up every few years to rubber-stamp the political flavour of the day. In a conservative Canada, immigration has been redefined as a problem, not an opportunity. Our immigration policy looks more like a job description drafted by a human-resource clerk than a vision for a great country. Maybe we shouldn't be surprised. For all the smug myths that make up our collective memory, Canada's past immigration policies have included a head tax on Chinese, a refusal to accept World War I refugees, total bans on groups deemed "undesirables," and an aggressive no-Jews rule. Even today, we deport Roma refugees back to Hungary, a country with anti-Roma fascists in its government. But we're too busy binge-watching *Game of Thrones* and *Orange is the New Black* to care. Let someone else fight for fairness in lonely battles with the government.

Vanier was standing in the waiting room of Henri Cabana, Luna's second immigration lawyer. Laurent had gotten his name from court records that showed the court had rejected Luna's bid to overturn the Refugee Board's refusal of her claim. Cabana had argued that the first decision should be set aside because Luna's first lawyer was an incompetent who had done a lousy job of presenting her case. The court had tossed that argument, along with Luna's hope of remaining in Canada.

In the waiting room, Saint Jacques had taken the last available chair. The others were occupied by two families sitting in silence with the patience of people too used to waiting in line. An old, white-haired man in a light brown kaftan and leather sandals fingered prayer beads and stared off into space. His wife sat rigidly beside him. A couple from Southeast Asia occupied two other seats, both dressed like they didn't believe the hot weather would last, the man in a thick brown sweater under a tweed jacket and his wife with a cardigan over her turquoise sari, and knee-length wool socks. Their two children were playing on the floor, dressed in shorts and T-shirts, like any Canadian kids.

Vanier passed the time reading the framed documents hanging on the wall, the Magna Carta, the Charter of Rights and Freedoms, and the Quebec Charter.

When Cabana's office door finally opened, everyone looked towards it. The lawyer filled the entire doorway. He was at least six and a half feet tall and barrel-chested, but he had a soft look about him, like someone who had once been powerful and now was settling comfortably into old age. He looked at Vanier and Saint Jacques. "I might as well see you two first. You're probably the only ones here with somewhere else to go."

As the two officers walked towards the door, Cabana stepped out, and leaned down over to the two kids playing on the floor. They looked fragile under his looming bulk as he tousled their hair with his huge paw. "Won't be long."

Vanier and Saint Jacques were already sitting when he came back. Cabana moved around and sat down heavily behind the desk. He leaned forward and rested his elbows in the semicircular clearing that was the only part of the desktop still visible among piles of folders, loose sheets of paper, magazines, and *The Gazette*. He reached under the newspaper and pulled out the regulation yellow notepad.

"Thanks for seeing us at short notice," said Saint Jacques. "I'm Detective Sergeant Saint Jacques, and this is Detective Inspector Vanier. We're looking for information on Sophia Luna."

Cabana's face changed, like a thick cloud crossing the sun. "Don't think I can help you there. But I am surprised that the Montreal police have taken to chasing down refugees. Isn't that federal jurisdiction?"

"She's been abducted, sir."

The news took him by surprise. He leaned back in his chair as though to get a better look at the two officers.

"Abducted. As in kidnapped?" He paused. "Have you

64

checked with CBSA?"

"CBSA?"

"The Canada Border Services Agency. They're the ones who hunt down failed refugee claimants. If you're high enough up their list, they'll do anything to get you. As soon as your appeals are exhausted, they can pick you up wherever you are and take you straight to the airport. But that's not kidnapping. It's called executing a removal order." Cabana leaned forward, looked at Saint Jacques. "You haven't checked, have you?"

"We don't believe this was official, that it was a government agency."

Cabana continued. "After the CBSA, I'd check the Guatemalans. She upset some very important people in Guatemala. That's why she filed for refugee status."

"Could you tell us about that, sir?"

"Did you read her file?"

"Just the Federal Court decision. That's how we got your name."

"I can give you the full-length story or the synopsis."

"Let's start with the synopsis."

He relaxed into his seat and brought his hand up under his chin. "Sophia was an investigative journalist in Guatemala. A pushy journalist and a successful woman. I suppose that was already two strikes against her. Just before she fled, she was writing a series of articles on how drug profits were corrupting the state. She was naming officials who were taking drug money—politicians, judges, police, the military. If you ask me, she was reckless, but we should all thank God for reckless people. She was getting threats on a regular basis, getting picked up for questioning, that sort of thing. A lot of powerful people wanted her to shut up and go away. One day her partner was hit by a car in the street. Just clipped, nothing too serious. But that night someone put a note in her mailbox. It said something like, are you brave enough to risk accidents to those you love? Which is worse, if you get killed, or you watch your family get killed? The next day she was arrested for theft. A police captain swore a statement that they had been lovers and that she had stolen $15,000 from a safe in his house."

Cabana looked at the two officers, held up his hand, "I know. Why does a cop have $15,000 in cash in a safe? Good question. He said it was official funds for paying informants. So it wasn't just theft, it was interfering with police business and theft of public funds. But it was all bullshit. She'd never met the captain."

"She wasn't his lover?" said Vanier.

"Remember I said her partner was clipped by a car? Her name was Lydia. Sophia's a lesbian. She doesn't like men. Even if she did, she'd go through a long string of men before she settled on a policeman." He looked up. "No offence."

Saint Jacques smiled.

"Was she found guilty?"

"No trial. Her publisher bribed someone at the prison, and she got out. She drove north to Mexico and took a flight to Montreal, claimed refugee status."

"Sounds like a reasonable claim, no?" Vanier asked.

Cabana looked at Vanier. "You're not an expert on our wonderful refugee system, are you? It's the Canadian equivalent of the Berlin Wall at the height of the Cold War, except we're keeping them out, not in. The administrative equivalent of minefields, barbed wire, and concrete walls, to make sure hardly anyone qualifies. They've written the rules so that half the people who make claims are automatically disqualified, then they stack the Refugee Board with people whose life mission is to keep Canada wholesome, white and Christian."

"In Sophia's case, there was another problem. She hired the worst immigration lawyer in the city. She got his name from a guy at CBSA. Imagine. That's like asking the police to recommend a defence lawyer."

Saint Jacques smiled again.

"It's a bit of a conflict, no?" Cabana said.

"So she lost her case," said Vanier.

"In a hearing, there are five buttons you absolutely have to push." Cabana held up his hand and starting counting off. "That you suffered persecution based on race, religion, nationality, social group, or political opinion. You must actually be afraid." He held up a third finger as though giving a lecture. "Your fear must be rational. The government can't or won't protect you and, finally, there's must be no safe place in your own country." He kept his hand up, the five fingers splayed. "If you don't push all five buttons, you're finished."

"And where did she fail?" Vanier asked.

"She didn't fail, her lawyer failed her. He's lazy, notorious for failed claims. He claimed she was unjustly accused. So, she came off looking like someone running from the law. A criminal fugitive and not a refugee."

"When she came to see me, it was too late. It's next to impossible to file new evidence in an appeal. You have to go on the evidence that was before the Refugee Board, and there was no good evidence before the Board. So she lost on a hopeless case, and it was a hopeless case on appeal. I tried to argue that her counsel was incompetent, but the court wouldn't even let me make the argument. The court said she had her opportunity to make her case and lost."

"What was the next step?"

"There was no next step."

"No appeal?"

"She could ask the Minister for a special permit. I told her that. But I also told her that there was as much chance of that happening as, I don't know, the Pope getting circumcised at the Wailing Wall. Showers, the current minister, is completely anti-immigration. He's done his best to rig the rules so it's next to impossible to qualify as a refugee. And he hasn't issued a single Minister's permit since he's been in office."

"What was the last time you saw her?"

"It would've been a few days after the Federal Court's decision. Two months ago."

"And you haven't heard from her since?"

"Not a word. Look, she was mad at me. Couldn't understand how I couldn't make things right. That's not un-usual. In any event, there was nothing I could do for her. I told her the process, there would be a removal order, and she could choose to leave. If she didn't leave voluntarily, she could be picked up and deported."

"Do you have her address?"

Cabana one-finger-typed on the keyboard and read out an address from the computer screen. It was Delaney's address on Oxford Street.

"We've tried there. She moved."

The lawyer raised himself up from his chair and went over to a grey filing cabinet. He flicked through the fold-ers, pulled a file out, and sifted through the papers. Then he pulled out a yellow sheet with handwritten notes on it.

"I have a note here from the last meeting." He was reading as he walked back to his chair. "She said if I want-ed to contact her, I should do it through David Reyn-olds." He picked up a pen and scribbled on a small pad of scrap paper that had been cut and stapled into an uneven notepad.

"Here are the coordinates of Mr. Reynolds. He's a good guy, works with refugees."

They drove west along Saint-Antoine and crossed At-water. The condominium developments were spreading like weeds, and there was construction on every block. Once, the land had been too close to the expressway for anything but cheap apartments, rooming houses, and in-dustrial buildings. Now it had become prime real estate, shuttered factories waiting their turn to become beehive condos or lofts for hipster artists, and rundown apartment blocks destined to become piles of bricks. The people who had lived in the area for years were under pressure from the encroachment, but nobody cared. They were only tenants, and all it took to move them was money. There was a sadness about it all. Neighbourhoods in decline die publicly, like roadkill.

The house they were looking for was on Saint-Augustin in the Saint-Henri neighbourhood. It was the kind of street city planners have nightmares about, a mixture of single family homes, duplexes, triplexes, apartment buildings, a factory and a couple of workshops. On the west side, all the buildings backed onto the train tracks. Vanier parked in front of a factory that had been converted to artists' studios. The address Cabana had given them was a white two-storey home. It had a small porch in the front, and a white picket fence low enough to step over. If it hadn't been for the green carpet of fake grass and the iron grilles on the ground-floor windows to keep the addicts out, it could have been a postcard house in the country. Two women were sitting on folding chairs on the porch, watching Vanier and Saint Jacques as they approached. Vanier tried a smile. "Is Mr. Reynolds home?"

The women said nothing, just stared back. Vanier reached down and fiddled with the latch on the gate. When it swung open, the whole fence shook with the movement, the wood rotting under the daily showers from neighbourhood dogs. The front door opened before they got to it, and the guy in the doorway surprised Vanier. He was wearing grey cords, a black T-shirt and a black cardigan. He clutched a worn black book in his hand. He couldn't have looked more like a priest if he'd worn a collar.

"Mr. Reynolds?" Vanier said.

The man nodded but the rest of him was immobile.

"Can we come in?" Vanier said.

He stood like a wall, didn't say a word.

"We're here about Sophia Luna. We'd like to talk to you."

Reynolds took a breath. "I have no idea where she is."

"That's the point, sir," said Vanier. "Neither do we."

Reynolds looked at Saint Jacques. "We're investigating Sophia Luna's kidnapping."

"Kidnapping? Who are you?"

"Montreal police. I'm Inspector Vanier. This is Sergeant Saint Jacques."

Reynolds looked down at the two women, who had been following the conversation. "You better come in."

They followed him through a dark hallway and into a room at the front of the house, a tiny office with a desk, a folding metal chair, and a couple of filing cabinets. Reynolds lifted papers off the metal chair, dumped them on the desk, and looked around.

"I'll have to get another one."

"I can stand," said Saint Jacques, but Reynolds was out the door before she finished.

Vanier was trying to make sense of the mess of papers

on the desk. Every manila folder bore someone's name, and there were court documents lying around, some marked up with pencilled notes. Saint Jacques was studying the National Geographic map on the wall, half covered with red, green and yellow tacks.

"I've always loved maps," she said.

Reynolds came back with another folding chair in his left hand, the black book still clutched in his right. He saw Vanier leaning over the desk. "I thought you were here to talk about Sophia." He unfolded the steel chair for Vanier.

"We are. You work with refugees. She was a refugee."

"Let's get something clear, Inspector. Here at Welcome House, we help refugees. That's what we do. The authorities don't like us. So if you're here to probe the organization, I'll just fold the chairs back up and ask you to leave."

"All I care about is Sophia Luna, nothing else," Vanier said.

Reynolds sat down behind the desk, piles of paper between him and his guests. He moved a couple of piles off to the side, put the black book down on the desk, and leaned forward. "So what's this about her being kidnapped?"

"Sophia Luna was kidnapped last night, sir, in Old Montreal," Saint Jacques explained. "Snatched off the street."

"And we're trying to find out who snatched her," Vanier added. "To do that we need to know about her and about who might have kidnapped her. I understand your organization may have been helping her, so you may know something that will help us."

Reynolds leaned forward, placed his palm on the black book. "Sophia Luna upset many important people in Guatemala. She managed to escape to Canada and claimed refugee status. She told me, and I believe her, that she'll be killed if she goes back to Guatemala. There's no question in my mind. If she was forced to return she would be killed. So perhaps those people have decided to follow her to Canada. Who else would want to kidnap a refugee?"

"What were you doing for her?"

"We helped her find a new place to live."

"You helped to hide her?" said Vanier.

"We helped her stay alive."

"When did you last see her?"

"Four days ago."

"And how was she then?"

Reynolds thought for a moment. "Now that you ask about it, it was unusual. She sounded upbeat. She's been under a lot of pressure, and most days she went from subdued to depressed. I remember I was surprised at how well she was doing. It was almost as though she had found hope. There was nothing specific that I can think of, it was just the way she talked, the way she sounded."

"And she said nothing specific about any changes in her life?"

"Nothing. We just talked about general stuff. I reassured her of our support, we talked about the heat. It was very warm in her room. But nothing specific, I'm afraid. I can't think of anything that might help."

"Where was she living?" Saint Jacques brandished her notepad.

Reynolds turned back to Vanier for assurance.

"I gave you my word." Vanier said. "This is just between us. I'm not working for immigration. We need to see where she was living, look through her things. We're investigating a kidnapping and murder. We need to search her room."

"Murder?" He picked up the book.

"She went to see a lawyer on the night she was kidnapped. He was killed."

Reynolds stood up. "I'll take you there. It's not far. But please, people's lives are at risk."

"It's between you and us," Vanier said. "No one else."

Vanier and Saint Jacques followed Reynolds north and east for about twenty minutes, and parked outside a three-storey building on Milton that looked like it was still standing only because the adjoining buildings were propping it up. The brickwork was sagging to fill the gaps left by crumbling mortar, and what paint remained was peeling in big flakes.

Reynolds fingered a fat bunch of keys as he mounted the steps. He chose one and opened the front door, beckoning over his shoulder at the two officers. They followed him into a dark hallway. Nothing happened when Reynolds flipped the light switch. "It's a rooming house.

Nobody puts any money into it. Don't even replace light bulbs."

Saint Jacques pulled out a flashlight and went in front. "Which floor?"

"Our people are all on the third floor," he said.

With the front door closed, the place was quiet as a mausoleum, except for the faintest noise of a radio playing somewhere. Vanier fought the urge to cover his mouth and nose from the smell, the wet sweetness that sets off alarms in everyone who's dealt with cockroaches. Reynolds followed them up to the third floor and pointed down the hallway. "Hers is room 34."

Reynolds pulled out the bunch of keys and opened the door.

The room had been ransacked. Clothes had been tipped out of drawers and piled in the middle of the floor. Anything with a lining had been slashed open. The mattress and boxspring were propped against the wall, each cut open with long slashes. Pieces of a small plastic radio lay beneath the window, as though someone had brought a heavy boot down on it.

Vanier looked around, trying to make sense of the disorder. "First Bélair's place. Then this? I wonder if they found what they were looking for?"

The room was small even for one person. With the three of them, it felt like standing in a wardrobe. Vanier noticed a black cable plugged into the wall outlet. "Her computer is gone. She's a journalist. She would have had a computer."

"She owned a laptop. I've seen it," said Reynolds.

Vanier turned to Saint Jacques. "I don't see any pads either, or paper."

A quick inventory turned up nothing to do with a journalist's trade except a beaker on the floor with pencils and pens spilled out of it. "Sylvie, get a team up here to see what they can find."

Saint Jacques pulled out her phone. "Sure."

Vanier turned to Reynolds. "Where's the bathroom?"

"It's not much, I know. But we don't have money. This place is a last resort, but usually temporary, until we can find a more permanent place. She was going back to a prison cell, maybe worse. It's better than a prison cell."

"Where's the bathroom?"

"It's communal."

"Show me."

They went back out to the hallway. Vanier didn't need a guide; his nose was good enough. The toilet had developed its own presence over the years, and you could have found it in a blackout.

It was cramped. Sitting on the toilet seat, you could lean your chin on the tiny sink. The toilet bowl was discoloured and pitted, with black hairline cracks. The cistern was high up on the wall, with a chain hanging down. Vanier stood on the edge of the toilet bowl and lifted the cover of the cistern. It was empty, except for water and rusting parts. He climbed down, sat on the toilet and leaned forward to look under the sink. He reached up and around the underside of the sink. Again, nothing.

Then he got up and moved into the bathroom. The smell was less intense, only the lingering odour of soap. The bathtub was an ancient claw-foot, with a yellow stain running down from the dripping tap. The shower curtains seemed to be held together by soap scum and mould. There was no cabinet, no place to store anything. Vanier imagined the tenants carrying all they would need to the bathroom, and then carrying everything back again to their rooms. He waved Reynolds outside and closed the door to make more room. Then he got down on his hands and knees to look under the bathtub and the sink. Nothing.

He opened the door. Reynolds was standing there. "The people in the other rooms, can we talk to them?"

"Sure, but maybe it's best if I ask the questions," Reynolds said. He led Vanier back down the hallway, knocked on the first door, and spoke quietly against the frame. "Philippe, it's me, Dave."

After a few moments the door opened a few inches, and a gaunt, middle-aged man peered out through the crack, both hands holding onto the door. He had sunken eyes and cheeks, but managed a half-smile at Reynolds. He ignored Vanier.

"Philippe, sorry to bother you. It's about Sophia. You know, the lady in 34?"

"Yes, Sophia. Such a wonderful person."

"She's missing, Philippe. And Mr. Vanier here is trying to find her. Someone has been in her room. We were wondering if you saw anything unusual, or heard anything."

Philippe shot a glance at Vanier and turned back to Reynolds. "You know me. I have nothing but my music. If I'm not playing, I have my headphones on. I would go mad otherwise. I went out for food yesterday but that was all. I have been here all the time, but not here. I am in my music, waiting." He looked at Vanier. "But Sophia, are you going to find her?"

"We'll find her," Vanier said.

"If she's missing, I don't think this is good." He withdrew back from the crack. "I'm sorry. I can't help." He took another step back, slowly closing the door, as though ready to stop if they forbade it. They didn't.

Reynolds turned to Vanier. "Philippe played violin for the St. Petersburg Philharmonic. But he's gay, and sick. AIDS. Not a popular combination in Putin's Russia. Of course, Canada refused his application for refugee status. Said he would not be in any danger if he were sent back to Russia."

Nobody answered at the second door, and Reynolds opened it with his key. The room was empty.

"I'll talk to him later. I'll let you know if he's got anything useful."

The third door opened even before they got there and a short, muscled African man stared at them through thick glasses. Vanier tried not to stare. The man's ears weren't big, but they stuck straight out of his head.

"I saw the men who did that. Who were in Sophia's room. I saw them through the hole." He gestured to a spy hole in the door. "I put that in myself. For safety."

78

He turned his head, alternating between Vanier and Reynolds, as though he had no peripheral vision. When Saint Jacques arrived up the hallway he almost turned his whole body.

He looked back to Reynolds. "Police?"

"Yes, police. But don't worry, Sékou. Nothing to do with immigration. Your neighbour Sophia has disappeared. Mr. Vanier and his partner are looking for her. They are helping." He turned to Vanier. "This is Sékou Camara. He's from West Africa. Guinea."

"She was scared these last days. First she was okay, like everything was going to be fixed. We talked. She is a very good person. I thought she was just scared like all of us. You know, just ordinary scared."

"Can we come in?" Vanier asked.

Camara backed into the room and the three of them followed.

Camara's room had the look of a train station waiting room after the last train has left, a place suspended. The single bed was made up, and two suitcases stood beside it. A mug sat on a plate on the countertop next to the sink, with a knife, fork and spoon standing in it. Vanier was willing to bet the cupboards and drawers were empty. There was a yellow nylon rope, knotted at intervals, coiled on the floor under the window, one end tied to the radiator.

The man saw Vanier looking at the rope. "I've been running for a long time. You always need an escape route. One is good, but the more the better."

The rope was ready to be dropped out the window. He could probably leave with his suitcases anytime and you'd never know he had ever been there.

The only place to sit was a wooden chair pushed up against a small desk and the bed. Saint Jacques pulled the chair out and sat down. Reynolds and Camara sat on the bed, and Vanier leaned against a wall, then slid down into a crouch.

Camara reached down and pulled the zipper back a few inches on one of the suitcases. He reached in and grabbed a plastic bag of tangerines. Then he took the bag over to the counter and quickly peeled four tangerines, putting them on the plate and handing the plate to Saint Jacques.

"Please. Share these with your colleague." He went back to the bed and sat down.

"Mr. Camara, you said you saw the men who went to Sophia's room. Could you tell me about that?"

"It was last night. When you are hiding like me, you get to recognize footsteps. Official footsteps. You know the kind that can't be quiet, or don't need to be. About six o'clock last night I heard them coming up the steps. I was looking at the door before they were in the hallway. I thought, maybe they were looking for me."

He pointed to the door. There were two sets of chains on it, and a steel lock that allowed him to prop a bar against the door when he was inside. If anyone had been looking for him, he would have had plenty of time to escape through the window before they made it through the door.

"They went straight to Sophia's room. They were in there for maybe half an hour. Two men. Both very big."

Vanier was thinking that just about everyone Camara met would fit the description of very big.

Camara seemed to pick up on Vanier's thought. "Bigger than me, of course, but big."

"You're sure?"

"I don't see that good around the edges, but through the peephole, looking straight, I see pretty good."

"And what did they look like? Apart from big."

"One looks like a business man, you know? Suit and a tie. The other guy, he looked like he was going to play football."

"You mean soccer?" asked Saint Jacques.

"Yes. Football. But not a football uniform. More for training."

"Track suit?" said Vanier.

"That's it. Track suit. Adidas. And a baseball hat."

"You ever see these guys before?" said Vanier.

"No. That's all I saw. I can't tell you anything else. They come here, go into Sophia's room. They stay for about half an hour and leave. I only see them for a few seconds. Once when they go in and once when they leave. I don't see faces. It was too quick."

Vanier sensed he was backing away, not wanting to get involved. The African looked at Reynolds. "I think I need to move."

Reynolds thought for a few moments. "We'll see

about it, Sékou." He turned back to Vanier. "You think there's a danger for the others?"

"I don't know. I don't think so. But until we know what's going on, your guess is as good as mine."

Vanier had Saint Jacques take Camara through the story again in the hope that something else would come out, but it was the same. At six o'clock two men had gone by in the hallway. He was sure they had gone into Luna's room and they left about half an hour later. One was in a business suit, the other in an Adidas track suit with a baseball cap. He didn't see their faces.

Vanier was sure Camara was holding back, but there was nothing he could do, not with two witnesses in the room.

As he was standing to leave, Vanier's phone went off. He looked at the screen, Sarah Delaney. He let it go to voice mail.

In the car, they waited while Reynolds pulled away. Vanier switched on the engine.

"Who called?" said Saint Jacques.

"Delaney. I'll drop you back to headquarters and call her then."

Before he could pull away from the curb, his phone rang again. He looked at the screen and put it back in his pocket, letting it ring until it eventually went to voice mail.

"Delaney?"

"No. Personal."

"You know that you can send calls straight to voice

mail, right? You don't need to let it ring six times."

He looked at her. He was constantly amazed at how many people assumed that he was technologically inept. "It's rude. The caller will know you could have answered but didn't."

Saint Jacques smiled. "A man of etiquette."

"No point in being rude if you don't have to."

It took ten minutes to drive back to headquarters. At seven-thirty it was still warm. The streets were filled with people out wandering for no better reason than to get as much of summer as possible. Every restaurant and bar had makeshift terraces on the sidewalk, and they were all full. Vanier started thinking of supper. A cold beer and a decent meal on a terrace was looking good.

After Saint Jacques drove off in her own car, Vanier pulled out his phone to check the missed calls. He had three: Delaney, Laurent, and Anjili. They had all left messages, but it would take him as long to go through the voice-mail procedure as to just call them back. He started with Laurent. When the detective answered, Vanier could hear children in the background.

"I hope you're having a barbecue."

"Exactly. We're out back."

"Well, enjoy. Enjoy the family."

"I am. So, what's up?"

"You called."

"Yeah, but like I said in the message, there's nothing yet. *The Gazette* said they will be able to tie the Luna cheques to a project, and then they'll know who she was working with. They should have it tomorrow."

"That's it?"

"That's all."

Vanier felt guilty keeping him from his family. "Okay. So call me when you hear something."

"For sure."

Sarah Delaney answered immediately. "Thanks for calling back, Inspector."

"No problem."

"Two things. First, I've got the name of the translation company. I had forgotten that one of the cheques bounced. The bank sent it back to me. Sophie got a replacement, but I kept the bounced one."

Vanier pulled at his notepad and leaned it on his leg, grabbed his pen. "And the name?"

"A. L. Translations Ltd." She sounded like she was reading. She gave him an address in Lachine.

"That's off the cheque?"

"Yes. The signature's hard to read but it looks like Antoine Lepage, maybe Anthony."

"Thanks. Could you hold on to the cheque? We may need it."

"Of course. The other thing was that about a week ago I had a call for Sophia. I completely forgot because it seemed like nothing at the time."

"How so?"

"It was just someone calling for her. They called my home number, the landline, and asked for Sophia. It was a man's voice, very friendly. I said she wasn't there but offered to take a message. He said no message but asked if I knew where she could be reached."

Vanier heard a beeping sound that announced a second call coming in. He took the phone away from his ear and checked. It was Anjili. He resumed his conversation with Delaney. "So you said no. You didn't know where she was?"

"Well, I didn't know. And that was it. He said thanks and hung up. I guess that was why I completely forgot about it. It was so, well, normal."

"Thanks for this, Ms. Delaney."

"Call me Sarah. Please."

Vanier was about to hang up. "One last thing, Ms. Delaney. Sorry, Sarah. Could you ask Bell or whoever your phone company is to give you the number? Maybe ask them for all the numbers that called yours in the last two weeks."

She agreed. She would call Vanier when she got the information.

Vanier was nervous about the third call, dreading another day of condo hunting. He knew that he would eventually break down and agree to something, anything, just to avoid having to keep looking. He punched one on his speed dial and waited. It rang several times.

Anjili picked up. "And there he is," she said. "He hasn't left the planet."

"How are you doing?"

"Better than you, I imagine. I actually sleep at night."

"I'm going to sleep tonight. Catch up. It's been busy.

Going to get something to eat and head home. Want to join me?"

"It's too late tonight, but what are you doing Thursday?"

He thought of condos. "What time Thursday?"

"Evening. If we're efficient, we could do three or four visits."

Vanier said nothing.

"Just kidding. How do you feel about a picnic in the park?"

Vanier smiled. "Seriously? That's the best idea you've had in ages."

"You're saying I don't have good ideas?"

"I'm saying, of all the good ideas you have, and there are lots, this is the best."

They made the arrangements. He would get the chicken and the wine and she would supply everything else. He would call when he got to her place, and she would come down.

"You get distracted when you come up, and we'd never get to the picnic."

"I'm distracted already."

"Just stay in the car and I'll come down."

EIGHT

Vanier and Saint Jacques were sitting in Vanier's car outside a high-rise apartment building in Lachine.

"Maybe it's not the right address," Vanier said.

Saint Jacques was staring at the door. "It's the one you gave me, and it's the same as the one on the website. He must work from home."

Vanier climbed out of the car. "The new normal. Everyone's self-employed because nobody wants employees. That way you never have to fire anyone or lay them off, just stop giving them work. So what do we know about this outfit?"

"It's a small translation company, A. L. Translations. I assume it stands for Antoine Lepage. He's the owner."

"That's original."

Saint Jacques was reading from her notebook as they walked. "It's been in business for ten years. Lepage is the sole owner, and there are no employees. According to what I could find, the company makes a couple of thousand a year."

"That's it? You can't live on that."

"That's the profit. He probably pays himself a salary. The profit is what's left over. Enough to keep the taxman happy."

"But he's not getting rich."

"He's a translator, boss. Translators don't get rich."

They walked into the lobby, and Saint Jacques pressed the button for apartment 301. "It's listed as Suite 301 on the website," she said.

"Fancy."

The voice box on the wall burst into life. "Hello? *C'est qui?*"

Vanier bent towards the box. "It's the police, Mr. Lepage. We'd like to talk to you."

There was a hesitation. "Give me two minutes. I'll come down."

"No. Buzz us in and we'll come up."

Vanier counted to three. The voice box squawked. "Okay."

A buzzer sounded, and Saint Jacques pulled the door open.

They took the elevator to the tenth floor. Vanier knocked on the door. When nothing happened he knocked again, louder. Then the door opened wide, and a cloud of cigarette smoke passed over them. Lepage stood in the doorway in a neon green T-shirt, striped boxers, and the brain-dead grin of a frat boy on a bender. His pupils were dilated. He stepped back and ushered them in.

The apartment was steaming hot and smelled of pot, stale beer, and pizza. He seemed to have made an effort to clean up, and empty pizza boxes and take-out trays were piled up on the kitchen counter next to a collection of empties. The picture windows were closed, and the air conditioning was off. The air was fetid, a mixture of stale food and body odour.

He gestured for them to sit on the sofa. "Excuse the mess. I don't get many visitors."

Walking past him, Vanier recognized the whiskey breath. Vanier kept walking, past the sofa and over to the window. He unlatched it and slid it across so that air could come in. It didn't seem to make a difference.

"You know, that's always the first thing my mother does when she visits. She always opens the window."

"Mothers know stuff," Vanier said, and joined Saint Jacques on the sofa. Lepage dropped into the armchair. The glass-topped table between them was decorated with different-sized ring stains.

"So what can I do for you?" Lepage managed.

"We're looking into the disappearance of Sophia Luna."

The grin disappeared. "Sophia? I haven't seen her in two months, at least. But if you find her, tell her she caused me a lot of trouble."

"How so?" said Vanier.

"She fucked up, and I nearly lost a great client. I gave her a real simple job to do for Essence. You know Essence, right?"

"Big engineering company, right?" said Saint Jacques.

"Yeah. That's them. It was a small job. Just a simple contract to translate into Spanish. Five pages, that's all. She did it in a day, and I flipped it back to the client. That's it, until a week ago. I get a call from the client. He says he needs to talk to the translator. He says there was a lot wrong with the translation and he wanted to get it fixed."

"Who called? What was his name?" said Saint Jacques.

"I don't know. Normally, the only one I speak to at Essence is Lynn, Lynn Gagnon. She's the one who gives out the translation work. But this was a guy. He mumbled a name, but I didn't write it down. I only spoke to him once."

"And you gave him what he was looking for?"

"Yes. I gave him Sophia's name and the address."

"When was this?" Vanier asked.

"Like I said, a week or maybe ten days ago."

"We'll need a number for Lynn Gagnon, and the address. What address did you give them for Sophia?"

"I'll have to look it up." He reached under the armchair and pulled out a laptop. "But don't worry, keep asking the questions. I can multi-task." He bent his head to look at the screen and started typing. Suddenly he looked up. It was as though a light had gone on, like he was coming back to life.

"Just a second. You can't tell Lynn that you got this information from me. There's such a thing as client confidentiality, isn't there?"

"It's a bit late for that, Mr. Lepage," said Vanier.

"But no. I mean, shit, business is bad enough. They're already pissed at me. Can't you work around it somehow?"

"Let's finish the interview first. You help us and we'll see what we can do to keep you out of things."

Lepage shifted forward in the chair.

"Please. It's important."

"So tell us about the translation."

"Essence needed a contract translated from English to Spanish. And they wanted it quick. I remember that. Sophia is a freelancer that I use sometimes. Her previous work was good, people liked it. No complaints. So I emailed her the contract, and a day later, I got the translation back. I sent it to the client and that was it. Sent the invoice, got paid, and sent a cheque to her."

"Can we get a copy of the contract?"

"No. I don't have one. The day after I got the call from the guy looking for Sophia, Lynn called. She was reminding me of our contract. I'm supposed to delete all Essence documents after the work is done and send an email confirming that it's been done."

"Is that unusual?"

"Not at all. Confidentiality. Lots of clients want me to destroy the documents after the work is finished. I guess they don't want copies of their documents all over the place."

"And did you do it for Essence?"

"Of course."

"What was the contract about?" said Vanier.

"You think I read the stuff if I'm not paid? I did a word count for pricing. That's how I price it. It's twenty-five cents a word. That's all I need to know."

"You don't remember anything about the contract?"

"The title. It was called something like *MOU – Compensation*. That's how I saved the document in my system."

"MOU?" said Vanier.

"Memorandum of Understanding, I suspect."

"Memorandum of Understanding. That's a contract?"

"A type of a contract, yes. But it was only a draft."

"And you're sure you don't have a copy?"

"I told you, I sent them an email confirming that I destroyed all the copies."

"Certain?"

Saint Jacques scanned the mess in the room and took a chance. "Including the one you attached to the email to Sophia?"

"The day after I sent the email to Lynn a tech guy from Essence showed up at the door. He said he was doing a spot check to make sure all Essence documents were deleted. What could I do? Essence is one of my biggest clients. So the guy spent half an hour playing with my computer and that's the end of it."

"So you have nothing related to the contract," said Saint Jacques.

"I have the invoice. I sent them. I told you, they paid. The invoice would have the job number. Lynn would be able to track the contract through the job number. It's on the invoice."

"Could you print it out for me, sir?" said Saint Jacques.

"I don't know. I should call the client first. For permission."

"Remember what we said about being cooperative?" said Vanier, who was standing now, with his back against the window. He was bathed in light from behind.

Lepage squinted up at him. "You promise you'll keep me out of this? Like I'm a source that needs to be protected."

"We'll do our best. Can we have a copy of the invoice?" asked Vanier.

Lepage typed on the computer and they heard the printer engage. When it stopped making noise, Lepage collected the single page and handed it to Saint Jacques.

"So. Is that it? Can I get back to work?"

"One last thing. You were going to tell us Lynn Gagnon's coordinates and the address you gave them for Sophia."

"Whatever I have in my address book. I can give you a printout."

Lepage punched some keys on the laptop and the printer clicked into action again. Saint Jacques and Vanier were already heading for the door when Lepage handed over the page. The address for Sophia was Delaney's house on Oxford.

Vanier's phone rang as they were walking to the car. It was Laurent.

"We've got news from *The Gazette*. Luna's cheques

were all booked as source payment by Nick Angus. I think you know him, right?"

Nick Angus had been *The Gazette's* crime reporter for over twenty years, and he and Vanier had a history. Angus's contacts with the gangs were better than with the police, and he was always looking for a big conspiracy, preferably one involving crooked cops.

"I do indeed. I can't miss a chance to ask that old bastard questions instead of the other way around."

"There may be a problem with that, sir. He's on leave of absence. He's in rehab."

"And a drunk can't have visitors?"

"Not that kind of rehab. It's physical. He got a really bad beating two weeks ago, in the stairwell of his apartment building."

"Where is he? You have an address?"

"*The Gazette* wouldn't say. Apparently it's a big secret."

"Shit. Okay. See if you can get us an address. I want to see him." Vanier disconnected.

It didn't take long for Laurent to track down Angus. He called a buddy of his who was involved in the police union, and the buddy called a union rep at *The Gazette* to compare medical plans. Apparently, *The Gazette's* health plan was still rich enough to pay for private care for staffers like Angus who had been at the paper so long, it was cheaper to keep them employed than to buy them out. When there's hardly any staff left to insure, you can be generous with insurance. The corporate strategy seemed to be that time would cure everything, and eventually the newspaper's content would be generated by cut and paste from the wire services and underpaid freelancers.

Within an hour, Laurent had received a faxed list of the approved rehab centres in the *Gazette* plan. He kept the original for the next round of negotiations with the city, and gave a copy to Laurent.

Laurent worked his way through the list of phone numbers, asking for Nick Angus every time someone answered. On the seventh call, he was told to wait while he was connected. He hung up and called Vanier.

The black SUV had been double-parked outside the bank for five minutes. Sékou Camara had been watching it from a dépanneur across the street. He hadn't been able to sleep the night before. Now he was sweating, and his stomach was acting up. He had been calming the ulcers with Pepto-Bismol lozenges and was almost finished his second package, but his stomach still felt like he'd been drinking vinegar. He put another lozenge on his tongue and sucked. His hands were shaking, and he felt like he was going to vomit. He took one last look at the clock above the cashier, took a couple of deep breaths and walked out into the street.

The SUV was parked with the arrogance of people who don't have to abide by rules. Traffic had slowed down to one lane, with motorists in the blocked lane sounding their horns. The man standing beside the SUV ignored the noise. Camara knew authority when he saw it, and authority had never been good to him.

Camara recognized the man standing beside the SUV as one of the pair that had searched Sophia's apartment. He looked like a banker, in a dark suit that contrasted sharply with the white shirt and red tie. A tough banker, but more banker than gangster. Camara fingered the safe deposit key in his pocket like a good-luck charm, waited for a break in traffic, and stepped out into the street. The banker made him out immediately, giving him a long appraising look. Camara tried to look confident. It was a farce, and he knew it. When you've spent too much time running, you can only look hunted. When Camara was halfway across the street, protective muscle got out of the back of the SUV. He was about twice the size of Camara, wearing a loose windbreaker. It was the second man from the search. The driver stayed in the SUV.

"You have the key?" the guy in the suit asked.

Camara swallowed, looked him in the eye. "You have Sophia?"

The way it came out, it sounded like he was asking a favour, like he should have said *Mister* and *please*. The suit nodded to the guy in the windbreaker, who opened the back door of the SUV. The suit pointed to the opened door.

"Look for yourself."

Camara moved past the suit and leaned into the dark interior. Sophia was sitting in the far corner. Her eyes were shut and her face was puffy. In the shadowy light he couldn't tell if she had been crying or beaten.

96

"Sophia," he said. Then, louder, "Sophia, it's me, Sékou."

The woman struggled to open her eyes.

"Sékou?" she asked, turning towards his voice, unable to focus on his face. He could see she had been drugged. She was barely focusing.

"Yes, Sophia, it's Sékou."

"Sékou. Don't do it. It won't work."

The guy in the windbreaker grabbed Camara by the collar and hauled him back out of the slamming the door closed. Camara looked back to the suit.

"She's not well."

"So let's get this done and you can take her home."

Camara knew he was lying. They were not going to let either of them go. They just wanted him to have enough hope to go into the bank, open the box and deliver the contents. But there wasn't going to be any exchange. He'd experienced enough betrayal, and he knew the futility of false hope. The hope that made people give themselves up because they were promised safe passage, or sign false confessions in return for promised immunity or protection. The key in his pocket and his ability to get access to the box were the only leverage he had. They needed him to cooperate. But if he gave them what they wanted, they would both be dead.

"Okay. The box. I can sign for access. Then you give me Sophia, right?"

"That's the deal. You go in with Carlos here"—he gestured to the muscle—"you open the box, and you give the contents to Carlos. You both come back. Then you get to take Sophia home and screw her."

Carlos laughed at the joke. The suit didn't laugh. He reached out and grabbed Camara's ears and pulled his face close.

"But don't try anything clever. Two, three minutes and it's all over. And you and your girlfriend can go home. But if you try to fuck with me, you're both dead."

The suit let go of Camara, nodded to Carlos. "Move it."

Camara went in the revolving doors first, his shoulders drooping. Carlos followed.

Inside the bank it was quiet as a temple, with deep carpets muffling all sound except the background click of keyboards. There were high-definition screens on every wall flashing the mantra to waiting clients: all your problems would be solved if only you borrow more money.

Banks had changed since the days of cheap pens chained to countertops and high-glass barriers to keep out thieves. Now the pens have disappeared, and the thieves are in charge of the banks.

They turned right. A security guard sat behind a cheap desk reading a newspaper. Camara spoke. His voice was shaking. "I need access to my box."

The guard put down the newspaper without folding it closed, and tapped the space bar on the keyboard to wake the computer. "Sure. I need the number of the box and some identification."

Camara put the key and his passport on the desk. The

guard looked at the passport and then at Camara. He typed the box number into the computer and squinted at the screen. Then he pushed a clipboard across to Camara. "Sign here."

The guard looked at the signature, then back to the computer. Camara willed him to find a problem, to deny access.

"Thank you, sir. You're good to go." He waved his hand in the direction of the safety deposit room.

Camara took one step forward, then his legs folded underneath him and he was lying on the carpet. Carlos leaned down, grabbed his collar and pulled, whispering in his ear. "Get the fuck up and open the box, or your friend is dead."

Camara turned his head to face Carlos. "You tell your boss. He calls me again on the same number and we arrange a safe transfer. Not like this. You deliver Sophia somewhere safe, and then I can open the box. You call me. I will tell you where to deliver Sophia."

Carlos pulled again at Camara's collar. "Get up, asshole."

"No. This is not safe. You call and we arrange something else."

The security guard was on his feet. "Is he all right? I'll call an ambulance."

Carlos was already on his way to the exit, leaving Camara on the ground. The guard pulled out a cellphone and dialled 911. Camara counted off four minutes on the floor and pulled himself to his knees. He looked at the guard, smiling. "I feel better."

"No, sir. Stay where you are. The ambulance is on its way."

A small crowd had already gathered. They parted as Camara walked slowly towards the exit. Outside, the black SUV was nowhere to be seen. Camara heard the ambulance siren and began to run.

NINE

Nick Angus's rehabilitation facility was actually a wing in a retirement home. Vanier and Saint Jacques waited for him next to a small fountain in a glass-domed atrium. When Angus eventually appeared, shuffling towards them behind a walker, he looked old and tired, more like a retirement home resident than a rehab patient.

Saint Jacques pushed her chair back to stand, but Vanier motioned for her to stay sitting. They sat and watched Angus shuffle up the hallway to their table, a pained expression on his face.

"He can't be more than fifty-five," said Vanier.

"He looks older."

He was dressed for bed, in pyjamas too big for him. His face was pale and he had an unkempt Yasser Arafat stubble that would never become a full beard. Vanier pushed a chair out with his foot and gestured for the journalist to sit down. As Angus shuffled in a small circle to line himself up with the chair, Saint Jacques stood up again.

"Leave it. I can look after myself."

"At least you haven't lost your charm, Angus," said Vanier.

Angus said nothing, other than maybe the *fuck you* glance he gave Vanier as he dropped into his seat.

"Thanks for agreeing to see us, Mr. Angus," said Saint Jacques.

Angus didn't acknowledge her. He turned to Vanier. "Like I said to your guy when it happened, Inspector. I've got nothing to say. It was a mugging. That's all."

"Mugging, my ass, Angus. I read the report. It must have taken a good ten minutes to do that much damage without killing you. Brutal, but careful. That's what I would say."

"I should be grateful they didn't kill me?"

"The report says they didn't even take your wallet."

"They were doing a Clockwork Orange. It was a bit of fun for them. And before you ask, I have no idea why they picked me."

"Did they say anything?"

Angus's eyes shifted off Vanier. He seemed to be studying the fountain. "No. Not a word."

"Sophia Luna was kidnapped. Snatched off the street. You think there's a connection?" The news shook Angus. Whatever he was doing in the care facility, he wasn't keeping up with the news. "You knew her, right?"

"Of course I knew her. She used to come to the Press Club."

"More than that. We got her phone records. She called

you regularly. Right up to the day you were beaten. For two weeks, you were exchanging calls all the time. What was that about?"

Angus looked away. "She was looking for help. You know, with the refugee problem. She was looking for some freelance work too. She's used to be a journalist in Guatemala. A good one."

"That's it?"

"That's it, that's all."

Vanier leaned forward. "Nothing about human trafficking?"

"She was working on a story, something to do with trafficking, something to do with prostitutes from Eastern Europe, that sort of thing."

"She didn't talk to you about that?"

"No. I told you. She just mentioned it offhand. She didn't want my help."

"Did you help her? Did you step on some toes?"

"The trafficking story, if there really was one, was hers. I know nothing about it."

"So why were you sending her cheques?"

"I felt sorry for her. She needed money. *The Gazette* can afford it."

"Over the years, Angus, you've given me lots of reasons to want to beat the shit out of you. But I've always restrained myself. Because I'm a good guy. Maybe the people who are into trafficking and prostitution aren't so restrained. Maybe they don't appreciate journalists asking questions. Maybe that's it, the connection to your beating."

This time Angus looked Vanier in the eyes. "I told you. I never worked with her on that."

"You see, what I don't understand is why would they kidnap her, but only beat the shit out of you."

"Exactly. Doesn't make sense. That's because there's no connection between the two."

"You sure?"

Angus just rolled his eyes.

"You know what I don't understand?"

"Enlighten me, Inspector."

"Here you are, the best-connected crime reporter in the city, and you're so scared you won't even help the police find a fellow journalist who just might still be alive. Who are you scared of, Angus?"

The reporter said nothing, just sat and fumed, staring at the fountain.

"We can protect you, sir," Saint Jacques said. "But if you've got information that could help us, that could help Sophia Luna, we need it. There's a chance she's still alive. If you have any information, anything that can help us find her, we need to know that. We can make sure no harm comes to you."

Angus looked at Saint Jacques like he had just noticed she was there. "If you believe that, you're naive. And I doubt very much that you're naive." He sat back in his chair. "Off the top of my head, I can think of three guys who were promised protection. They were killed while waiting to testify."

A man in a suit walked by, and Angus jerked his head

up to look at him before turning back to Vanier. "Leave me alone, Inspector." He clutched the handles of the walker and rose painfully. "Do me a favour. Leave and don't come back."

Angus didn': wait for a response. He turned slowly with the walker and shuffled off towards the elevator. Saint Jacques stared after him. Vanier got up. He caught up with Angus and started walking backwards in front of the journalist.

"I never liked you, Angus. You're a self-righteous prick, like you're the only one with right on your side. But chew on this. If you do nothing, if you crawl back to your room and close the door, you're already dead. Sure, the body will still be here, but Nick Angus, crime reporter, will be dead and buried." Then he pulled out his card and slipped it into the pocket of Angus's pyjamas, behind a filthy handkerchief.

"Think about it. Go up to your room and know you're dead inside, and all that's left to do is wait for your body to give up. Or call me."

Vanier walked away before Angus could say anything.

The Guatemalan consulate was on the fifth floor of an old commercial building on Saint-François. Once upon a time, when doing business in Montreal meant being close to the port, the building would have housed traders, transport companies, and customs brokers in a hundred small offices. Now the warren was occupied by the kind of businesses that needed some minimal physical presence to prove they existed. The large wooden board in the entrance hallway said it all—a long list of the ABC Limiteds and Acme Internationals that nobody had ever heard of.

The single elevator was out of service, and Vanier and Saint Jacques took the stairs to the third floor, where a plaque on one of a dozen identical doors announced the Consulate of Guatemala, with office hours from 9 a.m. to noon, Monday to Friday.

Saint Jacques knocked on the door and listened for movement inside. Vanier punched numbers into his cellphone and listened while the message asked for his preferred language. Then the recording began listing options: *For information on Guatemala, press one…* Vanier pushed zero to override the list. *I'm sorry. You have made an invalid selection. Goodbye.*

"Fuck." He knocked on the door, a lot harder than Saint Jacques had done. He got the same silence.

"Let's go," said Saint Jacques. "Don't we have a consular section? Maybe someone can give us the home address for the Consul General."

"Some hope," said Vanier.

They started back for the staircase. When Vanier pulled the stairwell door open, a young dark-skinned girl with a coffee in one hand and a stuffed briefcase in the other stumbled forward into the hallway, trying not to spill the coffee.

"Guatemalan?" said Saint Jacques.

She looked up, unsure. "We're police," Saint Jacques continued. "We're looking for someone at the consulate."

The girl hesitated. "Me too. The office is just over here."

"It's closed," said Vanier.

"Ah. Maybe I come back tomorrow." The girl turned to the staircase.

"Why don't you open the door instead?" said Vanier.

"What?"

"With the keys." He nodded to the bunch of keys she was clutching in the same fist that held the briefcase.

She smiled, gave a shrug. "Can I see some identification?"

They pulled out their cards and held them for her inspection.

"You can't be too careful," she said. "I was alone."

"It's all right. Here," Vanier said, handing her his cellphone and relieving her of the coffee. "Call your boss and tell him I need to speak to him urgently."

"My boss? The ambassador? He's in Ottawa."

"No, I mean the Consul. Where's the Consul?"

"That's me."

Vanier almost blushed. "I'm sorry, I …"

"Don't be. People make that mistake all the time." She handed the phone back to Vanier, put the bag on the ground, and opened the door. She went in and turned on the lights.

Saint Jacques followed her in and Vanier leaned forward. "You lead," he told Saint Jacques. "I think I've pissed her off."

"Show her we're not sexist?"

"Something like that."

The room was little more than a wide hallway, with a window at one end and a door at the other. The furniture was lined up along one wall, leaving a pathway from one end to the other. The furniture consisted of two chairs in front of a desk, one chair behind the desk, and two filing cabinets. The consulate was a one-woman operation. The consul dropped her bag and took a seat behind the desk, motioning to the two empty chairs.

"Sorry about that, but I'm nervous about unannounced visitors. I'm on my own here." She pushed two business cards across the desk.

Saint Jacques picked up a card and studied it. "I understand, Ms. Valencia. I would have done the same thing in your position. We'd like to talk to you about a Guatemalan citizen living in Montreal, Sophia Luna."

Valencia stiffened.

"I know Ms. Luna. Well, not personally. We've never met. But I am familiar with her."

"You knew she was in Montreal?"

"Of course. Everyone in the community knows that. She has made quite a name for herself."

"In what way?"

"Let's start with basics. Sophia Luna is a criminal. She is wanted on a number of criminal charges in Guatemala, and is using your refugee process to avoid having to face those charges. She is also doing her best to destabilize the government by spreading malicious lies. She appears to be popular among the more radical members of the opposition movement."

"When you said she's facing criminal charges, could you be specific?"

Valencia got up and went to the second filing cabinet. She came back to the desk with a thick folder. When she sat down again, she pushed her chair back so she could balance the folder on her legs and against the desk. All Vanier and Saint Jacques could see was the manila folder.

"Here we are." She ran her finger down a list. "Fraud, conspiracy, drug trafficking, money laundering, and theft."

"She's been busy," said Vanier.

The Consul gave Vanier a practised diplomatic look: *Exactly what hole did you just crawl out of?*

"The government of Guatemala takes her case very seriously, even if you don't. In fact, the Ambassador has lodged several complaints with your government about the delays in the Canadian system. We want her back in Guatemala to stand trial on these charges."

"She says the charges were fabricated, politically motivated. That was part of her refugee claim," Saint Jacques said.

"And if I am not mistaken, those claims were rejected." Valencia closed the folder and put it on the desk.

"You said that most people in the community knew her," Vanier said. "Do you have the names of any of her contacts?"

"I'm sorry. I knew she was in Montreal, but that's all. As I said, we never met. She never attended any community function I attended. I know she kept in contact with people in Guatemala, but I have no idea who she mixed with in Montreal. Her stories still appear from time to time in certain newspapers, and she sometimes did radio interviews from Montreal. That's all I know."

"Is there anything you can tell us about her that might help us find her?" Saint Jacques asked.

"Is she wanted here, too?"

"She was kidnapped and we're trying to find out who did that."

Valencia raised her eyebrows.

"I'm sorry. I assumed you knew. It was in the newspapers."

"I've been out of town. No. I didn't know. You think it was someone from the community?"

"Did she have enemies in the community?"

"Enemies? Probably. I mean, this woman was a criminal. I would think it more likely her kidnapping was the result of her criminal activities. That would make sense, no?"

Vanier was already on his feet. Saint Jacques kept trying.

"So there's nothing specific you can give us?"

"Nothing at all. I can email you a list of the charges she faced in Guatemala, but that's it."

"That's a thick file for nothing," Vanier said, nodding in the direction of the folder.

She looked up at him, another practised look. "Surely, Inspector, in your job you know how paper accumulates."

She placed her hand on the folder like she was swearing on a bible. "All that's in here is the usual banal stuff. Records from the refugee process, copies of articles she wrote, that sort of thing."

"Could I look through it?" Vanier reached forward.

"Absolutely not, Inspector. This is the property of the Guatemalan government. I couldn't possibly release it to Canadian police officials. But rest assured," she turned to Saint Jacques, "there is nothing in here that would help you with your investigation."

As they were leaving, Valencia called after them. "Inspector, you will keep me informed of the progress of your investigation, won't you?"

Vanier was holding the door for Saint Jacques. He turned and smiled. "Why don't you make that request through official channels?"

Vanier was staring across a desk at Denis Tremblay, a sergeant with the vice squad. Vanier wondered if dressing like a C-list celebrity was part of the job description. Tremblay looked like a Justin Bieber wannabe, his peroxide hair cropped close at the bottom and longer at the top, with an extra-long piece in the front like a backwards ponytail. The ponytail kept falling into his face, and Tremblay never tired of flicking it back into place.

"So, man, if the issue is trafficking, that's me. If it's smuggling, you're in the wrong place. We do trafficking, not smuggling."

"And the difference?" Vanier asked.

"Free will. Consent. People want to be smuggled into Canada and smugglers help them get in. Truth is, most people start out thinking they're dealing with smugglers and things change. Border Services deals with smuggling. All we see in vice is trafficking. It's a fine line. Truth is, most of the cargo never sees it coming."

"Sees what coming?"

"The shit."

"What shit?"

"The shit that happens after they book their ticket. Recruiters. They entice people with job offers. Canada is the dream destination, man. Then when they get here, there's no real job, and they're forced to work off the debt. They have no choice. They owe the money, they're in a strange country illegally, and the traffickers have their passports. They're fucked. Lots of times the gangs threaten the family back home. So you've got someone who has to do whatever the hell they're told to do."

"And there's a lot of this?"

"More than you think."

"And they all go into the sex trade?"

"Some do. I'm only looking at vice, that's my area, but any shit job you can't outsource to India, you can insource. You bring the cheap labour here. Construction, restaurants, cleaning companies, agricultural work. Go into some of these fancy restaurants downtown and half of the staff is from Bangladesh or some other shit hole. They do the work nobody else wants to do, cleaning dishes, peeling vegetables, washing toilets. There's always a team of them, with a team leader. The whole group comes from an employment agency. The team leader keeps them in line, and the restaurant pays the agency and doesn't give a shit if the workers don't get paid. But I don't do that stuff. Like I said, I'm in vice."

Tremblay sat back in his seat and swept strands of hair out of his eyes. He'd given enough. He wanted to listen.

"I'm investigating a kidnapping, a failed refugee claimant lifted off the street. She was a journalist back in Guatemala. We think she was working on a piece about trafficking in the sex trade. Eastern European girls being used as prostitutes in Montreal."

"That's it?"

"Pretty much."

"It's not exactly news. Montreal is the United Nations of prostitution. As if we didn't have enough homegrown, we get them from all over. Yeah, we've got lots of Eastern Europeans."

"Who organizes this stuff?"

"You think I've got the resources to find out? All I'm doing is busting the street-level transactions. I stake out a rub-and-tug for a few hours to understand the traffic. Someone'll go in and see what's on offer. Then we do a raid and arrest everyone on the premises. They get bail, don't show up for trial, and that's the end of it. We keep going."

"Sounds like all you're doing is mopping the floor."

"Hey, man, I could take that as an insult. But you're right. I'm mopping the goddamn floor. I don't have the resources or energy to find where the water is coming from."

"But you said you had jurisdiction over trafficking. Remember? Trafficking is yours and smuggling is the CBSA."

"True. That's true. But there's only so much we can do. I can't launch any international investigation. So, if I find a girl who's been trafficked, I call the RCMP."

"How can you tell?"

"If she's illegal? No papers."

"Then you turn her over to the RCMP?"

Tremblay cracked a smile. Vanier wondered why. "Yeah. The politicians decided sex trafficking was a major problem, so they set up this national task force run out of RCMP Headquarters in Ottawa. And you know how it is with the boys in red: nothing better than a task force. They'll be busy for years, until finally someone tells them to get off their asses and charge some poor fucker. And they'll say they're not ready. The team is headed by some dickhead that helped screw up the Air India investigation. You want his number?"

Vanier knew the Mounties specialized in big investigations that took years to get anywhere, and usually got bogged down at trial. Their greatest value was giving federal politicians a chance to say that something was being done. He took the number anyway.

"So you can't help?"

Tremblay looked at him like it was an accusation.

"Like I said, I'm busy. So are the other guys. Every

month we charge twenty or thirty girls and a couple of boys, and close three or four shops. Sometimes we even throw a couple of johns into the mix. You know what that means for the court appearances and the interviews with the prosecutors? I get maybe twenty, thirty hours of overtime every month." He leaned across the desk. "I am a garbage collector. I collect it and send it for processing. That's it, day after day. Every morning I start again, and there's always more garbage. You think I should be trying to stop prostitution?"

"No. Just shovel shit from one day to the next and wait for retirement."

Vanier got up to leave.

"Fuck you, Inspector. You think you could do better, put in for a transfer."

Vanier shrugged. He understood the frustration. Tremblay might have been ambitious once but the system had worn him down, or maybe he had let it wear him down. People weren't going to stop paying for sex anytime soon. He grabbed the door and turned back to Tremblay. "I think I'll stay where I am."

Tremblay had started writing on a notepad. "Not so fast, Inspector. You want to talk to somebody who has foreign girls, go see these guys." He passed the sheet of paper to Vanier. It said Whole World Entertainment. "They started out importing films. They specialized in really nasty stuff. I heard that they've started making their own stuff here in town."

"What kind of films?"

"The kind that wake you up at night crying. Violent shit."

Passing through the heavy velvet curtains, Vanier's first impression was of an inky black lake with islands of light. The small stage was lit up like Broadway, and each table had its own red lamp. As his eyes adjusted to the darkness, furniture came into view, tables with chairs and velveteen-lined booths along walls lined with dark red textured wallpaper. Vanier glided across the thick carpet like he was wearing slippers. He sat at a table in an alcove where he could see the whole club. Within seconds a young girl approached, balancing a tray on one hand, her other hand decorated with folded notes between her fingers, twenties, tens, and fives. She was wearing more tattoos than clothes and flashed a smile that dazzled white in the black lights, the kind that made some people look like toothpaste advertisements, and others like commercials for out-of-control dandruff.

She bent down close to Vanier's face. "What can I get you?"

"Export."

"And a dance?"

"Maybe later."

She filed it away for reference and turned back to the bar. Mid-stride she looked back over her shoulder and caught him watching. She flashed him another smile.

The club was half empty. Most of the tables were occupied by lonely hearts, guys on their own in the only place pretty women would even look at them. One raucous table had a bunch of college kids out for the night, trying to act cool around more naked flesh than they'd seen in a lifetime. In front of the stage, six Chinese guys were nursing beers, grinning like they had taken a rare night off from their convenience stores and wives, absorbed in the contortions of a naked girl on a throw rug.

Vanier was on his second beer when he saw what he was looking for. She was carrying beers to the Chinese guys. When she bent down to unload the beers, they started to search their pockets. Their body language said they were lousy tippers, counting out change as though it mattered and forcing her to shame them into leaving a little extra. She gave one old guy a deep bow and kissed the top of his head to distract him while she picked coins out of his outstretched hand. It didn't take long for her to notice Vanier.

She made a point of giving him plenty to look at as she slowly approached the table. She was wearing a Little Red Riding Hood costume that did nothing to hide what was available to any wolf. She would have stopped a fire truck.

"If it isn't my favourite policeman," she said.

"Marie-Anne. It's been a long time."

She reached out and ran her fingers through his hair. "So you finally decided to relax. You want a dance?"

"You're still hustling?"

"I'm a dancer. I don't hustle. It's art."

"No dance. Just some questions. Think of it as repaying your debt. Remember?"

"I remember, Inspector. But business is business. I need a reason to hang around, and the only reason that works is that you buy a dance."

"Marie-Anne, I said, it's business."

"Inspector, I can't talk to you if you don't buy a dance. The boss will be all over me."

"How much?"

"For you, thirty. Special price for my favourite policeman. I'll be back."

She put the tray on the table and walked off. He couldn't help watching her leave, and she knew it. She came back with a white pedestal table and pushed Vanier's legs apart with her foot to make room for it. She pushed the table between his legs and climbed up, leaning forward to rest her hands on his shoulders, waiting for the next song to start. Vanier tried not to look at her breasts.

"So what do you want to talk about, Inspector? And did I ever tell you that you get me hot?"

"Eastern Europeans. Eastern European prostitutes."

The music started and she began to dance.

"You mean like Russians? You like Russian girls? I thought you liked me." She moved her hands over her breasts, and down past her hips to let them rest on her thighs, all the while looking him in the eyes.

"Not just Russians. From that part of the world, could be Ukrainians, Belarusians. Do you see Eastern European girls working?"

He was keeping eye contact deliberately, and she was enjoying it. She reached behind and unclasped her skimpy top, pulling it free, her breasts inches from Vanier's mouth.

"I don't see them dancing, if that's what you mean. You know, they're not in clubs like this." She turned away from him and bent low, looking back at him through her legs. She held her ankles and slowly pulled her hands up the back of her legs, still keeping eye contact, still smiling. "They don't have the people skills. Most of them don't even speak English or French."

"But they're working in Montreal?"

She turned to face him again, bending low and moving her hands up from her waist to her breasts, pushing them towards Vanier's mouth. "Oh sure. But only special markets."

"Marie-Anne, can't you just tell me what you know, instead of me having to drag it out of you? What's the story on Eastern European sex workers in Montreal?"

She smiled, held her right breast up and bent to lick the nipple slowly. She stopped licking and leaned in.

"Men are shit, Inspector. You know that. And there are all kinds of shits. The ones that come here, they like beauty, the kind you find in the magazines. The best looking girls in high school, and the kind they could never have, and never will have. But we smile at them, take our clothes off for them, lie to them about how great they are. They own us for a few minutes and then go back to their apartments and jack off on that for however long the memories last."

She closed her hand in a fist and moved it back and forth in a lewd pantomime.

119

"I get it," said Vanier.

"Other guys prefer older women, someone like a friend's mother or some high-school teacher they had a crush on way back when. There are places for that too. There are the races. You like black girls? Asians? Spanish girls? You name it, there are places to find it. Then there are the massage parlours, the swingers' clubs, and the escort services, where you order whatever you want, like a pizza. Down at the bottom, there are the street workers who will give a blow job in an alleyway for whatever they can get."

She stood up, grabbed the waist of her short skirt and pulled it down. All that was left was the tall latex boots that came to mid-thigh, and boy-style red panties that accentuated the curve of her cheeks.

"You don't have to."

"Of course I do, Inspector. The boss will wonder, otherwise."

Her breasts were a teenage fantasy, silicone reinventing evolution. She leaned in until they were an inch from his mouth, whispered in his ear. "Then there are the special needs."

"Special needs?"

"Special needs, Inspector. I told you all men are shit, right?"

"Yeah. I got that."

"The special needs are the real shits. They're the ones who didn't grow up with normal fantasies from an underwear catalogue. Normal doesn't do it for them. They need something forbidden. Men who like children, men who like to hurt women. The scum."

She turned her back to him and bent low, slowly lowering her panties, sliding them carefully over the red boots. She kicked them off, and straightened up and turned to lean both hands on his shoulders.

She leaned in, close to his ear. "They import girls from Eastern Europe for those people. Whatever perverted fantasy you have, save up your money and you can have it delivered. The European women are the specialist import and you can have one of your own, to do whatever you want." She pulled back from Vanier. Stood up, looking him in the eyes.

"Put your clothes on."

She had stopped smiling.

"Any names?"

She leaned forward. "No names. It's just what I hear. What we girls talk about now and then. You want to know more, why don't you talk to that woman that runs Protect, Diana Prince. She should be able to tell you more. If she talks to you, that is. I hear she doesn't like police that much."

"Thanks, Marie-Anne."

"You want another drink? Another dance?" She was playing with her breasts as she talked. "Maybe I could do you a special price, Inspector. You make me very hot."

Vanier grinned. "No thanks." The music had stopped. There was a girl wearing nothing but thigh-high red latex boots standing on a pedestal between his legs, fondling

121

her breasts.

That's when the camera flash went off.

"Shit," said Vanier, jumping to his feet. The camera-man was out the door before Vanier could reach him. Vanier was on the street just in time to see the man pulling the passenger door closed on a red Toyota as it pulled out into traffic.

TEN

It had been a long night. At two o'clock, Katya thought it was over, until her door burst open and Pavlov stumbled in. He had been drinking. Now he was drunk, slurring his words. But he didn't need words to tell her what he wanted. He undid his pants and stood in front of her. She reached forward to fondle him, but no matter how hard she tried, it didn't work. Pavlov swore, blamed her for his softness. He pulled his pants back on, and she lay back on the bed. He slipped his belt off and wound it around his hand. As it lashed again and again across her breasts, Katya grunted, biting her lip. She knew better than to cry out. He stopped with the belt, pulled her up to a sitting position with a fistful of hair, and delivered a hard punch to the side of her head, where the bruising wouldn't show too much. He let go of her and she dropped back onto the bed. He punched her once more, in her stomach, before staggering out the door. He pulled the door closed behind him. Through the haze of pain, Katya listened for the key in the lock. She heard nothing.

It takes time for hope to die, but its death can be liberating. Hope keeps us going in the bleakest of times, defying logic and evidence. It stops you from lying down and waiting for your heart to stop beating. When you've lost hope, you're free.

Katya had known for weeks there was no way out, that she would never be allowed to walk away. She was going to be used until she lost her value and that would be the end of it. She had always thought about escape, but she knew it was stupid. They would catch her before she even had a chance to get out the window, and even if she did get out the window, she would fall five floors to the ground and die, or worse still, she would fall and only get injured. And they would bring her back.

She had gone through any number of scenarios, and none had a happy ending. In the end, escape meant nothing. She was illegal in Canada. She knew no one, and would be deported. If she stayed where she was, she was going to die, and if she escaped, the best that could happen was that she would be sent back to Ukraine, and they would find her and kill her. Staying or leaving, it was all the same. If death was inevitable, nothing mattered.

When Pavlov left, she knew at once that he had forgotten to lock the door. She made a decision. The fire escape in the hallway was padlocked, but there was a window about three metres past the fire exit that wasn't screwed shut. She had seen it every time she walked by. She was sure it would open.

She waited on the bed for two hours, listening intently for the slightest sound. When she was convinced that everyone was asleep, she got up and checked the door. She went back to the bed and reached under the mattress. She had found her passport three weeks ago in a drawer and taken it back. No one had noticed it was gone. She slipped it into her bra and turned back to the door. It opened soundlessly. She slipped out into the dark hallway, stopped and listened again. Nothing but four-in-the-morning silence, a silence that made her breathing sound loud.

She moved slowly down the hallway, sticking close to the wall, past the emergency exit, until she was in front of the casement window. It was chest-high and looked out over the parking lot five floors down. She reached up and pulled at the latch that held the two panes together. It opened with a soft click. It sounded like a sigh of relief. The two panes swung open. Katya leaned out quickly to grab them before they swung all the way out and hit the wall. One at a time, she let each one rest against the wall as she breathed in the night air, looking down to the asphalt—the only thing that would break her fall.

Just below the window was a four-inch ledge that wound around the building. If she could hang onto it for about three metres, she could make it to the fire escape. She kicked off her shoes and threw them out the window, listening for the sound of them hitting the ground below. It took longer than she expected. Then she struggled up into the window frame and sat astride the opening. She leaned out and rested her foot on the ledge, using the support to pull her other leg out of the window. With both feet balancing on the ledge and her hands clutching the window frame, she shifted her weight and brought her right hand down to the ledge. Then she took her right foot off the ledge, letting it hang in the air. She braced herself and took her left foot off the ledge, hanging with one hand on the window and the other on the ledge. She braced again and let go of the window frame. She was hanging by one hand. Pain shot through her fingers and right arm until she managed to grab hold of the ledge with her left hand. She took a deep breath and started to move towards the fire escape, releasing one hand, moving it forward, then grasping again, doing the same with the other hand. It felt like hours, but in only a few minutes she was standing on the fire escape.

She stood there for a moment and contemplated the fire escape. Every shuffle made noise, no matter how careful she was. She started walking down. About ten feet above the parking lot, the last segment of the staircase jutted out horizontally, far above the ground. It was weighted, the bottom of the staircase high up in the air so that it couldn't be accessed from the parking lot. You had to stand on it to make it drop.

She put her foot on the first rung and felt her weight counterbalancing the staircase like a see-saw. As she inched out along the staircase, it began to descend slowly to the parking lot. When she was halfway down, an electrical contact was broken, and an alarm high up on the wall of the building shredded the silence with an electronic siren. The staircase was suddenly ablaze in light. She lurched forward, forcing the staircase down to the asphalt with a loud clash. When she stepped off the bottom rung, the counterbalance snapped the last section of the staircase back into the air with a loud crash of steel on steel.

Katya looked around for her shoes, grabbed them and started running barefooted away from the noise and light. She didn't know where she was going, just that she had to put distance between the building and herself. She hadn't thought any further than getting away from the building, and now she had no idea what to do other than run as far as she could. She turned right out of the parking lot and made some quick choices, staying away from well-lit areas, from streets with traffic. Keep to the shadows. Hide from everyone.

After half an hour, she realized she was travelling in a big circle, passing the same places time after time. She kept running.

The sun was already coming up and lights were turning on in the houses she passed. When she caught a glimpse of a man in a window scratching himself awake, she knew she had to find somewhere to hide. She was walking barefooted in a skimpy red dress that screamed hooker.

She ran down an alley lined on both sides with garden sheds and small fences. She started trying the doors on the sheds. The sixth door opened with a creaking noise, and she slipped inside, closing it quickly behind her. She waited for her eyes to adjust to the gloom. One wall was lined with wide shelves. The floor beneath the lowest shelf was empty except for two plastic bags of soil. She got down on her hands and knees, pushed the bags aside to make space, and crawled under the shelf, pulling the bags back into place after her.

After fifteen minutes she began to relax. In thirty, she was asleep.

ELEVEN

Vanier's first stop was at the local convenience store for a coffee. He sipped the coffee while leafing through a copy of the *Journal de Montréal* under the hand-scrawled *Vous lisez, vous achetez*!! sign. The photograph from the strip club was relegated to page six, and given only a quarter of a page with a small caption, *On ne Peut pas Dérober la Vérité*. He closed the paper without buying a copy. If his photo had only made it to page six, it wasn't a big deal. He just hoped Anjili didn't see it.

The squad room was quiet; people had their heads down in concentration, or were staring, fully absorbed, at their computer screens. They were as obvious as a classroom full of fourteen-year-olds waiting for a substitute teacher to fall into some juvenile trap.

Someone had cut out the *Journal de Montréal* story and pinned it to the notice board. Vanier made a show of stopping to read. He leaned forward to get a better look at the picture, felt a dozen eyes on his back. "Not the best likeness," he mumbled, turning away.

He carried his coffee over to his desk and sat down. "It was work. I was interviewing a source."

"Next time, take me with you," Laurent said.

Vanier's phone rang. He put it to his ear. "Vanier."

"Inspector Vanier. It's Madame Cantin."

The police chief's assistant, though assistant was the wrong word. Handler, keeper, watchdog, protector—all better described what she did. "Good morning, Madame Cantin. What can I do for you?"

"The Chief would like to see you, Inspector. About an article in today's paper." Even though she was only booking an appointment, her voice still managed to convey deep personal disapproval.

"Okay. I'm coming up."

"No. Not immediately. Chief Bédard is busy all morning. He asked if you could be available at two o'clock."

Vanier accepted. If he couldn't figure out a way to avoid the two o'clock, he'd be losing his touch, and a meeting put off with the Chief was always a problem avoided. His phone rang again. This time his shoulders sagged. He pushed connect. "Anjili. I can explain."

"Luc, not glad to hear from me?" Her voice was bubbly. She was playing with him.

"Of course I am. I was surprised, that's all."

"So what can you explain?"

"The photo. I was working." His voice was strained. He didn't want to have to explain.

She seemed to sense his anxiety. "Luc, you don't let

me have any fun."

"Fun?"

"I was going to toy with you. Make you squirm a little. How often do I get a chance like this? My man, caught in *flagrante delicto*. Think of the leverage."

Vanier slumped in his chair. "Anjili. I …"

"Luc. I'm the one who should be sorry. And I am. Sylvie Saint Jacques called this morning. She told me what you were doing. I thought I could have some fun winding you up. That's all."

"Okay. But I was worried."

"Don't be. We still on for the picnic?"

"Absolutely. Wouldn't miss it."

"Love you, Mr. V."

Vanier put the phone down. The day was turning out much better that he could have hoped. He looked over to Saint Jacques and mouthed a thank you.

TWELVE

Katya woke up after a few hours of deep sleep. She couldn't remember where she was. She lay still and listened intently, trying to make sense of the noises that filtered through the wooden slats of the shed: cars passing, bicycles, kids shouting and laughing—sounds she hadn't heard in months. A scuffling noise on the other side of the wooden wall made her freeze. She listened and heard water playing against the wall, more scuffling. When the smell hit her she realized it was a dog relieving itself.

The darkness of the shed was broken by razor-thin slices of light that pierced the cracks between the wooden slats, turning dust into tiny beads of light. There was enough light to make out some of the contents of the shed: tools hanging on the wall, plastic bags of soil and compost, a manual lawn mower with blades covered in dried grass, columns of old paint cans, the usual collection of buckets that gardeners accumulate. Everything was covered in a thick coat of dust. That made her feel more secure. If the shed wasn't used that much, maybe she would be safe for a while.

She convinced herself that her sleeping spot was invisible to anyone standing up inside the shed. To see her, you would have to stoop down and look under the bottom shelf. She felt safe. She pulled her arm up under her head, closed her eyes, and fell asleep again.

THIRTEEN

Diana Prince, the director of Protect, was like a Goth granny. Her hair should have been grey with age, but it was a fierce metallic red, and almost all the visible skin from her neck down was covered in fading tattoos, some professional, others looking like they'd been made by a short-sighted drunk with a toothpick.

When Saint Jacques called, Prince had refused to meet them at the organization's offices. They had negotiated a meeting at Prince's favourite restaurant, a co-op on Ontario Street that specialized in fair-trade organic ancient grains, hand-milled by peasants with stone tools. The dress code seemed to be anything handwoven by poor people. Vanier had eaten lunch there a few times. He liked the food and the beer, but had trouble with the attitude: more self-righteousness per square foot than a born-again Christian convention.

Vanier and Saint Jacques were doing their best to lighten the mood, but Prince was intense. She had spent over thirty years fighting for the rights of sex workers. More often than not, that meant fighting the police. Now two of the enemy were sitting across from her, wanting her help.

"So what is it? Not enough homegrown girls to abuse, now you want to go after the weakest of them all? Is that it? A new efficiency measure, two arrests for the price of one? Whores and illegals?"

Vanier was trying to look non-threatening, facing away from her with his legs tightly crossed, both his arms hanging down by his side. He looked like a simple guy who had been waiting for a bus for hours and was resigned to waiting a few hours more. It wasn't working on Prince. The cop presence was still there. Even Saint Jacques was a cop first, and a woman when she got a chance. Their training focused on being imposing, on projecting an intimidating image. Nobody got trained on how to put people at ease. They were both improvising, though Saint Jacques was better at it than Vanier.

"We're investigating a woman's kidnapping and we think it involves people trafficking from Eastern Europe," Vanier said. "The woman who was kidnapped was a journalist. She was working on a story about the issue."

"Why should I help you? It's always the same. You go after the women, and the organizers are left alone. It's the women who always get shafted. It's what you guys do, harass the women and say you're fighting prostitution. That's bullshit."

"They say prostitution is a victimless crime," Vanier

said. "You believe that?"

She glared at him. "Do I look stupid? It's never a victimless crime. The victims are the girls, or the boys for that matter, the commodity. The johns sure aren't victims. It's the way the system works. It's like banning pork and punishing pigs when someone eats a sausage."

"Good one," said Vanier, smiling. "But I'm after the butcher."

Prince thought for a moment. "Ask some questions and we'll see what happens. No guarantees."

"Are there many Eastern European prostitutes in Montreal?" said Vanier.

"Define many." She almost cracked a smile.

"Come on. Give me a break." He turned to face her.

"One hundred, maybe two. It's hard to tell. All I've got to go on is what I hear. Very few of them come to me for help."

"Some have? Can you give me names?"

She leaned forward in her chair. "Put that aside for the moment. I may be able to ask someone to call you. It depends."

"On what?"

"The rest of the interview. Don't worry. You're doing all right up to now."

"Thanks." Vanier said. He didn't feel it. "What's the pipeline for getting these girls into the country?"

"No idea. I doubt even the girls know. The girls get moved. They don't know where, when, or by whom."

"Who runs the trade?"

"It used to be the Hells. Now it's the Russians."

"Names?"

"Jesus Christ. Don't you guys know anything?" She leaned back in her chair, looked at Saint Jacques. "You see the problem? You guys bust massage parlours, arrest six girls and maybe the guy who mops the floor. Maybe even a john if he talks back, or doesn't get his pants on fast enough. Then you go on TV and say what a great job you're doing fighting prostitution. The parlour's back in business the next week with six new girls and a new broom. Or maybe one of the girls has to mop the floor when she's not jerking a john. A policy like that can only be stupid, or deliberate. It would be nice to believe it's just stupidity."

Vanier said nothing, accepting the whipping.

Prince took a deep breath, leaned forward. "To answer your question, I don't know. Only suspicions. Got it? I think the biggest pimp is a bitch called Kedrov."

Saint Jacques was writing. "How do you spell that?"

Prince's shoulders sagged. "I can't believe you don't know this." She spelled out the name, Oksana Kedrov. "She's a very dangerous and violent woman. Worse than a lot of men, and that's saying a lot."

"These girls. Where do they work?" Vanier asked.

"Some are in the massage parlours. Some are escorts. They get delivered to your door by some heavy. You fuck her, give her a hundred dollars, and the heavy picks her up when you're finished. He takes the hundred dollars and delivers her to the next job. Those are the lucky ones, the ones that can speak some English or French."

"The others are on the street?"

She rolled her eyes at the question. "Girls on the street have to hustle, they have to negotiate. You need language skills for that. No, the ones who don't speak the language get the rough trade, where talking isn't required."

"And this is what Kedrov does?"

"From what I hear, she has a thriving business catering to the rough trade, and nobody messes with her."

Saint Jacques was still writing. Prince looked Vanier in the eye. "Wouldn't it be good if I didn't have to tell you who the bad guys are? If you knew that yourselves?"

Vanier treated the question as rhetorical. "Where could we find Madame Kedrov?

"No idea. I hear her name from time to time, but she has nothing to do with me."

They got up to leave. "If you can convince someone to talk to me, or to my partner, have them call."

They both dropped their cards on the table. Prince didn't move.

"She's angry," Saint Jacques said when they were in the parking lot.

Vanier thought back to the conversation. "She has good reason to be. See if you can get an address for Kedrov."

FOURTEEN

Laurent was sitting across the desk from Vanier, shuffling papers. "So, boss, we started with driver's licences. In the whole of Montreal there are only three Kedrovs. All of them guys. First one's an eighty-two-year-old living in a seniors' residence in Longueuil."

"He's still got a licence?"

"Seem so. Some eighty-year-olds still have it."

Vanier briefly wondered what he'd be like at eighty, and quickly put it out of his mind. "The others?"

"A guy living in a condo tower downtown, twenty-nine, and a fifty-year-old guy in Rosemont. The fifty-year-old in Rosemont is Oscar, a human resources manager in an insurance company. Been there for 25 years. He owns his own house and pays his taxes on time. Looks clean."

"And the other guy?"

"That's where things get interesting. His name's Pavlov, and he's living in a condo that's registered to a numbered company. He's one of the directors, and an Oksana Kedrov is the other. The numbered company is owned by a company called Golden K. So I searched the corporate database for all Quebec and Canadian companies owned by Golden K, and there are a dozen or so. They all have the same registered office, an accountant's office on Décarie Boulevard. He's probably just keeping the books for them."

"So, apart from the condo, there's no location?"

"Wait for it, chief. One of the companies is called Whole Earth Productions. Whole Earth Productions got a city grant last year to convert some space in Saint-Henri into a film production studio. We've got an address for the studio."

"I always said you were a genius, Laurent."

Whole Earth's office was in an old industrial building on Lacasse, its off-white paint peeling in large curls except where the walls were covered in graffiti tags. A sign hung over the main door announcing lofts and studio space for artists. The ground floor was unoccupied, but the listing at the door showed Whole Earth Productions on the fourth and fifth floors. The door was locked, so Vanier pushed the buzzer and waited.

The box squawked. "Yeah?"

Vanier leaned closer. "We're here to see Oksana. Oksana Kedrov."

"She ain't here. You have to come back." The box went dead.

Vanier pushed the button again

The box squawked again. "I said she ain't here. No visitors without an appointment. So call back and make an appointment."

"Excuse me."

Vanier and Saint Jacques turned around. The voice came from a hipster wheeling an old bicycle. Saint Jacques stood back to give him room and watched as he punched numbers into the panel, waited for the click and pulled the door open. He went through with his bike, and Vanier held the door for Saint Jacques and followed her in. All three got into the elevator. The hipster pushed for the second floor. The sign in the elevator showed Whole Earth Productions on the fourth and fifth floors, but a small sign said *Card Access Only* for the fifth floor. Vanier pushed the button anyway and a tiny light on the panel glowed red. He pushed four.

Two men were waiting for them when they stepped out of the elevator. The first guy would have stood out in any crowd, with a shaved head the size of a pumpkin. He dwarfed the guy next to him, who looked like a skinny kid dressed up for visiting relatives, in a blue checked shirt, cardigan and tight jeans. They were standing in front of a door with a small Whole Earth sign.

Vanier flashed his badge. Before he could say anything the kid spoke. "Like I said, officers. Mrs. Kedrov's not here."

"So who's in charge?"

"Mrs. Kedrov."

"We'll go in and wait for her."

141

"You've got a warrant?"

"No warrant. Just a social call."

While Vanier was talking to the kid, Saint Jacques wandered off towards the fire exit. The muscle watched her, torn between staying next to the kid and following Saint Jacques. He decided to follow Saint Jacques. Vanier advanced on the kid, backing him against the wall. He reached down, grabbed his crotch and squeezed. The kid yelled and his face screwed up in pain. Pumpkin-head turned and started back down the corridor.

"Tell your friend to stay where he is," Vanier said.

There was a split second hesitation and Vanier squeezed again, harder. The kid squealed. "Olag. Don't move."

With his free hand, Vanier reached into his jacket pocket and pulled out a business card. He folded it and stuck it into the kid's open mouth, sliding it into the gap between his front teeth.

"You tell Mrs. Kedrov to call me, and soon. You understand?"

The kid nodded and Vanier let go. He turned to Saint Jacques. "Let's go."

Olag walked back down the hallway, put his hand on the kid's shoulder. The kid shrugged it away. They both watched the doors close on Vanier and Saint Jacques.

"There was a bolt on the fire exit door," Saint Jacques said when they were in the elevator. "It was locked. You'd need a key to open the door. That's a fire code violation, isn't it?"

"A serious one. Someone should report it."

Vanier and Anjili were sitting on the grass in the Parc Maisonneuve. They had walked about twenty minutes from the entrance into the park. Vanier had brought Portuguese grilled chicken, goat cheese, and an ice-cold bottle of Vino Verde. Anjili had brought the best baguettes Vanier had tasted in years, three kinds of salad, and a Tupperware of strawberries and sliced peaches.

It was one of those warm summer evenings made for evening picnics. While they were eating, scattered groups of families and couples gradually left, leaving them alone, sprawled out on their blanket under a tree, overlooking a gentle slope down to an open green space.

Anjili was wearing a white cotton dress tapered at the waist, contrasting sharply with her tan. Vanier had done his best to dress the part too, with a pair of khaki pants he hadn't worn in years and a casual shirt over a vintage T-shirt.

She had kicked off her sandals as soon as they arrived, and Vanier followed suit, taking off his shoes and socks. Now they were lying at right angles to each other, Anjili's head resting on Vanier's stomach. It had been hot all day, and the warmth from the ground seemed to rise up and envelop them.

"There isn't a cloud in the sky," said Vanier. "Reminds me of when I was a kid. You know what it was like back then, when days lasted forever? Remember when summer was a lifetime? You grow up and you don't feel that anymore. Every day is short as a heartbeat."

"Hmmn."

"I'm glad we came."

Vanier reached down and ran his fingers through her hair. "My dad was stationed at Trenton one summer. I had a buddy on the base. We must've been nine or ten years old. Before girls, that was, well before girls." Vanier drifted off into memory. "Those were the days."

She lifted her head and let it drop back on his stomach.

He grunted. "Outside the base there was a small forest with a gully running through it. There was this huge tree, maybe an oak."

"Like you would know, Luc."

"I know some trees. And I think this one was an oak. It was huge. You know how the branches on the best climbing trees always start too high up for kids?"

"Maybe. I think."

"It's impossible to start climbing them. You can't reach the first branch. But you can see that if you could just get to the first branch, the rest would be easy. But you can only stand at the bottom and imagine what it would be like to climb to the highest branches. Well, this tree was growing on the side of the gully, so you could get onto the first branch with a short jump. Every day, Frank— that was my buddy's name—Frank and I used to go there. We spent hours in the tree. You could get really high up and see for miles."

He traced his fingers through her hair in long slow strokes.

"When I think of Trenton, that tree is the first thing that comes to mind. And it's the sense of time that I remember. We would go off in the morning and spend forever just messing around, making up stories. Sometimes the tree was a fort, sometimes a ship, sometimes a spaceship. And when we finished, we'd walk back to the base and it was eleven o'clock, a lifetime to lunchtime. Is there a name for that? That different sense of time?"

"I don't know. But I think it happens to all kids. Sometimes to adults too, like when I'm with you, Luc, sometimes ten minutes feels like a couple of hours." She laughed.

"Hey."

"No, seriously," she said. "There are moments when my awareness seems to be at a different level. Like everything is slow. I can hear everything. Colours are brighter. Like now."

He shifted a little to get a better view of her face. Her eyes were closed, and a small smile played on her lips. He traced the outline of her jaw with his finger, drew his finger across her lips. She opened her lips slightly to touch his finger with her tongue, and when it lingered on her lips, she parted them, until her teeth could reach up and gently bite.

His hand moved slowly down and slid under the light cotton, tracing the outline of her bra, floating over her breasts, cupping them through the sheer fabric and feeling them in his hand, squeezing gently, feeling the rising shape of her nipples under the rasp of lace beneath his palm.

She made low sounds of approval, letting his hand

roam. After a while she sat up and reached behind her back to pull the zipper of her dress. "Can you help me?

He said nothing. Undid the clasp. She pulled her arms through the straps to remove her bra without removing her dress.

"That's better," she said, resting her head back on his stomach. Vanier moistened his fingers and slipped his hand in again, caressing each of her naked breasts, drawing circles around her nipples, making sweeping touches until the nipples rose to meet his fingertips.

Anjili reached down under her dress. He watched as her hand traced the outline of her panties and then squeezed her mound through the fabric. She slipped her hand inside and played her fingers up and down. She spread her legs slightly, bending her knee and bringing one foot up closer to her body. He watched her fingers explore, spreading moisture over her lips, stopping every now and then to sink in and then pull out. She brought her hand up to Vanier's mouth, put two fingers inside and felt his tongue. Vanier sucked on her fingers until she pulled them back.

He brought his own fingers up to his mouth and moistened them, rubbing the wetness on her hard nipples, taking one nipple between his fingers and gently squeezing, pulling and releasing. When his fingers got dry, he wet them again, and resumed playing with her nipples.

Anjili was groaning now, a deeply felt groan of pleasure. They were alone and there was no hurry. She had all the time in the world. Her breathing was deeper and louder, mixed with moans and half-words. Vanier helped her on the way, rubbing wet fingers over her nipples, pulling gently at them, squeezing and releasing them as she climbed. He could tell when she was near, but he couldn't tell how close, so he followed her, each peak a stepping stone to the next, until finally she lost control, her fingers moving frantically in her panties and then the explosion deep within her, and the release of air, of tension and mumbled words all mixed up.

She lay still on the blanket.

He had almost fallen asleep when he felt her stir, rolling onto her side, her head still resting on his stomach. She reached for his belt and had it open in seconds. She needed two hands for the button on his pants, and slid the zipper down. She had him raise his hips slightly so she could pull his pants out of the way, just a few inches down from his waist. Then she reached and guided him into her mouth. Now it was Vanier's turn to groan. She held him and turned to smile up at him, another one of those moments when time stood still.

She was taking her time, enjoying the feeling of having his complete attention, knowing that all he was thinking about was what she was doing to him. When she stopped it was to move herself up. She straddled him, pushed her panties aside and took him inside her. She leaned forward and whispered, "I don't think I'll be able to come again. So this one's for you. All yours. Just enjoy yourself."

He did. He lay on his back with Anjili slowly moving on top of him. She looked fully clothed from the outside but he could make out the shape of her breasts moving under her dress, could feel her skin bouncing on his thighs. They stayed like that for several minutes, hardly moving, skin on skin. He watched her face, eyes closed as she concentrated on moving back and forth on top of him, as if nothing else mattered. He motioned for her to roll over. He reached up under her dress and grabbed her, pulling her closer with every stroke until he couldn't hold back.

She reached around him and pulled him in, then started whispering in his ear. It didn't take long. Vanier felt like screaming, but managed to keep it to a low moan.

After, they lay on the blanket. It was as if they were the only ones in the park, the only ones for miles around. For the first time in days, Vanier felt a tremendous peace.

FIFTEEN

Vanier's phone rang. He didn't recognize the number.

"You are looking for me, Mr. Vanier." A woman's voice, heavily accented. A smoker. Vanier took a chance.

"Oksana Kedrov herself. Yeah, I want to talk to you."

"I'll be at my condo for the next three hours. Why don't you come by? And bring your pretty assistant."

The line disconnected before he could say anything. He considered bringing Laurent, but he was busy. Instead, it was Saint Jacques leading the way up the carpeted hallway to Kedrov's apartment.

The door opened before they walked up, and a burly guy who could have been Olag's brother nodded in the direction they should go. Kedrov was sitting at a glass and chrome table working on a laptop. She had short hair, dyed blonde, and a body that was straining to escape through every seam in her pantsuit. A cigarette was burning in an ashtray that overflowed with lipstick-stained butts. The woman's heavy perfume mixed with the cigarette smoke to make the place smell like a 1950s broth-el. She didn't look up as they crossed the deep carpet.

The condo was like all the condos Vanier had seen recently. He could guess the layout. The view was the best thing it had going for it, and everything went downhill from there, unless you wanted your home to look like a quickly built three-star hotel.

Vanier and Saint Jacques sat down at the table. Kedrov still didn't look up.

"You like it here?" said Vanier.

Kedrov took her eyes from the screen, glanced at Vanier for a second, and turned to Saint Jacques. "I love Canada."

"I mean this place," Vanier said.

"It's a place to stay." She was still talking to Saint Jacques. "But you didn't come here to ask about my living arrangements."

"Just wondering. I'm in the market."

"It's not for sale." At last she turned to Vanier. "What you want?"

"Nick Angus. Ring a bell?"

"You haven't introduced us," said Kedrov.

"Detective Sergeant Saint Jacques, Oksana Kedrov."

Kedrov turned to Saint Jacques again. "And you like working with Detective, ah … Vanier?"

"Answer the question," Vanier said.

"No. I don't know any Nick Angus. Should I?"

"He works for *The Gazette*. He was writing a story about your business."

She turned to face Vanier. "Then he should have asked for an interview. Very poor journalism. It shows what a rag *The Gazette* is. I read *Le Monde*."

"What about Sophia Luna?"

"Who is she?"

"Another journalist. She was working on the same story."

"And who says they were working on a story about my business?"

"One was badly beaten. The other kidnapped. Do you know anything about that?

She fixed him with a stare. "Why should I? I am a movie producer. Assaulting and kidnapping journalists is not good for people in my business. In the long term, that is. It makes for bad publicity. These journalists should have called me for an interview. Publicity would benefit me. My movies are very successful. They appeal to a discerning clientele."

"Prostitution? Human trafficking? Not the kind of business you want publicity for."

She turned back to Saint Jacques. "Rumours. I'm sure you know how it is. As soon as a woman is successful, the men tried to find fault. If there were any serious evidence of this, I would be charged, no?" She smiled.

Saint Jacques said nothing.

Kedrov turned back to Vanier, the smile gone. "If this is what you wanted to speak about, you're wasting your time. More importantly, you are wasting my time." She pushed a business card across the table to Saint Jacques.

"If you ever want to appear in one of my movies, give me a call. A woman like you, so beautiful. We could make a wonderful movie. It would capture you in your prime, and you would have that image forever."

Saint Jacques finally spoke. "And you would hire a police officer?"

"Ah. First we would have to establish trust. Trust that I would not hurt you and that you would not hurt me."

"Trust?"

"I know. It is such an elusive thing. We would have to get to know each other's weaknesses, so neither is tempted to hurt the other."

"Or they will get hurt back?"

"You see. You understand."

Saint Jacques stood up. "No thanks."

"I'll think about it," said Vanier.

Kedrov ignored him and began typing on her laptop. The bouncer reappeared to show them out.

FOURTEEN

When Katya woke again she was hungry and thirsty. The inside of the shed was bright with blades of light streaming through the slats in the wood, so she continued to lie in the dust under the shelf, and listened to the noise of people outside: summer noises, the shrieks and laughter of children playing, creaking pedals propelling rubber wheels on asphalt, dogs barking, and the footfalls of the occasional jogger.

Everything seemed normal. She could smell the smoke from outdoor cooking and imagined people sitting on the balconies and in the gardens she had seen earlier. Her bladder was bursting, but she was too afraid to move. She waited another two hours, until she couldn't wait any longer. She crawled out of her hiding place, stiff and sore, and stood up. Even in the half-light of the shed she could see she was filthy, covered in dirt. She looked around for something to empty her bladder into and saw a bucket in a corner. She pulled her panties down to her knees and squatted over it. It sounded like she had turned on the garden hose. When she finished, she pushed the bucket further back into the corner, crawled back under the shelf and waited. She noticed how hot it was in the confined space, the air close and thick, the musty smell of dust giving way to her own odour of day-old sex and sweat.

Hours later, when the outside noises had subsided except the occasional passing car, she crawled out again. She found a large pair of rubber boots and put them on. She knew she looked terrible, ridiculous even, in a whorehouse-red dress and oversized rubber boots, covered in dirt. She needed to wash and find something to wear.

She opened the shed door a crack and peered out into the night. The alley was deserted. In a garden a few houses up, someone had left a full line of washing and she headed for it. She had picked out what she wanted even before she got to the clothesline. She pulled jeans, a T-shirt and a flannel shirt off the line, grabbed a pair of men's y-front underwear and white socks, and ran back to the shed. The jeans were too big, but she used garden string for a belt and rolled up the pant legs. The flannel shirt over the T-shirt looked like a conscious fashion choice, and you would hardly notice the rubber boots under the jeans. She rolled the hooker dress into a ball and threw it under the shelf. In her new clothes she felt safe enough to think about food. She had no money, and knew her best chance would be the same as in every city in the world—a dumpster behind a fast-food restaurant.

Walking away from the shed she felt adrift. It was the

only anchor she had, and she didn't want to lose it. She walked in careful but expanding circles around the block, turning right, then right again, then right again until she was back at the alley. When she completed the first tour and arrived back at the shed, she started out in the opposite direction, all the while seeking out landmarks that would tell her where she was in relation to the shed. She wasn't tired now, but she was starving.

After about an hour she saw a giant cheeseburger over a storefront. The restaurant was closed, and she peered through the darkened window. It looked the same as a hamburger restaurant she used to go to in Poltava, thick plastic tables and chairs fixed to a steel beam bolted to the floor. At the back, above the counter, there was a picture menu, which would be lit up when the place was open. She looked up and down the street; it was deserted. She walked around to the back. Two rusting steel dumpsters guarded either side of the back door. She pushed up the lid of the first and looked in at a pile of black garbage bags. Resting the lid on her head, she grabbed the first bag she could reach and pulled it out. Then she got down on the ground and ripped it open. The greasy smell made her mouth water. Almost every cardboard container had some leftover fries and she began stuffing them in her mouth. They were cold, salty, and loaded with grease, but hunger made them taste good. Now and then she'd find a half-eaten burger. She ate the first three bread and all, and then started picking the good parts out, breaking off the obvious bite marks, eating pieces of cold hamburger and fried chicken patties. She worked through the bag fever-ishly and finished in ten minutes.

She searched again in the bag and collected two fistfuls of paper napkins, used and unused, and then heaved the torn bag back into the dumpster. She stood up; the smell of grease from her hands was beginning to sicken her and the food was lying heavily in her stomach. She pulled one of the dumpsters out from the wall and backed into the emp-ty space. She pulled down her pants, squatted and emp-tied her bowels, using the paper napkins to wipe herself.

She went back out to the street and started wandering again, always keeping a sense of where the alley was.

The salty food had given her a fierce thirst, but it took her two hours before she found somewhere to drink, a coiled hose in a fenced-in garden. She climbed over the fence, turned on the faucet and put her mouth down to drink the cold water. After she had finished drinking, she leaned forward and aimed the water through her hair, us-ing her free hand to wash her head and face and neck. It cooled her off, but she wasn't any cleaner. Without soap she was just moving the dirt around. When she reached to turn off the tap she caught sight of her hands, grimy and streaked black with dirt. She stared at them for a few moments, turning them over as though to be certain they were hers. She hooked the hose over the tap and plunged her hands into the water, rubbing them back and forth, using her nails to scrape at the skin. When she was satis-fied, she put her head under the flow and scratched and rubbed at her scalp until she felt she was clean. Then she did the same to her face, splashing it with the cold water, rubbing, and splashing again.

When she had finished, she felt like someone who had crossed a river, emerging exhausted on the other side. She felt ready to continue.

FIFTEEN

Vanier was strap-hanging on an articulated bus that had left the Guy Concordia metro station at 11:47 a.m. Camara had called him at ten to tell him exactly what bus to take. The bus was standing room only. Vanier knew the route vaguely, but he had studied it again while waiting for the 11:47. The 165 followed Côte-des-Neiges almost the entire way, up the side of the mountain, past the Montreal General where Bélair had been killed. Then it swept along the ridge close to Westmount, before descending through a thick mix of neighbourhoods that covered the northern flank of the mountain. After passing through low-rent immigrant areas at the north end of Côte-des-Neiges, the bus crossed Jean-Talon and entered the leafy Town of Mount Royal, a moneyed suburban enclave of large homes on large lots. Jean-Talon was a border, as effective as a barbed wire fence, and Vanier was sure Camara would make contact before they reached Jean-Talon.

As they were stopped outside the Montreal General,

Vanier watched an old woman pull herself into the bus with one arm while the other dragged a wheelie bag filled with groceries. She bumped her way through the crowd and ended up next to him, glaring up and down at the people occupying seats. Nobody seemed to notice her, or care.

In front of Vanier, a kid was sitting with his back to the window, absorbed in a video game, listening to the sound through ear buds. Vanier reached for the wire and yanked out an ear-bud. The kid glowered up at him. Vanier leaned down into his face, close enough to let the kid know what he'd had for breakfast.

"Get up and give the old lady your seat, asshole."

The kid looked at the woman and shrugged, then he looked back at Vanier and decided it was wiser to stand. The woman sat down without making eye contact with either of them, pulled her basket close to her knees, and stared ahead. The kid was trying to manoeuvre past Vanier, to move back down the bus, but Vanier blocked his way and pulled the cord to ring the bell. "This is your stop."

"It's not my stop."

"It is now. Maybe you'll find your manners out there."

The kid knew when he was beaten, and got off the bus. Vanier watched and waited for the finger. He got it as the bus pulled away. He hadn't noticed Camara getting on, and only saw him as he was negotiating his way through the thicket of people.

Camara stopped when he was level with Vanier, and reached up for a strap. He leaned close. "Don't look at me. Just listen."

Vanier stared out the window.

"You know who I am, Inspector?"

"Of course." Vanier didn't tell him the ears were a dead giveaway. "I recognized the accent on the phone. Sékou Camara, the rooming house."

"Yes."

"Sophia trusted me. Before she disappeared, she was very scared. She gave me the key to a safe deposit box. She said what was in the box will save her. She told me she gave my name to the people at the bank, and only she and I can open the box. She gave me the key and a phone, a special phone, not for me to use. Just to keep. If anything goes wrong, she will call, or someone else. She said she will exchange her freedom for what is in the box. She acted like it was certain. So I kept the key and the phone."

Vanier did the lost-on-a-bus routine, bending to look out the window and then scanning his surroundings idly.

"So right after the people search her room, the next day, I went to the bank to open the box. Inside I find a data stick and some papers. I made copies. Then I put them back. She was right, the information maybe will save her life."

"What kind of information?"

"Can't say that. Just listen."

"Maybe two hours after you left the rooming house, they call me on the phone. A man's voice, a Canadian. He promised to give me Sophia for the key. I must meet them at the bank the next day. I went there, but he was lying. No way he would let Sophia go free. She was in the backseat of the car. Drugged, maybe. Like she had no idea what was happening.

"I went crazy. What was I supposed to do? Me against two men, big men, no way. And Sophia, like drugged in the back seat. But they needed me to open the box. No way Sophia could go into the bank like that."

Their eyes met for a second, then they both stared out the window.

"I know if they get what they want, they will kill Sophia. Me too. So when we went in the bank I pretended to have a heart attack. I fell down on the floor. The man who was with me, he shouts to get up, but shit, no. I stayed on the floor. I told him to call me back on the same number. We will make a fair meeting for an exchange of Sophia."

The bus stopped at the Côte-des-Neiges metro station. People flooded off, and even more people got on. Camara was pushed closer to Vanier.

"So I escaped. I still have the key, and I still have the phone. But now I'm scared. I need help."

"We can protect you," Vanier said.

"No, you won't protect me. Maybe you will help for a while. But after, they will send me back to Guyana."

Vanier knew he couldn't stop deportations.

"This way, maybe I can stay in Canada. Sophia too."

"What do you want me to do?"

"I want you to help. In the exchange. They will call and say where Sophia is. When you have her, you call me to say she is safe. Then I will go with them to the safety deposit box and give them the stuff."

"Shit. That's not a plan." Vanier looked him in the eyes. "Why don't we get off, go to the station. We'll find a way to make this work."

"No. This will work. It must be this way." Camara had a piece of paper in his hand. "Here is my number. I will call you soon and tell you where to wait for Sophia. When she is safe, you call me and tell me."

The bus had stopped, and Camara didn't wait for a response. He moved behind Vanier and stepped off the bus. Vanier watched as Camara disappeared into the crowd.

Vanier got off at the next stop, pulling out his phone while looking for a taxi to take him back to his car. Flood answered. He explained about the safe deposit box and Camara's heart attack.

"Banks these days have more cameras that Hollywood. If we can find the bank, we can get pictures, and a warrant to open the box."

"Any idea which bank?"

"He wouldn't say. All we know is the date. And that Camara signed in and dropped to the floor like he was having a seizure. That must ring a bell with someone. And they have to have records of who owns the boxes. Start calling all the security people for the banks. Tell them it's urgent. Camara is trying to set up another exchange. We need to find the bank before that happens."

"Right. I'll get started."

Lynn Gagnon met them at the elevators and led them through a maze of cubicles, heads popping up every now and then as the occupants checked out the visitors. Gagnon found two spare chairs and placed them in the passageway outside her own cubicle. The two detectives sat down, looking into the tiny box where the head translator of Essence spent her days, surrounded by padded walls covered with hand-drawn birthday cards and family photos printed on photocopy paper.

On the phone, Gagnon had tried her best to dissuade them from coming; she thought they could do everything by phone. Whenever someone suggested something could be done on the phone, Vanier preferred eye contact.

"I'm sorry, but I don't have the authority to book a meeting room at short notice. Everything has to be done forty-eight hours in advance. Only management can do last-minute."

"Not a problem," said Saint Jacques.

Saint Jacques had declined the offer of a coffee, and Vanier was wishing he'd done the same thing. He was nursing a cup of the cheap institutional stuff with clumps of powered creamer floating on the surface.

"Like I said on the phone, Inspector, we do all kinds of translations. Some we do in house and some we subcontract. Antoine Lepage is one of our regular subcontractors. If he doesn't do it himself, he's got a list of people he uses."

"So who do I need to talk to if I'm interested in a particular contract?" said Vanier.

"That would be me."

"What can you tell me about job number 14-0629.

That's what it said on the invoice."

"Let me look."

She rolled her chair back inside the cubicle and started punching keys. She looked at the screen and screwed up her face. She threw Vanier a quizzical look. She typed some more, and turned back to the detectives. "It's not showing up. Are you sure it's the right number?"

"Certain," said Saint Jacques, handing her a copy of ALT's invoice. "14-0629."

Gagnon studied the invoice. "Let's try something else."

They waited while Gagnon tried different permutations. She looked up from the screen. "The records show the number wasn't used. It's a cancelled number."

"What does that mean?" Saint Jacques asked.

"Nothing. Just means it wasn't used. 14 is for the year, and the 629 is the number in the queue. This would have been the six hundred twenty-ninth translation job in 2014. But it's not unusual for numbers to be cancelled. When that happens, the cancellation is normally cross-referenced with another number. For instance, if the job changes, you might want to change the job number to make the charge to a different account. But just cancelling it altogether probably means someone screwed up. There's no work associated with it."

The explanation was lost on Vanier, and Saint Jacques looked like she was having trouble keeping up.

"So there was no work done on the file?" asked Saint Jacques.

"The system wouldn't allow any work to be done."

"And nobody got paid? Mr. Lepage said he got paid," said Saint Jacques.

"The system can't generate a cheque on a cancelled job number." She looked from Vanier to Saint Jacques like a schoolteacher.

"What if the job number was cancelled after the work was done? After the payment?" said Vanier.

"I don't know how you would do that. Maybe the technical people could do it but it would be difficult."

Vanier scratched his head. He was losing patience. "Can you tell what department the number was associated with?"

"You're not understanding me. The number is in the system, but there's nothing associated with it. It's a mistake. It's simply a dead number."

"This is the job you called Antoine Lepage about two months ago. First to get the work done and then to make sure he had destroyed the Essence document. You remember that?" he asked.

Gagnon thought for a while. "Kind of. Vaguely."

"He said you were very insistent on destroying the documents and wanted confirmation that all copies had been erased. Doesn't that ring a bell?"

"That's unfair. It's company policy. I was just reminding him of that. I remember the call. Not the details, but I remember reading him the instructions over the phone. But it couldn't have been the job number you're asking about."

"Why not?"

Now she was focused on Vanier like he was a kid needing special attention. "Because, as I told you, there's nothing in the system associated with that job. If any work had been done before the number was cancelled it would show up in the system. Even if the job was cancelled, the various steps before cancellation would have been logged."

"Who asked you to call up Mr. Lepage?"

"No idea. People don't call me. Everything is automatic. If someone has a job, they go into the system and place the order, if you will. They write out what they need, attach the document and enter the job number. Then the job is cued for translation. Every day, I get messages cued up for action. Even if they only want to check on the progress of a particular job, they don't call, they log a message into the system. If I have questions, I have to ask it through the system and wait for a response. It's rare that I talk to the person who's looking for the translation. Every morning, I get a list of job numbers that need action, I pull them up and I do whatever is necessary. That's all."

"And do you know who went to his office to make sure all copies were destroyed?"

"Somebody went to check?"

"Yes. Any idea who?"

"Not me. I called him, reminded him of the duty to destroy copies and that was it. I would have logged into the system to confirm that I had spoken to him and given him the instructions. Again, that's the sort of thing that would be listed in the job log."

"If you did that, shouldn't you be able to track down that note in the system?"

"Of course. That's what I did earlier. When I was looking for a record of the job. I searched all my entries. There was nothing."

Vanier felt like banging his head on the cubicle wall but was afraid it would topple over.

Saint Jacques stood up. "Let's try something else. If I asked you who in the company might need Spanish translation services, who would come to mind?"

"It could be anyone. We operate in several countries in Central and South America, and we've got four groups—transportation, infrastructure, resource development and power generation. There must be more than a thousand employees who could need Spanish work on a regular basis."

"So you're saying there's no way to identify the documents that were sent to Lepage?" said Vanier.

"If he doesn't have them, and he shouldn't, and there is nothing in the system log, it's impossible."

"So who are the people in charge of Central and South America? Can we get those names?" said Vanier.

"Latin America, that's Richard Susskind. He's vice-president for Latin America. But he wouldn't be involved in this sort of thing."

"Can you get us a meeting with Mr. Susskind now?"

Gagnon looked surprised. "Really? Mr. Susskind is responsible for all of Latin America. I doubt he can help you with this."

Vanier stood up. "We would like to meet him. Now."

It took half an hour, but Vanier and Saint Jacques were eventually put in a small, windowless conference room lined with whiteboards. The plastic table was too large for the room. The receptionist pointed them to seats at the far end of the table, farthest from the door, but to get to them, they would have had to walk sideways along the side of the table, so Vanier chose for himself, taking the chair nearest the door and pulling another chair out for Saint Jacques. Whoever came in after would have to squeeze along the table.

It was another ten minutes before Richard Susskind showed up. He was short and heavy, well on the way from fat to obese, his jacket cut like a tent to hide the bulges. He was not happy about having to shuffle sideways up the table to squeeze into a small plastic chair. Two women followed him and sat down to his right. He introduced them as Adriana Menendez, his personal assistant, and Sylvie Nadeau, one of Essence's lawyers.

"Always need a lawyer when you talk to the police," Susskind said with a grin. The two women pulled out business cards and pushed them up the table to the two officers.

"Thanks for seeing us, Mr. Susskind," said Vanier. "We're investigating the kidnapping of Sophia Luna. Does that name mean anything to you?"

A grimace passed across Susskind's face, but Vanier couldn't tell if it was because of the name or Susskind simply trying to get comfortable with his belly squeezed under the table. He made a show of giving the question serious thought. "No. Of course, I cannot be certain. I meet hundreds of people every year. But no, the name doesn't mean anything to me. Should I know her?"

"She did some work for Essence."

Both women were scribbling notes, trying to get everything verbatim.

"It's possible. But I don't know her. We could do a search of the human resource records if you want." He turned to his Menendez. She nodded and wrote something on her pad.

"No," Vanier said. She wasn't an employee. She did some translation for Essence, freelance, English to Spanish. That would be your group wouldn't it?"

"I'm responsible for Latin America, if that's what you mean. But that doesn't mean she was working for my group. It could have been the Europeans. They speak Spanish in Spain, don't they?" He gave Vanier a salesman's laugh.

"Does Essence have work in Spain?"

"It's possible. There's no major contract that I'm aware of, but maybe we bid on work from time to time. If there was a bid, they would need translation."

"Who should we speak to?"

"George Lautaud is VP Europe. He works out of the London office. Adriana can give you the number."

"Is it likely that he'd be using a Montreal translator for an English to Spanish job if he's in Europe?"

"Now that you mention it, I suppose not."

Vanier sat forward in his chair. "We're investigating an

abduction, Mr. Susskind. Madame Luna was a journalist from Guatemala and she did freelance translation work for Essence. But it seems all traces of what she translated have disappeared. We just want to make sure that her work for Essence had nothing to do with her disappearance."

"Well, I know nothing about her or any work she did for us."

"Whatever work she did, it seems to have disappeared from the system. Any ideas about that?"

"Officer, just because I'm in charge doesn't mean I know everything that's going on. I don't micromanage."

"Is Essence doing any work in Guatemala?"

"None for the moment. We have a mine there, in Chajul, but there was an incident about a year ago ago. The mine's been closed since then."

"An incident?"

"Yes, Mr., ah …" Susskind picked up the business card. "Mr. Vanier. There was a mudslide. Unfortunate accident."

He was getting to Vanier. First officer, then mister. Now Susskind was looking down at his lap, staring at his BlackBerry. Vanier said nothing, letting the silence hang. Susskind was absorbed with his BlackBerry, and the other four were looking at him.

He looked up from the BlackBerry. "What? Oh, I'm sorry. What was your question?

"Am I boring you, Mr. Susskind?"

"Just not sure how much help I can be, that's all."

"Tell me about the unfortunate accident."

Susskind slipped his BlackBerry into his pocket. "There's nothing to tell. There was an accident about a year ago, and people were killed. But we made things right. We put together a compensation fund for the victims and survivors."

"How many people died?"

Susskind switched to concerned executive. "Too many. One death is too many. And my sympathies go out to the families. But Essence did what was needed to be done to help those poor people."

"How many people died, Mr. Susskind. Simple question."

"I don't have the exact number. I don't know if anyone does. But it was in the region of a hundred. Like I said, too many." Susskind looked at his watch. "I am not sure what this has to do with the woman who has disappeared."

"Sophia Luna."

"Listen, I would love to help, but I don't think there is anything I can do for you."

Vanier stood up. "Thanks for your time."

Susskind didn't move. It looked like he was going to have to shove the table away before he could stand up. "If there's anything else, just give Adriana a call."

SIXTEEN

As soon as the TV stations and newspapers began running the hospital images of the guy in the tracksuit, the calls started coming in. There were over eighty, and every lead had to be checked. One by one the leads were verified. It took time. But eventually there were only two left, and they both led to the same place. A ticket-taker at the Crémazie metro station had called in, and swore he used to see the same guy taking the metro most mornings around seven o'clock. The second call was from a woman who said she recognized the guy as her neighbour. The address was close to the metro station.

Uniforms had gone to the address a few times, but the suspect was never home. Eventually they talked to the landlord, who confirmed the resemblance. A door-to-door canvass of the building got another three positive identifications. Finally, they called it in to Saint Jacques.

Now Vanier and Saint Jacques were standing down the hallway from the apartment. Five SWAT officers were lined up against the wall, two on either side of the door, dressed for shock and awe in black bulletproof jackets and military-style helmets, and carrying Heckler and Koch MP5 submachine guns.

From the end of the hallway, they watched the lead officer put his boot to the lock of the flimsy door. The door cracked under the force and five officers streamed into the apartment, yelling "*Police! Par terre!* On the ground."

In seconds, the team leader was back, walking up the hallway to Vanier and Saint Jacques.

"Clear. The place is empty."

Vanier nodded and headed for the broken door, followed by Saint Jacques. The apartment looked like a by-the-month hotel room. Whoever had lived there had cleared out, leaving nothing personal. A quick tour confirmed there were no clothes, papers—any of the hundreds of things that people own. In the fridge there was a carton of milk, some eggs and a loaf of bread, two pizzas in the freezer.

"We'll have someone dust the place for fingerprints, sir," said Saint Jacques.

Vanier nodded. "We might have the guy. If only we knew who he was."

They both turned at a noise in the doorway. One of the SWAT team was leading a man in jeans and T-shirt past the broken door. He looked like he had been painting, his hair, skin and clothes flecked with small white spots.

"Mr. Chabot, sir. He's the landlord."

"Who lived here?" Vanier asked.

"Carlos. I don't know his last name. But Carlos. He's been here for four months. It's a month-to-month rental. All furnished."

"What do you know about him?"

"Quiet, no trouble. He paid the rent. What else is to know?" Chabot shrugged his shoulders.

"Is he from here? From Quebec? How old? Where does he work?"

"He paid cash every month. Like I said, he was quiet, no trouble. Didn't have parties, didn't destroy the place. What else do I need to know?"

Vanier walked over and put his face within inches of the landlord's face. "Listen. When I ask you a question, you listen, then you think, then you answer. Got it? Now, was he a Quebecer? Speak French or English? Height, weight, colour of hair and eyes? Any scars? Everything you know about him. Got it?"

The landlord took a step back. "Hey, don't get mad. The guy was dark-looking, you know, South American. He spoke Spanish. Tall and built like a shithouse, one of them gym freaks with arms the size of your leg. Always polite but never smiled. Curly dark hair, maybe close to black, and dark brown eyes. But a quiet guy, you know. Never heard nothing from his place."

"And his name was Carlos?"

"He said, 'Call me Carlos'."

"He had a job?"

"Most of the time he came back it was, like, four o'clock in the afternoon. So maybe he had a job, maybe the early shift. He always had a bag with him, like maybe he was carrying work clothes or something. But I never saw a uniform."

"Did he give references when he rented?"

"I don't ask for references. You pay, you stay."

"And he paid?"

"Like I said, every month."

"Cash?"

Chabot looked at Vanier like it was a stupid question. "I don't take cheques."

"So no last name. He never asked for a receipt?"

Vanier got the look again. "A guy like that doesn't need a receipt. This was the kind of guy you don't fuck with." He looked to Saint Jacques. "Excuse me, screw with. He was serious. So he pays me and I keep out of his life."

Vanier looked to the SWAT officer that had brought him in. "Get him out of here."

As Chabot was leaving, he turned around. "Who's going to pay for the door?"

"Put in a claim," Vanier said.

Vanier wandered into the kitchen. The window gave out onto an alley. It was wide open, but there was hardly a breeze. Vanier reached for the window and pushed it up slightly. As he did, a piece of cardboard that had been jammed in to keep the window up fell onto the sill.

Vanier picked up the folded cardboard, let the window slide down. The sash was broken. The cardboard was three business cards folded and refolded to make a wad to hold the window open. The business cards said Carlos

Santos GSC, and under the letters were the words Global Security Consultants. There was no phone number and no address. He turned to the SWAT officer in charge. "Close it up until the fingerprint guy gets here. We've got to go." He headed for the door, turned back to the SWAT guy. "Thanks."

"No problem. A nice change to go in and there's nobody home. More peaceful that way."

Saint Jacques had found an address for GSC on her phone in seconds. The drive took twenty minutes. When they got there, Vanier was surprised. The offices took up the entire floor of a downtown high-rise on Mackay Street, expensive real estate for a security company. The reception area confirmed that GSC was making serious money, all marble, steel and glass, with a receptionist that looked like she had just finished a photo shoot for *Vogue*.

The receptionist beamed a smile as they entered, appraising Saint Jacques's outfit at the same time and seeming to find it wanting. Vanier smiled back, introduced himself. They were looking for whoever was in charge, he said.

"That would be Mr. Merchant. I'll see if he's available."

Saint Jacques sat down, and Vanier paced slowly, stopping to look at the magazines lined up neatly on the low table, *Soldier of Fortune* and the *Economist*, along with several GSC brochures.

Eventually the receptionist took a call. "He'll see you

now. Follow me."

Merchant met them at the door to his office. "Thought we would talk in here rather than in a boardroom. It's more personal. After all, boardrooms are for clients and we're in the same business, aren't we?"

Merchant's office was a shrine to himself, photos on every wall showing him in uniform, half of them with the over-decorated military types you find in countries where the army still runs everything.

Merchant waved at two seats in front of the desk and dropped into his own, a fancy black model. His suit jacket hung over the back of the chair, and his shirtsleeves were rolled up. His eyes matched the greyness of his close-cropped hair. He started tipping slowly back and forth in the chair, apparently enjoying the swinging motion. He kept a polite smile on his face, but he was appraising them like a horse trader at an auction.

"We're trying to locate one of your employees, Carlos Santos."

The mention of the name didn't seem to register with him. "Doesn't mean anything to me."

"He worked for GSC," said Vanier.

"No, he didn't."

Vanier slid a five by seven print made up from the hospital video clip across the desk. "Do you recognize this man?"

Merchant looked at the photo without touching it. Vanier thought he saw a flicker of recognition cross Merchant's face, but it didn't last.

"This the guy you're talking about? Santos?"

"Might be. We're not sure."

Merchant picked up the photo and made a show of studying it.

"Do you recognize him?"

He shook his head and handed the photo back to Vanier. "Sorry. It's not the best photo, is it? I mean for identification. Could be anyone. But no. It doesn't look like anyone I know. And this guy, or Carlos Santos, doesn't work for me."

Vanier looked to Saint Jacques and nodded. She fished in her pocket and pulled out a plastic evidence bag with the Santos business cards. "The man we're looking for had these. Why would he have your business cards if he didn't work for you?"

Merchant took his time. Studied the cards. Looked up. "It's weird. But you're cops. There are a lot of strange people around. You can get a card like this at any printer. You can even make them on your computer. It's got our name and logo, sure. But like I said, he's not one of our employees. I know everyone who works for me and he's not one of them."

"Why would he have the card if he didn't work here?"

"You'll have to ask him, won't you? But look at it. It doesn't have a phone number, no email. It's not one of our cards. They have the phone, email, and address. What's the use of a business card if it doesn't have your contact information?"

Merchant grabbed two business cards from a small silver tray on his desk and handed one each to Vanier and Saint Jacques.

"See what I mean? That's my card. That's what cards are supposed to look like. You want to get in touch with me, it's on the card. You ask me, this Santos guy isn't too smart. Maybe he printed up the cards to impress girls. Who knows?"

"This is a big company. Maybe you could check." Said Vanier.

Merchant stopped the back and forth in the chair. "If you insist, but for the record, this is a security company. It's my company, and nobody works here without me knowing about them." He leaned forward and punched numbers into the phone, leaving it on speaker.

"Mr. Merchant?"

"Véronique, can you do me a favour? Do we have anyone by the name of Carlos Santos on payroll?"

"Doesn't ring a bell. But let me check."

Merchant looked at the officers. "Véronique is in human resources. If he works for us, we pay him. And if we pay him, Véronique will know."

Véronique came back on the phone. "Mr. Merchant?"

"Go ahead."

"No. We don't have anybody by that name on the payroll."

"Thank you, Véronique." Merchant pushed a button to disconnect. "Nothing wrong with my memory. He doesn't work for us."

Vanier looked to Saint Jacques. She shrugged imperceptibly and Vanier began to stand up.

"That's it?"

"For the moment," said Vanier. "If you remember anything, let me know. Or if Santos shows up for work, let me know."

Merchant remained sitting, rocking back and forth. Vanier slid his card across the desk. Merchant look at it but didn't make an effort to pick it up. He reached for the phone instead.

"You can see yourselves out, right?"

Vanier was sitting in the gloom of his apartment, high up on Redpath. The pale moonlight mixed with the lights from the city below was all he needed. He had a glass in his hand, half full. He closed his eyes and listened to the music.

He was sitting in a club in prewar Berlin listening to Coleman Hawkins and his orchestra, a collection of European session-men bolstered by some of the great US musicians who, like the Hawk, had been exiled to Europe when drug convictions got them barred from playing in the New York clubs. He imagined the club's dark interior, filled with smoke and heavy with the smell of alcohol, perfume, and sweat. A room filled with people who knew they were in the presence of greatness. The tracks all started early, and you could hear the conversations dulling to silence as the music began and the Hawk transported the audience into dreams they never knew they could have.

It had been too long since Sophia had been kidnapped, and they still had nothing.

He didn't know when he had started thinking of her as Sophia, but it had become personal, and he was failing her. Someone out there was holding her and would probably kill her, but all he kept getting were dead ends. He needed a break. If he knew what she wanted to trade, he could maybe figure out what was going on, but Camara had gone to ground.

He went back to the bottle on the counter and poured another drink, opened the fridge door for some cold water. The light from the refrigerator fell on the GSC brochure he had dumped on the counter with the takeout menus. He picked it up and settled back down on the sofa. He flipped on the small lamp, enough light to read by, not enough to destroy the mood.

The brochure was more photos than words, tough guys in uniform providing security in countries no tourist would want to visit. It had a map of the world with red dots on the places where GSC was working. Red dots for Montreal, Toronto, and Vancouver, and a sprinkling across the north, marking remote mines and oil fields. Further south, there were three cities in Mexico and one in Guatemala. The brochure said GSC had provided security for the Essence mine in Chajul since its opening in 2007.

Vanier got up and went to the computer. He Googled the Chajul mine. Most of the hits were from two years earlier, when the mine's tailings reservoir had collapsed, causing a mudslide that covered the village at the foot of the mountain. Susskind hadn't remembered exactly how many people the slide had killed, but all the reports put the number at over a hundred. The Guatemalan government had reacted quickly by promising everything to everyone: compensation and retribution, new attention to mine safety, health care for the injured, and schooling for the orphans. More promises than an election manifesto. More recent articles focused on the fact that nothing had been done other than burying the dead. The village had not been rebuilt, and the survivors had scattered. One article reported a Canadian government announcement of a $100 million compensation fund that would be paid for by equal contributions from the Canadian government and Essence.

When he tried Googling Sophia Luna and Chajul he got nothing. When the accident had happened, she was just starting her refugee odyssey and hadn't published a word on it. Searching for Sophia Luna on her own turned up a few results, but nothing recent. She had been keeping her head down in Canada.

After an hour of trolling through the search results, Vanier turned off the computer and refilled his glass. It was two o'clock in the morning.

SEVENTEEN

Katya was already shedding the fear that had been with her since she had fled. She wasn't relaxed, but she could go for a couple of hours without being overcome by dread. But she knew she couldn't stay in the shed much longer and had been searching for somewhere safer to stay.

The day before, she had spent hours walking the streets, trying to plan her next move. She had walked as far east as the Atwater market, where she found a trove of discarded food. She could understand the thrown-away fruit and cheese—it was rotting in places, or growing mould. But she was baffled by the unopened packages of good food that were discarded. She just accepted that in rich countries people throw food in the garbage. She had no trouble finding enough to eat. Market vendors threw away enough to feed an army.

Finding a new place to sleep was harder; all the good places were taken. Whenever she came across a hidden corner or an alcove, there was always a rolled-up blanket or large bags stuffed with clothes, signs that someone had staked a claim and was coming back.

On the morning of the third day she decided that staying in the shed wasn't an option. As she left and closed the door, she told herself she wouldn't be coming back.

She turned right on Notre-Dame and walked in the direction of the market. It was early, and the streets were quiet. She thought it might be a weekend. She heard a car slowing down behind her and turned her head slightly. It was a police car. Her heart started pounding, but she forced herself to look straight ahead and kept walking, doing her best to look calm. But if you're homeless, it doesn't matter what you do, you stand out. If you have spent nights sleeping in the open and days wandering the streets, you cannot hope to look the same as someone who has a home. Your skin has a layer of grime, your face is red from the sun, your clothes look old and dirty, and your hair is matted with filth. If you're homeless and on your own, you're particularly vulnerable, an antelope that can't keep up with the herd. Every predator has you marked as a victim. The police car was still keeping pace with her. She knew it was worse to pretend it wasn't there. Only guilty people did that.

She turned her head. The cop was alone in the car and she locked eyes with him, keeping a blank face, no expression, no communication. After a few seconds she heard the car radio bark to life and the car picked up speed and left. She breathed a sigh of relief.

The market was already bustling when she got there.

There were hardly any customers, but workers were putting displays in order; unloading fresh produce and piling fruit and vegetables onto tables, filling empty boxes with anything that was slightly damaged, and building piles of empty cartons.

Katya wasn't the only scavenger. Most of the others were street kids, wearing black on black on black. To Katya, their attitudes were as dark as their clothes. She wasn't one of them, and because of that she drew only hostile glares.

She walked along the back of the stalls where the throwaways were, always walking slowly, trying to look like she had somewhere to go, but giving herself time to see what was available. Every now and then she'd stoop to pick up some discarded fruit. The best were just blemished, thrown away because the upscale market crowd would only pay for pristine fruit. She found a loaf of stale raisin bread in the container at the back of the Première Moisson and ate half of it. Then she went inside the market building and washed herself at the sink in the ladies' toilets.

She spent the rest of the morning wandering, noting landmarks that would allow her to know where she was and where she had been. As time passed, there were more people in the streets and her fear evaporated. She concentrated on finding an alternative to the shed. The busier the street, the less likely it was to offer a safe place to sleep, so she walked up and down smaller streets, exploring laneways and parks, attracted by shadows and corners and hidden places where no one seemed to go. She walked aimlessly north towards the Ville-Marie Expressway. The elevated highway rested on concrete stilts running parallel to Saint-Antoine. The land underneath was fenced off to the public, a shadowland of dirt where nothing grew in the gloom, and the only colour came from the graffiti that covered the concrete pylons. Katya stuck to the south side of Saint-Antoine, looking across the street for a break in the wire fence. She was so absorbed, she didn't notice the skinny girl on the bench outside the metro station. As Katya drifted past, the girl called out. "Change? Spare some change?"

The voice startled Katya. It was the first time anyone had spoken to her in days. She stopped walking and turned to look at the girl. She looked worse than Katya. She was emaciated. The flesh had all but disappeared from her face, leaving only skin, with eyes bulging from their sockets. She was shivering despite the heat, dressed in a pair of ripped denim shorts and a dirty grey T-shirt stained black at the armpits. Her greasy hair was dark brown except for a two-inch strip of crimson at the ends.

"I said, you got spare change?"

"No. Sorry. No money."

Katya stood there, staring.

"You lost?" the girl said.

Katya looked up and down the street. They were alone except for passing cars. She studied the girl, sitting with her feet on the bench, arms wrapped around her legs.

"Not lost. Just walking."

"Oh."

Katya sat down on the bench. The girl ignored her, staring straight ahead at nothing, her body twitching as though she was cold.

"I have no home. I am looking for a place to sleep."

The girl motioned with her head to the expressway. "Under there. We all sleep under there."

"How you get in?"

The girl unclasped one shaking arm from around her legs and pointed. "There's a hole in the fence. Over there." She pointed to a road that led under the expressway and on up to the city. "On the other side. Up the road on the other side."

Katya looked over to where the girl was pointing. "Yes?"

"Lots of people sleep there."

"You sleep there?"

"Yeah. Sometimes."

"You can show me?"

The girl looked at Katya as though for the first time. "If I show you, you owe me, right?"

"I owe you?"

"Yeah. Like when you get money you give me some. Okay? I help you, you got to help me. Deal?"

She held out a dirty hand and Katya reached for it. "Deal. When I get money I give you some."

The girl held onto Katya's hand, she was staring at the eagle tattoo. "What's that?"

"Nothing. Is Russian eagle."

"You Russian?"

"No, Ukrainian." Katya was getting nervous. Too much information. She pulled her hand back from the girl's grasp. "You can show me now?"

The girl sighed. "Okay. Sure. Where's your stuff?"

"No stuff. I have nothing."

"Shit. Nothing. Okay. Then maybe I help you get a sleeping bag. Then you owe me big time."

The girl put her feet on the floor and stood up. She leaned forward and half tripped, half ran towards the road. Then she stepped out and crossed without looking at traffic. Cars swerved to avoid her, the drivers shouting abuse. She gave the one-fingered salute to no one in particular and continued unsteadily across the street without looking back to see if Katya was following. Katya waited for a break in the traffic and ran to catch up. The girl led her around to the north side of the boundary fence and, about thirty metres in from the road, she reached down and pulled the wire fence up and away from the post. There was a triangular opening in the fence. The girl got down on her hands and knees and climbed under, letting the fence drop back into place. Katya followed.

At two in the afternoon, the space under the expressway hovered in a shadowy dusk. There was a stench of rotting garbage. The ground was littered with junk: empty bottles, beer cans, cigarette butts, takeout containers, and discarded scraps of food. The sound of the traffic on the road above was soothing background noise compared to the loud buzzing of flies around them. Katya wondered if she could sleep here, but she told herself it was a step up. She would be sharing space with Canadians. It was almost like living in a community.

"Only one rule. No shitting here. You want to shit or piss you go to the end over there." The girl waved vaguely over to the southwest end of the fence. "Far away as you can go. Next to the fence."

Katya hoped she wouldn't have to go. "How many people here?"

"Maybe fifty, sometimes more. You need to come early to get a good spot."

The girl was already leaving and Katya ran after her. "You said for bag to sleep."

"Sleeping bag. Oh, yeah. Sure. I'll show you. Man, you're going to owe me big time."

"Yes. I owe you." Katya smiled.

The girl hardly talked as she led Katya east along Saint-Antoine. Then she stopped dead in the street, turned back to Katya and asked to see the tattoo again. Katya held her arm out.

"That's crazy," she said.

"Is nothing," said Katya.

When they got to Richmond Street, they turned south, and the girl pointed to an open warehouse door halfway down the street. "That's the Salvation Army warehouse. They give things away if you need stuff. Go in and ask for a sleeping bag and blanket. Say you have no money and sleep outside. Okay?"

"Ask for bag for sleeping."

"No. Ask for sleeping bag. And blanket."

"Sleeping bag. And blanket."

"Yeah."

The girl turned and walked off leaving Katya staring at the open warehouse door. She eventually mustered the courage to walk into the dark interior and found herself in a massive storage area. To her left were bales of used clothes, tied up and stacked high like so much hay. The rest of the place was crammed with all kinds of furniture, fridges, stoves, and televisions.

"Hi. Can I help you?" Katya jumped. She turned to see a young guy smiling at her. He looked like he was maybe fifteen years old, but he seemed to be in charge.

"A friend tell me to come here. I need sleeping bag. And blanket."

"Do you?"

"Yes. I need."

"Why is that?"

"I sleep outside. No home."

"Money?"

"No money. Please."

The man was taken aback. "Okay, I suppose. Follow me."

He led her up a flight of stairs and into a sorting room where the donations from collection sites across the city were separated and appraised. "Sleeping bags are over there, blankets two tables down. One of each, help yourself."

There were six sleeping bags to choose from, and Katya examined each one carefully. Finally, she took one that smelled okay, the one with the fewest stains. The blankets came in all sorts. She went for a light one, something portable.

The boy came over carrying an empty knapsack. "You'll need something to carry them in."

She smiled, took the bag and started stuffing the sleeping bag inside.

"No. Like this." He took the knapsack back and showed her how to roll the sleeping bag and attach it on the outside. Then he did the same for the blanket.

"Thank you. I have no money. But one day, I come back and pay."

"I know. It's okay. Some clothes?"

Her eyes lit up and she followed the boy to the other end of the room. He moved his arm over tables stacked with women's clothes. "Take what you need. Come down when you're finished."

He left her to wander around the tables and she chose things that would fit, shirts, underwear, two pairs of jeans. She even found sneakers that she liked and put them on. She put the wellingtons into the knapsack and carried everything downstairs.

The boy was piling cartons against a wall and looked up. "Got everything you need?"

She was grinning. "Very, very kind. You are very kind. Thank you."

He walked over to her. "You need help, anytime, come back here. Okay?"

He reached over to put his hands on her shoulders and

she recoiled from his touch.

"I'm sorry," he said, holding his hands in the air.

"No. Is me. I am sorry."

Now she was looking at the square of sunshine shining through the warehouse door, resisting the urge to start running towards it.

"Thank you," she said.

"You're welcome."

He smiled, and she backed towards the door.

EIGHTEEN

Vanier was having lunch in a tavern when Camara's call came. The waitress had just put down a plate of rare roast beef smothered in onion gravy. It came with mashed potatoes and limp broccoli that had been cooked for longer than it had taken to grow. He shoved a slice of meat into his mouth and clicked connect on his phone.

"Inspector Vanier?"

"Yes. Listen, Sékou we have to talk."

"It's happening. In half an hour. At the café in the food court at Place Ville-Marie. Can you be there?" Camara sounded excited. Scared and excited.

"Half an hour. That's crazy. Listen. We need time. We need to set this up."

"It's all they gave me. I am going to the bank now. Call me when you have Sophia. Then I will give them what they want."

"No. Listen. You have to ask for more time."

"I cannot. Can you be there?"

Vanier looked at the time. Put the phone pack to his ear. "I'll be there."

He stood up and pulled out a twenty, dropped it on the table and moved to the exit. If the traffic was good he could make it in twenty minutes, but the traffic was never good in Montreal in the summer. He dialled Saint Jacques as he was walking to the car, and she patched in Laurent. He told them what was happening and asked them to put together a team.

He made it to Place Ville-Marie in twenty-five minutes, mounted the pavement and parked his car outside the main entrance on University Street. He was listening to Saint Jacques on his cellphone.

"We'll be there in five minutes, boss. Wait for us."

"I'll meet you inside."

He clicked the phone and ran towards the building. The food court was the first level down. He pushed his way through the office workers crowding the escalator, scouring the crowd, trying to watch everyone, looking for anything out of the ordinary. He knew the café was on the south side of the food court; he went there sometimes in the winter to take in the sunshine that streamed through the skylights.

He saw her through the crowd as he ran through the food court: Sophia Luna, sitting in a wheelchair, looking like a retirement-home resident taking an afternoon snooze. When he got close he saw she wasn't asleep, but her eyes were staring blankly at nothing.

He squatted down next to the wheelchair. "Sophia?"

Only her eyes moved, she looked up at him, trying to focus. He pulled out his phone and dialled the number. "We have her," he said when Camara answered.

He turned back to the woman in the wheelchair. "Let's get you out of here."

He squatted down to flip the brakes on the chair when he noticed her eyes staring up at the skylight. He followed her gaze. A man was leaning against the glass skylight, holding himself steady with one hand against the glass. He had a gun in the other, raising it to aim.

Vanier shoved the wheelchair just as the flash of light exploded and a bullet hit the ground at his feet. A shower of glass rained down on them. The chair stopped rolling but Luna was still plainly visible from the skylight. Vanier pulled his gun and aimed just as the man took a second shot and disappeared. Vanier holstered his gun and went to Luna. She was lying on the ground bleeding, the wheelchair on its side next to her. He couldn't see where the blood was coming from.

Saint Jacques appeared as if from nowhere, and then Laurent. Both had their guns drawn. Vanier pointed to the skylight and turned to the staircase that led directly to the Plaza where the shooter had been standing.

"Laurent, you come with me. Sylvie, stay with her. Call an ambulance." Then he was gone, followed by Laurent.

Saint Jacques turned to Sophia lying on the floor in a pool of blood that was growing by the second. She leaned down to feel for a pulse. It was faint, but there was one. A few people were milling around her, while others slowly emerged from behind chairs and counters. She punched numbers on her phone and put it to her ear. A man in the crowd reached into his pocket, and Saint Jacques pointed her gun at him. "Nobody move!" she shouted.

The man pulled his hand out of his pocket and dropped his cellphone to the floor. It broke on impact, spilling plastic parts. Almost everyone froze.

Saint Jacques caught a movement out of the corner of her eye. She turned and aimed. Before she could get a shot off, she heard one, and dropped, her head smacking the marble floor. She heard another, and lost consciousness.

Officers Flood and Descartes had been assigned the job of tracking down the bank branch where Camara had tried for the first exchange, and had wasted days in an effort that increasingly seemed futile. The banks' security departments were uniformly useless, and everyone else they spoke to was politely helpful without breaking a sweat. None of the banks kept their closed-circuit images for more than forty-eight hours, and there were too many reports of people falling sick in various branches. It seemed people regularly had heart attacks in branches. It took time to follow up on all the reports, too much time, and trying to speak to a live person on the telephone was next to impossible. Bank staff hid behind voice-mail systems that were as effective as steel doors at keeping people away.

Now they were stuck in traffic on Saint-Ferdinand in Saint-Henri, heading to the Laurentian Bank on Saint-Jacques to interview the staff. Except they weren't going anywhere. People had gotten out of their cars and were looking up the street to see what the problem was. Others had decided to be more proactive by leaning on their horns.

Flood got out of the car. At the top of the street, a black SUV had mounted the sidewalk, and was trying to navigate around a truck. The SUV was travelling in the wrong direction, and the truck driver wasn't cooperating.

A cyclist swept by Flood. Descartes was out of the car at once. "That's him. Camara." Descartes was pointing. There was no mistaking the straight-out ears that Vanier had described.

They watched as Camara swerved through the jammed cars and disappeared onto Charlebois. Both detectives pulled their guns and ran towards the SUV. It had given up the chase and was reversing back up Saint-Ferdinand. They watched as it did a wide sweeping turn on Saint-Jacques and sped off.

NINETEEN

Each time Vanier pulled up outside the emergency room these days, the parking had gotten worse. This time he just parked up on the curb and cut the engine. Let them tow it, he thought.

He rushed past the sick and despairing in the waiting room and burst through the swinging doors to the trauma centre. He was tackled before he could even take a breath.

"You can't come in here." This from a tiny nurse that Vanier could have lifted and tossed into the nearest bed.

"I'm with the cop who was shot."

"Are you family?"

"I'm all she's got right now."

The nurse softened, turned and pointed to a curtained-off bed. "She's in bed three."

Vanier moved to the bed and pulled the curtain back. Saint Jacques opened her eyes at the sound and smiled. Her head was bandaged like a turban. He couldn't see any hair, just the smile under the bandage. He had a flash of

Elizabeth Taylor. Vanier opened his mouth, but no words came.

"I'm okay, boss. Just a flesh wound." She was trying for a cowboy accent.

"Ha!" was all he could muster. Loud and drawn out; he repeated it. "Yes. Yes. Yes." As though he was convincing himself it was true. Tears were dribbling over a shaky smile. "Jesus, Sylvie."

"Are you crying?"

"Of course not." He made no effort to wipe the tears away. "What happened?"

"Like I said. A flesh wound. The bullet grazed my thigh, and my leg collapsed. I hit my head on the floor and lost consciousness."

"So you're okay?"

"Define okay. They said I'll be fine in a couple of days. Rest and recuperation. It will hurt to walk at first, but that's all."

"You were lucky, Sylvie."

"I know." She took a deep breath. "This may sound strange, boss, but I think the Lord himself has saved me. For a reason. I think He has a mission for me."

Vanier didn't know what to say. He stared at her with his mouth open.

"I'm kidding. Jeez, you're in worse shape than I am."

Vanier looked around for a seat, but couldn't find one. "And Sophia Luna?" Saint Jacques asked.

"She's dead, Sylvie."

"Did you get anyone?"

"No. There were at least two, maybe three. They all got away. But we'll get them. Anyway, it's not your problem now. You just focus on yourself."

"I want to come back. Maybe in three or four days?"

"Sylvie, I don't think that's a good idea. Anyway, it's not my call. You need to be cleared by the medical guys. Getting back to active service is going to take time."

She laid her head back on the pillow. "Just don't rent out my desk."

The curtain parted, and Flood and Descartes approached. In a second they were transformed from heartbroken mourners to happy idiots. Everyone had assumed the worst, and seeing Saint Jacques grinning was like a resurrection. The three men crowded around the bed as though they were taking strength from her. Eventually, Vanier made a move. "We've got work to do."

None of them had the courage to attempt even a soft, cheek-brushing kiss; the turban was intimidating. They settled for high-fives.

The squad room was hushed. They were all staring at the TV screen waiting for Chief Bédard to begin talking. He looked grim and uncomfortable, which was understandable, given that he was about to give a press conference with only bad news and no answers. Vanier recognized Julie Laflamme, a communications specialist, standing at the podium next to the Chief. She grimaced as Bédard pulled out a large white handkerchief and wiped the sweat off his face, not realizing that the scene was already being broadcast live on at least three channels.

The TV commentator was droning on. "I don't know if it's nerves or the heat from all those cameras, but Police Chief Bédard is sweating, using an old-fashioned handkerchief to deal with it. They seem to be ready to get under way any moment now."

Laflamme stood behind the microphone and gestured for silence. It didn't take as long as usual for calm to descend on the room. The atmosphere was deadly serious.

"Ladies and gentlemen, if we can get started, please. I am Sergeant Julie Laflamme and I'm the contact point for all follow-up questions related to this incident. For those of you who don't have my coordinates, I've left business cards on the table over there. Now, Police Chief Bédard is going to read a statement and then he will take a few questions."

She turned to Bédard and gestured him forward.

"Good evening, ladies and gentlemen. This afternoon at one forty-five, a woman was shot and killed in Place Ville-Marie. Her assailants also shot and wounded a police officer who was at the scene. The murder occurred during a police action. We do not have suspects in custody. Our officers were shot at and returned fire but we do not believe any of the assailants was injured.

The victim's identity is being withheld pending notification of her family. For the purposes of the investigation, we are also withholding the identity of the injured officer and the names of the officers involved in the incident. Ladies and gentlemen, rest assured that we are putting the full resources of the police service into this investigation. We have several lines of inquiry ongoing and are confident that arrests are imminent. Thank you."

The room erupted into shouted questions. Bédard pointed to a reporter from *La Presse*. "Mr. Gallipeau."

"Can you confirm the nature of the police operation? Drugs, organized crime? What was it?"

"At this stage it would hamper the investigation to disclose that information."

Bédard pointed again. "Ms. Thibault."

"Was the victim under police surveillance at the time of the incident?"

"If you're asking if the victim was involved in criminal activity, the answer is no. She was not involved in any criminal activity."

Another shouted question. "How many police officers were involved in the action?"

"Once again, in order not to jeopardize the investigation, we are not releasing any details at this time."

Laflamme raised her hand to try to restore order, but Bédard didn't notice. Someone shouted another question.

"How do you know the victim was not shot by the police?"

"The information we have at the moment is that there were no shots fired by the police prior to the shots that killed the victim. Subsequently, during a chase, a police officer fired on one of the assailants."

Laflamme almost shouldered Bédard away from the microphone. "Please. Let's have some order." She looked at the crowd of reporters and picked the reporter from *Le Devoir*. A serious paper. "Mr. Beaulieu."

"Do we know how many assailants were involved?"

Bédard was back at the microphone. "There were at least two men involved. However, we are still reviewing the forensics and the closed-circuit footage."

"Was the victim specifically targeted?"

"We believe the assailant knew the victim and intended to kill her. Yes."

"Do we have a total number of shots fired?"

"Not yet. That's for the crime-scene people to determine, and they're doing it as we speak."

The *Gazette* reporter yelled into a brief silence. "Place Ville-Marie is a pretty crowded place. Was it wise for the police to start shooting in a public place?"

Bédard looked at the journalist like he was ready to kick the shit out of him, but you don't get to be Chief by giving in to your emotions. He took a deep breath instead, "Mr. Thompson." Bédard couldn't help rolling his eyes. "Our officers were being fired at. I should remind you that our officers were responding to a murder that occurred in broad daylight in a busy shopping centre. Our officers are highly trained in the appropriate use of their firearms. So I am confident their actions were correct, and the risk of not returning fire would have endangered even more people."

The shouted questions broke out again, and Bédard realized he was losing control. Laflamme stepped forward with both hands up. "One more question." She pointed to the reporter from the *National Post*. "Mr. Gauvin."

"Were the assailants Muslim? Was this a terrorist incident?"

Bédard looked back to Laflamme, and she stepped up to the mike. "There is nothing to suggest this was terrorism-related. That's the end of the conference. Anyone who has additional questions can call or email me. Thanks for your attention."

Bédard was already heading for the exit.

The TV channel cut to a commentator, and someone pressed mute on a remote. The squad room was silent as people tried to digest what they has just seen. Vanier broke the silence. "You heard the Chief. We have lots of leads, and an arrest is imminent."

He stood up. "Truth is, we've got nothing." He turned to Laurent. "Can you recap where we are?"

"Sure, sir. Seven days ago, we had a kidnapping. The victim was Sophia Luna, a failed refugee claimant. A journalist in her former life, she had lots of enemies in Guatemala, and clearly she had some here in Canada. Here she was working on a story with Nick Angus at *The Gazette* and doing some translation. Angus was badly beaten a week ago and won't tell us anything. He's scared of something, too scared to talk. We believe Luna was working on a human trafficking story, and may have pissed off Oksana Kedrov. Kedrov specializes in Eastern European women for the sex trade and is said to be very violent. The closest witness to the kidnapping was the lawyer she was meeting, and he was murdered a few hours later. His office was turned over during the night. Luna had wanted the lawyer to help in some sort of exchange she was arranging. We got an identification on the lawyer's killer from a business card. Name of Carlos Santos, but that may have been an assumed name. We have no record of a Carlos Santos that fits the description. In any event, our Carlos Santos has disappeared. The business card listed GSC, a security company, but they say they've never heard of him. Luna had been staying in a safe house on Milton, and her room there was turned over too. A friend, Sékou Camara, says he saw two men enter the room after the kidnapping. Camara went missing shortly after we talked to him. He seems to have gone into hiding."

Laurent turned to Vanier. "Next thing we know, he calls you and meets you. He said he had tried to do an exchange, Luna in exchange for the key to a safe deposit box. Camara figured they weren't going to let Luna go, so the exchange didn't happen. He said there were three men involved, and they were holding Sophia in the back of a black SUV. Camara wanted help in arranging safe transfer. This morning, Flood and Descartes missed the trade at the bank by a few minutes. We think Camara got away."

"And that's when things go wrong," said Flood.

"They've been going seriously wrong since the start," said Vanier.

"When Flood and Descartes got to the bank today, the street was blocked, and traffic was snarled. Descartes says he saw a black guy riding a bike the wrong way up the street in a hurry. Probably Camara. Both of them saw an SUV backing towards the intersection. It was pointed in the wrong direction. Maybe they were trying to chase Camara and got stuck. Witnesses say the SUV had been parked at the bank and had made a U-turn to go the wrong way up the street. Flood and Descartes were stuck in traffic but saw the SUV leave. Inside the bank, they were able to confirm that Camara signed in for access to the box with another man. They came in together and they left together. The box is empty. We have a picture of Camara and the guy with him. Both pictures will be on the news tonight."

"So Camara's alive," Vanier said.

"Alive but in hiding."

"If they got what they wanted, why shoot Luna?"

"Because she knew what was in the box."

"And Camara told me the first thing he did was to copy the papers and the information on the data stick. So he's still got the information, and he's still a target. Probably always was. He was lucky to get away."

"So where does that take us?"

"What was she working on?" Vanier said. "What was in the box? Find the guy who was with Camara in the bank, and find Sékou Camara."

TWENTY

Katya spent the rest of the afternoon wandering. She felt safer when she was moving and less conspicuous with her knapsack, as though carrying the knapsack invested her with purpose. It was still light at seven o'clock when she went back to the place the girl had shown her. She wanted to arrive early enough to find a good spot to sleep, but not so early that there would be a lot of daylight left. She wasn't looking for conversation, and daylight, even in the gloomy shadows under the highway, would invite contact. Contact made her nervous.

The space under the expressway looked like a campground. People were milling around, talking, arranging places to sleep, sitting around small fires. Within minutes of her arrival, just about everyone had looked in her direction, appraising her. Some looked away, others nodded. Nobody smiled. She picked her way through people settling in and found a spot at the outer edge of a large group. She kicked bottles and Styrofoam containers out of the way to clear a small place for the sleeping bag. Then she spread the blanket on the ground and put the sleeping bag on top of it. She sat down, pulled her shoes off, and stuffed them into her bag. She used her sweater as a pillow and linked one arm through the knapsack. Slowly, the darkness thickened and the small fires appeared brighter. It was getting louder. People were yelling, laughing and swearing. Guys were drinking beer from cans, crushing the cans and lobbing them down towards the fence.

Katya felt almost invisible inside the sleeping bag. She could look around without attracting attention. Even in the gloom, she could see that most of the people were younger than they looked at first. Most of them seemed to be children who had grown up too quickly. About two metres away, another girl was doing the same as Katya, scanning her surroundings, looking for signs of trouble. Katya watched her watching the crowd, both of them trying to be invisible, both of them alert and ready to jump and run. The girl looked no older than thirteen.

Katya was nervous, but she still felt a sense of security. Even at the far edge of the group, she was a part of them just by being there. Even if no one knew her or cared about her, she was still among people.

After what seemed like hours, the crowd began to still, some settling into sleep, others continuing murmured conversations. Gradually, the noise from the highway came to the forefront, rubber on asphalt sounding like a constant river. Real sleep was impossible—Katya's senses were overwhelmed—and she floated in a dreamy state just beneath wakefulness. She would sleep tomorrow. Tonight, it would be enough just to rest, to rest among others who were in as bad a situation as she was.

As the camp quieted, she felt something small run over the sleeping bag. Rats. They seemed to be everywhere, all at once, running furtively between the sleeping bodies, searching for food, avoiding anyone who was sitting up. Katya pulled her head inside the sleeping bag, leaving just enough room to breathe through a small gap in the material.

Hours into the night, an engine broke the quiet, driving alongside the fence farthest from the road. At the break in the fence that served as the camp's entrance, the pickup truck turned and backed up so that its lights were shining directly on the sleepers. People began to stir, but nobody said anything. The truck was invisible behind the glare of its headlights, but there was no mistaking the sound of doors opening and then slamming shut.

Katya didn't move, staring into the glare trying to make sense of the light and shadows.

The girl from the morning was the first one she recognized. She had ducked under the fence and was bouncing like an excited six-year-old, running from side to side, bending down to inspect the sleepers, checking everyone on the ground. Then a man Katya didn't recognize came into the light. Two more men. Katya froze. It was Pavlov and the guy she knew as Makar.

She wanted to run but couldn't. Running would mean standing up in the blazing glare. But she knew she couldn't just wait for the girl to find her. She dragged herself out of the sleeping bag and lay on the ground, still in the shadows, watching as the girl worked her way towards her through the sleepers. Then she rolled slowly down the slope, passing through the camp's communal toilet, until she reached the fence. She crawled along it until she was out of the main arc of truck's light. She stood up and began to climb. The fence shook and clattered under her weight.

"There she is," the girl shouted. "She's climbing the fence."

Katya was halfway up the fence when the light from a flashlight caught her. She scrambled faster, reaching the top before she saw the barbed wire. She told herself it didn't matter and reached up. Her yelp surprised her, as though it had come from somebody else. The pointed barbs did their work, slicing the palms of her hands and flooding her brain with pain. She reached up again and got enough of a grip to pull herself up, high enough to lean on the barbed wire. But she couldn't move, someone had a tight grip on her ankle. She tried to shake it free but then both her ankles were caught and she was pulled to the ground. She had barely landed before she felt a boot kick her in the stomach.

"That's her. That's her." The girl was jumping up and down, shrieking. She bent down and grabbed Katya's arm, held it up. "See. The tattoo. I told you. Where's my hundred dollars? Serge, where's my hundred dollars? Where's my money?"

The man slapped his hand hard across her face and the girl tumbled to the ground. She was back on her feet immediately, as though the slap had meant nothing.

"Come on. Serge. A hundred. You promised."

"Here." He pulled a handful of crack bottles from his pocket, handed four to the girl. "Make them last."

She looked at the tiny bottles for a second, trying to decide. Then she reached out and closed her fist over them. She took off, running back to the hole in the fence.

The kicking stopped, but Katya stayed on the floor looking at the three sets of shoes. Serge turned to Pavlov, holding out his hand. "I should get five."

"I should give you what you gave her," said Pavlov.

"No. I'm a businessman. She's just a junkie. Five hundred was the deal." He held his hand out and Pavlov put five notes into it, then turned to Makar. "Get the bitch into the truck."

Makar reached down and grabbed a fistful of Katya's hair and pulled her to her feet. He didn't let go as he marched her back towards the truck.

Katya's eyes were open and she was walking, but her brain was shutting down. Her life was nothing, just a series of moments, one placed after the other, leading nowhere. There is no journey without a destination and Katya was once again walking to nowhere.

TWENTY-ONE

Saint Jacques walked into the squad room on crutches, carrying her customary protein shake. Everyone in the room froze for a second and then rose to their feet and started clapping. Saint Jacques beamed, held the container up and did a theatrical bow.

"Okay, that's enough. Thanks, guys. There's nothing wrong with me."

Laurent grabbed a chair and brought it over. Saint Jacques couldn't refuse, and sat down in the middle of the room. Then Laurent and Flood lifted the chair up and carried her to her desk. She made a show of getting up and limping back to pick up her crutches off the floor. "I wouldn't be back if I didn't think I could work. So thanks. But that's enough."

She went back to her desk, looked over at Vanier, who was shuffling papers. "What are you looking at, boss?"

They had already had the conversation. If she wanted to come back, she could. And he was going to do his best to ignore the fact that she had just been shot. He'd promised to treat her like everybody else. It was easier said than done. "What was done to track down the guys who beat Angus?"

Vanier didn't reply. He was staring at the mound of paperwork strewn over the desk. It looked like he had printed out everything.

"And?"

"Nothing. Sweet fuck-all. The uniforms filed a report of what they saw and what Angus told them and that's it. The ambulance got there first. The two uniforms saw Angus on the stretcher just before he was put in the ambulance. They talked to him for less than five minutes. All Angus said is that it was two big guys. He said he had no idea who they were or what they wanted."

"There wasn't a detective? I mean, it was a pretty brutal assault," said Saint Jacques.

"Sure there was. One of Montreal's finest, André Beaudoin. He showed up at Angus's bedside two days later and interviewed him for half an hour. Then he wrote a report that's almost a photocopy of the uniforms' report. Sounds like it was a full day's work for Beaudoin. Shit, he probably put in for overtime."

Saint Jacques knew Beaudoin, and he was sloppy and lazy. "He didn't interview the neighbours?"

"He didn't do anything. Nobody did anything. Just another unsolved mystery. No wonder this city's going to hell."

"You really think there's a connection between Angus's beating and the killings?"

"It's possible. We know Angus was paying Luna, so they were probably working together on something. That could have made someone angry."

"Is it too late to interview the neighbours? It was nearly three weeks ago."

"Probably. Three weeks is a long time."

"But we don't have much else to do. What's the address? It would do me good to get out and about."

"You're not going anywhere. I'll take Laurent."

Saint Jacques was already on her feet. "Let's go, boss."

Angus lived in an apartment building on Atwater, the steep part that meanders up the mountain from Sherbrooke. There were sixteen buzzers in the alcove inside the front door, each with paper slips inserted in metal slots to show who lived where. Angus was still listed in 405. Vanier tried the main door. It was unlocked, and they walked in. They crossed the lobby to the janitor's apartment. The door was wide open, and the smell of cigarette smoke drifted out into the lobby. Vanier knocked loudly and walked in.

At the end of a short hallway, the guy who lived there was sitting at the table, a full ashtray in front of him like a dinner plate. He was wearing a white vest, no shirt. The vest was flecked down the front with tiny holes from burning cigarette ash. His hair was dishevelled, and he hadn't shaved in a while. The room was a crap magnet, every flat surface covered with junk from tenants who weren't coming back to claim it. Against the main wall, there was a huge, glass-fronted cabinet in some ancient wood. Once it might have been used to show off fine china, but now it was filled with baseball caps displayed like museum pieces. Two TV sets sat on top of the cabinet, showing black and white images of the lobby and the building's garage.

"Are you the janitor?" said Vanier.

"Superintendent." He didn't move to get up. "You looking for a place?" He gave Saint Jacques a once-over and turned back to Vanier. "A hideaway?"

Vanier smiled and Saint Jacques rolled her eyes. "I'm Detective Inspector Vanier. This is Detective Sergeant Saint Jacques."

"Well, are you?"

"No," said Saint Jacques. "We heard about the assault on Nick Angus. Were you here that night?"

"That's ancient history." The super crushed his cigarette in the ashtray and looked up. "How long does it take you guys to investigate an attempted murder? He could've died, you know."

Vanier looked around, feeling claustrophobic in the small room. There was nowhere to sit, every chair was covered in junk, the place was a cross between a mid-career hoarder's den and an overstocked thrift store.

"We know," said Vanier. "So you were here when it happened?"

"Course I was. It's my job. And he's lucky I was here. I saved his life."

"How so?"

"By calling the ambulance. If I'd been out drinking

he'd have bled to death."

Vanier nodded at the TV screens. "So you saw who did it?"

"I saw nothing. I decided to go sweep the stairs and I found him lying there."

Vanier looked at the super and tried to imagine him deciding to sweep the stairs at eleven o'clock at night. Before he could say anything, a voice yelled from the doorway. "Andy, my man. I need a bag. Now."

Vanier and Saint Jacques turned to see a guy in his early twenties walking up the hallway dressed in a game-ready Lakers uniform, a Dennis Rodman wannabe. He almost tripped over one of Saint Jacques's crutches before he noticed her. Then he froze. "Oh."

He looked around with wild eyes. "Andy, I can come back. Sorry. Didn't know you had company."

"No problem," said Vanier, then turned to the super. "Give him a bag, Andy."

Andy stubbed out his cigarette in the ashtray, locked eyes with Vanier. "Give me a break."

"You give me a break. What did you see?"

"Okay. Just a second." He swirled around in his chair and pulled open a filing cabinet. He grabbed a baggie bulging with weed and tossed it to Rodman, who grabbed the bag and smiled. "Got any papers?"

Andy nodded to a shelf. The kid reached up and shifted through a collection of bottles of cheap booze. He grabbed the packet of Rizlas. "Thanks, Andy."

The three of them watched one of the screens on top

of the cabinet as Rodman appeared in the lobby and then disappeared into the stairwell.

"It's medical. His mother pays me for it. He came here to study at McGill and went crazy. He's seeing a psychiatrist. So I make sure he takes his pills and keep him in weed. She comes to see him once in a while."

"Yeah. You should get a medal. Now what did you see?" said Vanier.

"All right. But you didn't hear it from me. Angus has a bad gambling problem. My guess is that he just ran the tab up too high."

"What do you mean?"

"The two guys. I know them. They work for Danny Maloney. One of them used to come by here all the time collecting from Angus. Even asked me if I wanted to make bets. Do I look like I've got the money to make bets?"

"You have names?"

"The regular. His name's Pat."

"Last name?"

"No last name."

"So what happened?"

"That night, they came into the lobby together, Pat and another guy. Pat makes a call on his phone and presses the elevator button. The elevator comes and only Pat gets in. The other guy takes the stairs."

"The way I figured it, Pat was checking that Angus was home. He takes the elevator and the other guy goes up the stairs in case Angus makes a run for it. I guess they met Angus in the stairwell. Ten minutes later they both came out of the stairwell and left. I went up to see what was going on."

"You know where I can find this Pat?"

"I see him hanging around the Peel Pub sometimes."

"What does he look like?"

"Average, nothing special. Always wearing jeans and a T-shirt and this leather jacket. Like he thinks it makes him look cool."

"Anything else?"

"Yeah. He has a mean streak. You know, short temper. I once saw him break a glass in somebody's face."

"No. I mean, how would I recognize him?"

"Like I said, average. Except his hair. He has a ponytail. A blonde ponytail. Maybe that's what makes him so sensitive. The ponytail. He's bald in front and got a ponytail in back. Weird."

"That's it?"

"You see him, you'll know what I mean."

Vanier figured he could check photos at headquarters. Maloney was well known to the police. He ran a gang that was into everything illegal in the West Island. If this Pat was an associate of Maloney, there would be a photo of him too.

"Okay. Thanks." Vanier looked at Saint Jacques. "Anything else?"

She shook her head. She was leaning on the crutches as though spending so much time with Andy was making her nauseous.

"Great place to deal dope," Vanier said as they were

walking to the car.

"How so?"

"Christ, I wouldn't search the place in a hazmat suit."

Vanier was scrolling through photographs of known associates of Danny Maloney when his phone rang. He winced, and for the hundredth time made a mental note to change the tone to something other than electronic beeps.

"Inspector Vanier?"

"Yeah. Who's this?"

"Sergeant Faubert, Terrebonne Police."

Terrebonne was a north-shore suburb of Montreal on the banks of the Mille-Îles River. Not one of those fresh-built dormitory towns, but an ancient place that had grown slowly over five hundred years.

"We found a body that's connected to you."

Vanier's mind started flashing through the possibilities. "A relative?"

"I doubt it. Are you black?"

He didn't need to answer. Faubert would have known a black detective on the Montreal police force was unlikely. "So who is it?"

"No idea. He has no ID on him, but he had your business card in his pocket."

"Describe him."

"Small, black guy. Big ears, well, not big, but strange looking. They stick straight out from his head. Maybe he wore glasses. He's got those marks on the side of his nose, you know."

"Shit. Yeah, I know who he is."

Vanier wondered what Camara had been doing in Terrebonne. Off the island of Montreal, Quebec was a white man's world. Unless he knew someone there, Terrebonne wasn't a place to hide.

"Where did you find him?"

"In the dump. The Lachenaie site, just out of town."

"The dump?"

"The garbage dump. He came in on a truck today."

"Okay. Don't move him. I'm on my way."

Vanier got instructions to get to the site from the highway and picked up Saint Jacques on the way out. It was highway driving almost all the way, and they were there in forty minutes. Saint Jacques had been doing research on the way, tapping on her phone. "It is the biggest landfill in Quebec. Takes almost half of Montreal's garbage."

"How much is that?"

"From the city, it's over a hundred trucks a day. All told, they get over five hundred a day, five days a week," Saint Jacques read on her screen.

"Holy shit."

"Apparently, Quebec produces more garbage per person than any other province."

"At least we're number one in something."

Vanier had prepared himself for the smell. He remembered the old Miron quarry in the Saint-Michel district and how it stunk up the entire neighbourhood during the summer. He expected the smell from Lachenaie to start early, that he'd be able to use his nose for the last ten kilometres. But there wasn't a smell. The only sign that they were approaching the dump was too many seagulls—they were everywhere, and there wasn't a fast-food joint in sight.

When they got to the entrance, Vanier held his badge out the window and the guard waved them through.

Three police cars, a funeral home van, and a dump truck were parked in a tight semi-circle, while dump trucks manoeuvred around them with the never-ending flow of garbage. A police officer came over, walking clumsily in large rubber boots.

"Sergeant Faubert," he said, holding out his hand to Vanier.

Vanier introduced himself and Saint Jacques. Saint Jacques had left the crutches in the car, managing to walk with only a slight limp.

"He's over here," Faubert said.

They followed him to the edge of a crater where the garbage was dumped. Close up, there was no mistaking the smell. It clawed at the nose and settled in the stomach. It was bad, but Vanier had smelled worse in alleyways behind Montreal restaurants. They were joined by someone who obviously knew his way around.

"This is Eugène Grimard. He's the foreman."

Grimard started into the guided tour. "You've probably noticed, it's not like the landfills you see on TV. We work hard to keep the place as clean as possible. It's not just a big hole in the ground, there are a series of huge cells, like a beehive. Underneath are ten metres of clay to stop leakage. So the garbage is dumped and then crushed immediately, flattened as much as possible. The compactor weighs fifty tonnes. The guy on the compactor is supposed to look at the stuff coming out of the truck. We only accept non-hazardous waste, so he's looking for electronics, paint, that sort of thing. Anyway, he saw this carpet unroll as it came off the truck, and then the body inside. It's over there." They looked over to where Grimard was pointing, and they could see Camara's body lying on a threadbare brown carpet. He looked like he was sleeping, except half his head was missing. There was a huge dark stain on the carpet around his head, like a halo.

"I mean, I thought they only did that in movies, you know?" Grimard said. "You know, wrapping a body in a carpet."

"Some people just don't have any imagination," said Vanier. He'd seen bodies wrapped in carpets before. He thought it was sloppy, but who knows how many body-filled carpets were decomposing in garbage dumps, gone forever, without a trace.

"The coroner has been here, right?" Vanier asked.

"Been and gone," said Faubert. "I got his card. I'll email you the details. Said it looks like a gunshot to the head."

"This is the truck?" said Vanier, pointing to the empty vehicle backed up to the edge.

"Yeah," Grimard said. "I told them not to move anything. I mean, right away, we checked if he was alive, but there's no way. It's awful. You could see his brains. The truck, it's evidence, right?"

"We'll take a look at it, but we're not going to hold onto it. We'll need the route though."

The foreman smiled. "I already asked for it. They're going to fax it to me. The truck is one of ours. The driver said he was doing commercial pickups in Côte-des-Neiges, businesses and restaurants."

"Can we walk over to the body?"

"Yeah, it's solid. But I brought some boots," said Grimard.

Grimard handed Vanier and Saint Jacques a pair of boots each. They went back to sit half inside one of the squad cars and pulled them on. Vanier stood up. "Lead on."

Vanier stepped up onto the pile of garbage. It was like walking on a rancid sponge. Grimard offered Saint Jacques his arm. "It takes a while to get used to it," he said to her.

She reached out and grabbed onto his arm, followed him onto the pile. "Thanks."

Camara was lying on his back, his blank eyes open. He had taken a shot to the head. The entry wound was through his forehead and the back half of his head was missing. Up close you could hear the buzzing of flies already crawling inside to lay eggs. Vanier leaned down and grabbed Camara's chin, working his head around to check for other wounds.

Then he stood back up and turned to Faubert, pointing at the corpse. "His pockets are turned out. Were they like this?"

"Yeah. My guess is someone already searched him.

But they missed your card."

Vanier looked at the ground, and then back to Camara. The smell was overpowering, like being trapped in a bag of rotting meat.

"We'll need to get a photographer out here."

"I called one. He's at a wedding but he said he'd come over."

"And someone is going to have to search around for the weapon."

"You're kidding, right?" said Faubert.

"I doubt the weapon is here. But someone has to put in an hour or two to look for it."

Faubert cracked a smile. He looked back to the parked cars where two uniformed officers were lounging on the hood, shooting the breeze. "I got just the guys for you. After we get the body out of here."

"I'm sorry." Saint Jacques said. They turned to look at her. Her face was bloodless.

"We're finished here, "Vanier said. Let's go back."

Saint Jacques turned, bent over and started retching. It took a while until there was nothing left. Then she stood upright, tried for a smile and bent over again to finish the job.

Back on dry land, Saint Jacques limped off, distracted and unsteady, her hands resting on her hips as though she had just finished a marathon.

Vanier turned to Faubert. "We'll need the photographs first, then the morgue can have him. Once he's gone, your guys can search for the weapon. We'll need to keep the carpet." Faubert nodded. "And Mr. Grimard, do you think it's possible to tell anything about the pickup location from where the body was when it came out of the truck?"

The foreman was enjoying himself. "Absolutely. With garbage, it's first in, last out. The body was at the back end of the load, so most likely he was picked up at the start of the route. Maybe not the first pickup, but early on. Everything gets compressed and pushed to the back as the truck goes through the route. If you're finished here, we can go over to the office and pick up the route map."

"Is the driver there?"

"Yeah, he didn't want to stick around here."

Saint Jacques caught up with them as they were walking. Some colour was coming back to her cheeks. Vanier slowed down for her. "Feeling better?"

"Yes. Sorry about that."

"Nothing."

The driver was checking emails on a computer. Grimard waved a hand in his direction "This is Louis Guérin. He was driving the truck."

Guérin's pupils were dilated, his eyes blinking up at them in the light. He still smelled of the joint he had just finished. Vanier couldn't really blame him, he would have killed for a stiff drink himself. Vanier nodded, didn't shake hands. "So, did you notice anything?"

"No, man. Come on. I drive up, push the dumpster into place, pull the lever and watch the shit go into the back. Then I push the lever, the dumpster comes down, I unhook it and push it back out of the way. I've got sixty-five stops. It all looks the same after a while.

"You drive stoned all the time?" said Vanier.

"I wasn't driving stoned, man. I had a stash. I've been driving around with a dead body all day. How would you feel?"

Grimard handed Vanier a list of all the stops the truck had made. Vanier glanced at it but was finding it hard to concentrate. His stomach was churning, the air smelled like it was rotting. He thanked Grimard and made for the door.

As they were walking back to the car, Grimard came out of the office and called after them. Vanier and Saint Jacques turned around. The foreman was pointing at their boots, he wanted them back.

TWENTY-TWO

Pavlov Kedrov was sitting on a sofa in the Whole World Productions office. Opposite him, on another sofa, a man in his late forties alternated between a humourless smile and a gloomy look, nervously pushing his hand through his hair every few minutes. He was wearing a tan jacket and jeans that looked like they had been pressed. An assortment of worn porno magazines were strewn across a cheap coffee table that separated the mismatched sofas.

Kedrov was sitting with his legs splayed out like he owned the place. "You have the money?"

"Yeah. I got the money." Tan jacket leaned forward and patted his back pocket.

Kedrov held his hand out and the man pulled a wad of bills from his pocket, fifties and hundreds. He counted $1,000 onto the table.

"They explained the deal to you?"

"Kinda."

"A thousand gets you one hour with the girl. We'll

tell you when you have fifteen minutes left. We film everything and we own the film. You want a copy, it's $500 extra."

"Can I see it first?"

"No. You give us the five hundred and we'll send it to you. That's the deal."

"Okay, but I'll have to come back with the five hundred."

"It's up to you. Some rules. You've got one hour, so try to make things last. Start off easy. An hour's longer than you think."

"I understand. Make it last." He grinned.

"Right. Start off easy and work it up. Pretend the cameras aren't there. Are you going to have a problem doing this in front of people?"

Tan jacket was still grinning. "No. I got no problem with that. Anybody in that room would probably like to be doing what I'll be doing anyway."

"Okay. We want lots of shots of the girl's face. So every now and then, you hold her head up and make her look at the camera. Don't forget that. It's important."

The man nodded. He understood.

"And remember. She likes it rough, very rough. She won't show it because she's acting. So don't worry about hurting her, she's enjoying herself."

"That's not really my issue, is it?"

"Okay. But remember, start slowly and build up. Try to avoid broken bones. If we tell you to stop, you stop. I don't want to deal with corpses. And lots of face shots to the camera. Got it?"

"Sure. When do we start?"

Kedrov reached down and grabbed the money. "Follow me."

He led the man down a hallway, pulled open a door, and walked into a small room, empty except for a table and chair.

"Take your clothes off in here. Then you come out through there." He pointed to a second door and left through it.

The man took off his jacket and placed it carefully on the back of a chair. He removed the rest of his clothes, carefully folding everything and placing them on the chair. When he was naked, he pushed the door open. The room on the other side was dark except for an igloo of light over a large bed. A boom microphone was hanging in the shadows and two mounted cameras were aimed at the bed. He counted four men moving around in the shadows. A skinny girl dressed up like a schoolgirl was lying face down on the bed, her eyes hidden in the curl of her arm.

"Okay, we're ready to run," he heard someone say.

He walked across the room feeling like he owned the place. It was a rush he'd never felt before. He approached the bed, leaned down, grabbed her hair and turned her head around to force her to look at him.

Katya opened her eyes.

He could see she was afraid; she was terrified. That's when he knew it was going to be worth the thousand bucks. He was going to enjoy himself.

TWENTY-THREE

Saint Jacques hung up the phone and yelled across to Vanier. "It's what we thought, sir. I just heard from Inspector Laframboise. They've finished the fire inspection at Whole Earth. He says the fifth floor looks like a whorehouse doubling as a movie studio. Ten small rooms that lock from the outside and a couple of rooms made up like movie studios. Five of the rooms were occupied, four women and one guy. He said when they were doing the inspection they were shadowed everywhere by two heavies. The rooms were not locked, but the women and the boy were obviously intimidated, like they were distressed, but too scared to say anything. I think we've got enough for a search warrant. Laframboise said he'd be happy to sign an affidavit."

Vanier was on his feet. "Great." He pointed to Saint Jacques. "You collect Laframboise and get him over to the Crown. Who's the Crown on duty today?"

"Pascal Dubois, I checked. He said he'll be in his office

all afternoon."

"Good. Tell him it's urgent. Lives are in danger. I want to go in this evening. Overnight if we have to. Make sure the warrant allows that."

"Yes, sir." She stood up and grabbed for her crutches. She realized she couldn't talk on the phone and walk with crutches at the same time, and sat down again to call Laframboise.

Vanier looked over at her. "You okay to drive like that?"

"I said I'm fine. Only thing I can't do is dance."

"Or run," said Laurent.

She ignored him, grabbed her crutches and moved to the door, faster than most people walked.

"I'm going down to Whole World." Vanier yelled over to Laurent. "I'm going to park myself outside the building until the warrant arrives. The fire inspection probably spooked them, and I don't want them moving people out. You need me, call me."

Vanier had been sitting in his car for hours watching the parking lot at the Whole World building. It was eleven o'clock, and they still didn't have a warrant. It had been quiet since he had arrived. All he had been doing was sitting and watching, and thinking. He knew finding a connection to Luna was going to be a long shot, but he still wanted to go in. He wanted to shut the place down.

He pulled out his phone and punched Saint Jacques's number again.

She answered immediately. "I'm still waiting for Dubois to finish the paperwork. He says he needs another hour. Then we're going over to the judge's house. Dubois says we could have the warrant in about two hours."

"Isn't there anything you can do to speed it up?"

"I wish there were, boss. But he's slow. He's doing the typing himself. And he keeps telling me he'd rather be home."

Vanier was frustrated, but there was nothing to say. The Crown prosecutors worked at their own speed, and that was that. He changed the subject. "Remember you once said that nothing on the Internet disappears, that everything exists forever?"

"It's not my idea. It's the way it is," said Saint Jacques.

"I've been thinking. Luna's computer has disappeared, and Essence cleaned up everything from Lepage's computer."

"You mean have someone go through Lepage's computer to reassemble what was deleted?"

"No. Could you even do that? I was thinking of the email provider."

"Google?"

"Yeah, Google, or whoever his email is with."

"Wait a second." Saint Jacques put him on hold and did a search for Lepage's email on her phone. He had sent her an electronic copy of the invoice after the meeting. "He's got two email addresses, one tied to the website. The other's a Gmail address. You want me to get Google to turn over the records?"

"It's worth a try, no?"

"We'd need a warrant, I think."

"Or consent. What if Lepage consents? We could ask for a search without a warrant."

"I suppose. I'll send him an email."

"Wait a second. There's movement at the gates." Vanier could see Pavlov's minder, pumpkin-head, opening the gates to the parking lot. Inside the lot, a large white van was waiting to leave.

"Shit, Sylvie. I think they're leaving." Vanier watched as pumpkin-head pulled the metal gates back. The white van pulled out of the parking lot. "Sylvie, I'm going to follow them. You keep working on the warrant, and execute the search as soon as you get the warrant. Don't wait for me. My guess is they're moving people out."

Vanier turned on the ignition and pulled out. It didn't take long to figure out that the white van was heading for the highway. He checked his gas; he had almost a full tank.

Following the van on the 401 was not difficult. The highway was flooded day and night with trucks ferrying containers between Montreal and Toronto. He spent the first hour and a half behind large trucks, occasionally pulling out into the fast lane and speeding up to make sure the van was still in front. He figured they were going to Toronto, and he could hold back to avoid being seen.

Somewhere outside of Kingston, he lost them. When the van didn't show up two trucks ahead of him, he roared down the highway for fifteen kilometres. The van was nowhere to be seen, and he realized it must have taken an exit without him noticing. It was fifteen minutes to the next exit. He took the bridge over the highway and got back on, towards Montreal.

He called Saint Jacques. "I lost them. I'm just east of Kingston, and they must have taken the last exit. Any news on the warrant?"

"We're at Whole Earth now," Saint Jacques said. "The place is empty. It's been cleaned out. The only one here is the son, and he's saying nothing."

"Did you find anything on him?"

"Nothing, just the usual, credit cards, ID, scraps of receipts from ATM machines. Wait, there was something, an address and phone number on a notepad. I think Laurent already boxed it. Give me two seconds."

Vanier held his breath as he sped eastwards along the highway.

"I've got it. I have a phone number. It's a 613 area code. Where is that?"

"Ottawa. That's not going to help. What's the address?"

Saint Jacques read the address. It meant nothing to Vanier.

"Let me check it, boss. I'll call you back."

The line disconnected. She called back two minutes later. "Two things: 613 covers Kingston as well as all the territory up to Ottawa. Second, the address is not far from where you are. What was the last exit you passed?"

"I turned around. I'm heading east. I got on at exit

632, and haven't passed another since then."

"Okay. According to the map, at the next exit, you'll be maybe fifteen minutes from the address."

Saint Jacques relayed the instructions, and Vanier followed. Twenty minutes from the highway he was there. The house was in darkness. Vanier parked on the road, and walked towards the house on the grass, staying off the gravel in the driveway. It didn't take long for his eyes to adjust to the dark. He moved around the house, looking in the windows. If anyone was home, they were fast asleep upstairs. When he got around to the back, he saw the dock. He pulled out his phone and called Saint Jacques.

"I need you to look up a phone number for me."

TWENTY-FOUR

Katya had been sitting in the back of the van for about two hours with three other women and a boy barely out of his teens. At first, there was no conversation, each of them imprisoned in recent memories. Finally, one of the women turned to her neighbour and asked, in Russian, "What did they tell you?"

"Nanny. I was going to be a nanny, looking after rich kids. I would work one year, maximum. Earn some money to send home and the rest to pay the cost of coming to Canada. After that I would be free."

"I was going to work in a language school," the boy said. "A tutor for Russian. Same thing, one year, that was it."

"Liars," Katya said.

They fell into silence again. "Where do you think we're going?" the boy asked.

"The firemen. I think we're being moved because the firemen came and checked. They want to hide us."

"It's a long way," said another woman.

The conversation was stilted. None of them wanted to talk about what they had been through. None of them knew anything about where they were going. And they were all scared—their entire landscape was a prison.

After what seemed like two or three hours, the van slowed down to take a curve. They could see out the back window that they had left the highway. Half an hour later the streetlights ended, and there was only the blackness of the country and the brief lights of small villages. Eventually, they came to a halt, gravel scratching beneath the wheels. They waited, listened as the driver's door opened and slammed closed. The back door of the van opened and the man called Makar gestured them outside.

They stood on the gravel, stretching and staring around in the night. They were in the driveway of a large house that sat on its own in the gloom. The only light came from a single bulb above a garage. Beyond the building, the darkness had a different character, freckled with grey spots that appeared and disappeared at random. The night was loud with crickets, and Katya remembered how good fresh air could taste. She sucked it in and tried to imagine where she was.

"A river," one of the girls whispered, nodding to the darkness beyond the building.

The front door of the house opened and they turned in that direction. Katya could make out two figures coming down the steps, carrying flashlights, the beams of light pointed straight ahead at the group in the driveway, the gravel crunching as the men approached.

Katya listened hard to distinguish words in the mumbled conversation between the two men and Makar, but could understand nothing. Then the three men broke like sheepdogs around the group and herded them up the driveway along the side of the building. Soon they were walking on grass, and the river came into view. They were led to the edge of the river, onto a wooden dock. One by one, they were hustled onto a boat. Makar stayed on the dock. There was another brief conversation between the three men, and Katya watched as Makar returned to the van.

One of the men led them into a small cabin and motioned for them to sit on a bench that ran along the wall. He left, and they heard the door being locked shut. Katya stood up and looked out through a porthole, but there was nothing to see beyond the small circle of light coming from the boat. She jumped when the boat's motors exploded into life and they pulled away from the shore. Seconds later the lights on the boat went out. Katya kept watching out the porthole, leaning her hands against the wall to steady herself. The shoreline disappeared quickly.

In the dark cabin, the boy broke the silence. "America. The river is the St. Lawrence. It's the border. We're going to America."

All five of them stood, peering through the portholes, but there was little to see except the occasional pinprick of light in the blackness. In fifteen minutes the boat had passed through a series of islands. It looked like they were on the open sea.

Almost imperceptibly at first, they heard the noise of another motor. It seemed to be getting louder, coming closer, until there was no mistaking the noise of a helicopter. It was directly over the boat, and its heavy, pulsing noise was the only thing they could hear. Night turned to day as the boat was bathed in light from the helicopter, then turned back to darkness when the boat swerved violently, and began weaving across the water in tight curves like a skier descending a mountain. Katya and the others had to sit down to be to avoid being pitched to the floor of the cabin. They heard a rattling and the door was flung open. A man played a flashlight into the cabin as though checking that they were still there.

."Out. Fast," he shouted, gesturing them to follow him.

The boat was speeding across the waves in wide curves to avoid the helicopter. They filed out of the cabin like drunks, grabbing at anything to keep their balance, following the beam of the flashlight on the floor, and climbed the staircase leading to the deck. Katya was the last one to start climbing. When she was halfway up, the flashlight clicked off. The man was behind her, pushing her to move faster. On deck, Katya watched the helicopter trying to keep up with the speeding boat. Every few minutes the helicopter's light swept across the deck. Each time, the boat changed course, and the light was lost.

At a loud hissing sound, Katya turned. It was an orange dingy, inflating on the deck. The man grabbed a rope, lifted the dingy and pitched it over the side, holding the rope. The dingy landed upside down and the man struggled at the rail to right it. He turned back to the five passengers and pointed to a ladder that led down to the water.

Someone screamed. "No. We will die. Please."

The man yelled to be heard over the noise. "Into the fucking boat. All of you." He pointed at the boy. "You first. Climb down the ladder and turn the boat up. Then you get in."

The boy didn't understand. Out of nowhere, the man suddenly had a gun in his hand. He pointed it at the boy and waved towards the ladder. The boy pulled himself along the boat's rail to the ladder, holding on desperately to avoid being thrown over the side as the boat rose and crashed through the waves. He put one leg over the rail and started down the side of the boat.

The man watched him go, and then turned back to the women. He waved the gun again, pointing at one of the women. "You next. Faster."

She pulled herself along the rail towards the ladder and looked down into the water. The boy was perched on the ladder as the boat ploughed through the waves. One second he was at the water line, and the next second, a metre above. The man on the deck pulled on the rope to manoeuvre the dingy towards the boy. The boy reached out and grabbed the rope, but he couldn't manage to turn the dingy right side up. He hooked one leg over a rung on the ladder and used both arms to right the dingy. As it settled right side up on the water, they were bathed in light from the helicopter. The boat swerved violently, hit a wave and lurched out of the water before slamming back down. The impact dislodged the boy's leg from the ladder, sending him into the water. Katya screamed. She watched the boy surface, already far behind the boat, watching the dingy being pulled away in the night. The woman at the top of the ladder froze. The man on the deck pushed her in the back with the gun.

"Okay, now you."

She climbed down the ladder and half-jumped, half-fell into the dingy. As she did, another woman was already climbing down the ladder. She tried jumping for the dingy but missed, her hands slipping on the plastic sides before she managed to grasp the rope that ran around the side of the dingy. She held on, her body trailing behind in the wash. The third woman froze on the ladder, riding it up and down in the swell, unable to leap into the dingy. The man screamed at her. "Jump. Jump!"

She kept looking back and forth from the man to the dingy but she couldn't find the courage to jump. The man put his leg over the rail and climbed down two rungs. He leaned down. "Jump!" he screamed at her. "Jump, I said. Fucking jump!"

She froze on the ladder even as he brought his heel down on one of her hands. He did the same to the other hand. Still, she kept her grip on the ladder. He tried harder, six or seven times on each hand until finally she let go. She dropped into the water and was lost in the swell. The man climbed back into the boat, pointed the gun at Katya.

"Now you," he screamed over the noise. "Move it."

If she stayed high enough on the ladder, Katya thought, she could leap over the woman clutching the rope on the side of the dinghy and then be able to pull her to safety. She waited for the right moment and jumped. At the same time, the boat swerved violently and the dinghy fell into a trough. Katya landed on her belly on the rubber side. The impact dislodged the woman's grip on the rope, and Katya could only watch as the woman disappeared into the blackness. She pulled herself onto the dinghy. The other woman was vomiting, half into the dinghy and half over the side. They were still being pulled alongside the boat, and Katya looked up to the deck. The man caught her eye as he let go of the rope. The dinghy stopped moving and settled in the water as the boat roared off.

Katya lay on her back looking up into the blinding light of the helicopter. At least she wasn't going to die, she thought. Then she felt coldness at her feet. A growing puddle of water gushed in through a rip in the floor.

TWENTY-FIVE

The steel door closed behind Vanier and locked with a metallic finality. He was standing in a neon-bright cell looking at a shivering girl perched on a fold-down metal bed attached to the wall. She hadn't looked up when he came in, or at the noise of the door closing behind him. She was staring at the floor, huddled under a silver hypothermic blanket, her legs drawn up to her chin.

"I'm Luc."

No response.

She looked fragile, like he could have tipped her to the floor with a slight push and she would have tumbled and shattered into pieces. Water had pooled around her on the metal ledge. He noticed a flash of yellow beneath the silver blanket. She was still wearing the clothes she had been wearing when they pulled her out of the St. Lawrence. He reached over and pulled at the blanket around her.

"You should take the wet clothes off, just keep the blanket."

Again, no response. He turned back to the door and rapped it with his knuckles.

The door opened with the noise of grinding steel, and Vanier stepped into the hallway. "She's freezing. She's still wearing her damned clothes," he said to the uniformed officer.

"I was told to wait for a female officer to come on duty. We don't have anything to give her."

Vanier didn't slow down to listen, pushed past the uniform. "Give her a proper blanket at least," he yelled over his shoulder as he strode off. "I'll be back."

Thirty minutes later Vanier returned, carrying two plastic Walmart bags. He took them into the cell. The girl was curled in a fetal position on the ledge, wrapped in a coarse brown blanket, her clothes and a towel in a wet pile on the floor. She was still shivering.

"It's me again. Luc. I got you these."

She was staring blankly into some middle distance. He put the two bags on the floor in front of her and pulled clothes from the bag—underwear, a shirt, jeans, a thick sweater, gloves and a woollen toque. He took the toque and pulled it onto her head.

"Put the clothes on, you'll feel better. I'm going to get a coffee. I'll be back in a few minutes. Can I get you something?"

He rapped on the door again. As it opened he heard a small voice. "Coffee."

He turned. She hadn't moved.

"Cream and sugar?"

"Sugar," she said.

When he came back with two coffees, she was dressed and sitting with her back to the wall. He pulled the lid off one and offered it to her. She reached out and took it, clasping it in her hands, blowing on the surface and sipping at the same time. He put his own coffee on the floor, gathered the wet clothes into an empty plastic bag and sat down on the floor, his back to the wall.

"My name's Luc. I told you that, didn't I? What's your name?

"Yes. You said."

"You speak English?"

"Some. Not much."

"So what's your name?"

She sipped at her coffee, head down. Stole a glance at Vanier. Vanier was resting his head against the wall, his eyes closed. He was exhausted. After a few minutes he reached for the coffee, took the lid off and sipped.

"Good coffee."

She looked him in the eye for the first time, like she had made a decision.

"Katya. Katya Babyak."

"What were you doing on the boat?"

Her eyes flickered. Vanier recognized fear.

"The others. How are they?" she said.

"What others?"

"We were five. Me, three women and a boy. They made us leave the boat."

"I'm sorry. You were the only person. Only you."

"They kill the others."

"Who's they?"

"Two men. One, he drives the boat. The other, he makes us go in the water. There was a helicopter and he said to go in the small boat. He killed them."

"They have not found any bodies. Maybe they survived. Did you have life vests?"

"What is that?"

"You know." Vanier made like he was putting on a life vest. "Orange vest. You put it on to help you float in the water."

"Oh." Then she shook her head. "No."

"Look, Katya, let's start at the beginning. Tell me what happened."

"Food. I need food. It is long story."

"Okay. I'll order food. Then you tell me the story."

Vanier got to his feet and rapped on the door again. When it opened, he gave $20 to the officer. "I know. It's not your job. But we're both starving. Can you see if you can find us something to eat? Anything, doughnuts, muffins, McDonald's breakfast. Just get something, okay?"

The officer took the money and closed the door without smiling. Vanier slid back down the wall to his place on the floor.

"I am prostitute. I did not start out to be prostitute. They forced me. In Ukraine, I pay money to come to Canada. Only half, but lots of money. They say there is a job for me in Canada. Nanny. They say when I start to work, I pay the rest of money. But when I come to Canada they say they own me. They give me this." She rolled her sleeve up and held out her arm to show the tattoo. "It means I am property until all money is paid. But it is not true. I am property forever."

She rolled her sleeve back down.

"I must work to pay money. And they made me prostitute. But I am no good for this job so they sell me for men who like to beat women, who like to rape. This is my job. To be raped. Yesterday—no, maybe before yesterday. Two men in uniform came to place. Pavlov, he said not to talk, not say anything. So we say nothing. When they leave, we go to our rooms and are locked in there. But no work that night. Usually, there is work every night. But this night, nothing. After many hours we go downstairs into back of truck."

"So we drive for a long time. Then we stop and go to boat. We are on boat maybe thirty minutes and then we hear helicopter. The man, he is scared. He says for us to get in small boat. The others. They die, no?"

"I don't know. Maybe. Yes. They are probably dead."

Katya nodded.

Vanier stood up and passed her a photograph of Sophia Luna. "Did you ever see this woman?"

She looked at the photo and shook her head. "She is beautiful. But I never see this person."

He took the photograph back and handed her one of Oksana Kedrov. "You know this person?"

Katya shuddered, made a grunt-like sound. "This is lady who owns me. This is lady who made me tattoo. She is boss, Mrs. Kedrov. Pavlov is her son. Very bad people."

She gave the photograph back to Vanier. "What happens to me?"

"I don't know, Katya, but I'll find out."

TWENTY-SIX

Sylvie Saint Jacques was leaning on her crutches in front of the reception desk in Google's Montreal offices. The company had taken a couple of floors of a stately building on the corner of McGill College and Sainte-Catherine and transformed the space into a cross between a kindergarten and an upscale frat house.

Saint Jacques had dressed for the part, less cop and more woman, playing for sympathy with the crutches.

She heard a whooshing sound, and turned to see a guy in jeans and a T-shirt emerge feet first from a green and red plastic chute. An alternative to taking the stairs. He stood up and raised his hands in the air like a circus performer signalling the end of a trick.

"Sergeant Saint Jacques?"

She nodded and reached out her hand, balancing forward on the crutches.

"I'm Khartapuka Khalsa. You can call me Kharta." He shook her hand, smiling all the time, her squeeze harder than his.

"I heard you had a problem," he said.

"I was hoping you could help us."

"That's what Google does. Come with me," he said.

He led her down the hall to a fishbowl conference room. What wasn't glass was painted in playroom green and yellow. A laptop was open and ready on the glass table. Saint Jacques leaned her crutches against the wall and limped to a seat. She explained the problem: a lost document attached to an email. She had the email address of the sender and the receiver, and the approximate date it would have been sent.

"Big problem," he said.

"No. I've got the sender's permission. It's his document." She was fishing in her bag for the email from Lepage.

"No. No. That's not what I meant. I assume you're not asking me to do anything illegal. You wouldn't do that, would you?" He gave her a wide smile.

"Of course not. It's perfectly legal. The sender consented," Saint Jacques said. "I know it's difficult. But we're investigating the murder of the recipient." She pushed a sheet of paper across the table with the details.

"Exactly. What I meant is that it's more work to find individual documents. Imagine a warehouse filled with paper. No, imagine six warehouses, all of them filled with documents, and you want me to find one page in all that paper. The big agencies, CSIS and the RCMP, those kind of guys, they don't ask for individual documents. They get the metadata. That's like asking for the keys to the warehouse so they can go looking themselves. That's a lot easier. We just do a massive download over to them and that's the end of it. Let them go searching through the warehouse."

"I didn't realize it would be so difficult. I really appreciate the effort."

He smiled at her again. "Not a problem. We have a shortcut. Why don't you wander down the hall and get a coffee. I should have something when you get back."

Saint Jacques got to her feet and reached for the crutches. "Can I get something for you?"

"That would be wonderful." He beamed at her. "I'll have a tea."

Saint Jacques followed his directions to the kitchen, resisting the temptation of the pinball machine. Two guys were playing foosball. The pool table was free. She wondered how anybody got work done.

In the kitchen, she didn't even have to make the coffee. Another techie, who introduced himself as Kevin, showed her how the machines worked. He insisted on carrying her coffee and Kharta's tea back to the boardroom for her.

Kevin settled in like he was part of the meeting. "Did you know Kharta is still looking for a wife? He's getting worried. If he doesn't find one soon, his family has lined one up for him. Right Kharta?"

Kharta ignored his colleague and turned to Saint Jacques. "Is there anything wrong with trying to meet your soul partner? Call me a romantic, but I know there is someone out there for me. I just have to find her. What do you think, Sylvie?"

He had stopped what he was doing and looked at Saint Jacques, waiting for an answer.

"Great coffee." She held the cup up for emphasis. Then she relented. "I suppose so, yes. There's nothing wrong in believing."

Khalsa smiled again.

"There you go, Kharta," Kevin said. "Keep trying."

Kharta turned back to the screen, punched the keyboard and a huge screen on the wall lit up. Saint Jacques saw an email from Antoine Lepage to Sophia Luna.

"Is this what you're looking for?"

"Wow. That was fast. Is there an attachment?"

Kharta was grinning. "Two attachments. This." A Word document flashed on the screen. "And this." An Excel spreadsheet popped up. "Should I email them to you?"

Saint Jacques was distracted, trying to take in what she was seeing: a contract and some sort of schedule. "Sure. Email's great." She gave him her card. "I'm impressed."

Kharta typed in her email address, sent the documents and closed the laptop. He sat back in the chair, beaming. "Done."

His smile was contagious. "I'm impressed." Saint Jacques said. "Really."

"Now that your business is done, tell me, how did you injure your leg? It's not the season for skiing accidents."

Saint Jacques leaned forward. "Gunshot wound."

Kharta's eyes opened wide. "Wow."

"No way," said Kevin. It wasn't a denial, more an amazed approval.

"Just a flesh wound. Nothing serious."

"You are a very brave woman." Kharta said.

"In the line of duty?" said Kevin.

"In the line of duty. Took one for the team."

Both men were in awe.

"And speaking of duty, I have to go," she said. She stood up and grabbed the crutches. Kharta walked with her to the elevator.

"It was very nice to meet you, Sylvie." He reached over. "Here is my card. Call me. Maybe we can have coffee together sometime."

Saint Jacques smiled and took the card. "Thank you. It was really great coffee."

"I mean it. Really."

"Me too."

If you want to know what's going on in a police station, you talk to the desk sergeant. They are the gatekeepers, watching who comes in and who leaves. They have the pulse of the station. Vanier had been talking to the desk sergeant every time he passed him, cultivating the relationship.

Three RCMP officers from the human trafficking task force had arrived to question Katya, and now the sergeant gave Vanier directions to the boardroom where they were setting up.

Vanier found the Mounties arranging recording

equipment on the table. It didn't take much to figure out who was in charge. He was wearing a grey suit, white shirt, and blue tie. His suit was the cheap, off-the-shelf kind that showed he hadn't made it yet, but it was pressed and clean—like he was still trying. He looked up and shot Vanier a questioning look. "Can I help you? I'm Inspector Robert Brown. This is Sergeant Bob Kaminski and Corporal Julian Carter." He didn't offer a handshake.

Vanier said nothing, taking in the three officers.

"What's your business here?"

"Detective Inspector Vanier, Major Crimes, in Montreal. I was following the van that took them here. I heard about the operation and I wanted to question the survivors."

"Survivor. There's only one. If you leave me your card, I'll send you a copy of my report."

"I already talked to her. Do you want a copy of my report?"

"You don't have any authority here. You shouldn't have interfered with the witness."

Vanier walked across the room until he was within touching distance of Brown. "If I find a potential witness in a murder investigation, I'll ask them any questions I want."

Brown had been bending over the table, pulling papers out of a briefcase. He stepped back from the table and straightened up. "You listen to me. I'm leading a national task force. The woman is likely involved in human trafficking, and she's my witness. Get that straight. I want to know what she's been up to."

"Mind if I sit in on the interview?" Vanier asked.

Brown hesitated, exchanged glances with the two others. "If you do, you can't say anything. Not to her, not to us. We won't acknowledge your presence on the tape, and I don't want you to appear on the transcript."

"I'll be a fly on the wall."

"Seriously. I don't want your shadow on the transcript."

Brown picked up the phone and punched some numbers. "You can bring her up now. We're ready. And send up some coffee." There was a pause while Brown listened to the voice at the other end. "No, I don't think this is a fucking hotel. Fine, we'll get our own damn coffee." He paused again, listening. "Yeah, I got it. Turn right outside and there's a Tim Horton's on the next block."

Brown slammed the phone into the cradle. "Asshole." He turned to Carter.

"Julian. Go get us some coffee, will you." He looked at Vanier. "I suppose you want one too."

"That would be great. But, Julian, turn left outside. Two blocks down there's a decent coffee shop. They roast their own beans."

"What, Tim Hortons isn't good enough?" Brown pulled a twenty from his pocket and handed it to Carter.

"Get five," said Vanier. "One for our guest."

Julius hesitated, looked at the boss. "Okay," Brown said. "Get her a coffee too."

Five minutes later, the door opened and a female constable led Katya into the room. Brown gestured to a chair, and Katya sat down, turning to watch the constable leave. Then she looked at Vanier and managed a thin smile. He was sitting at the far end of the table, out of the witness's sightline while she was being questioned. Brown and Kaminski sat directly opposite Katya. She leaned forward and folded her arms on the table.

Brown got straight down to business. He put a small microphone in the middle of the desk, switched on the recorder and did a sound test. He played it back, heard himself, and was satisfied. He held his hand in the air and switched on the recorder.

"This is Inspector Robert Brown, and I am in conference room 2 at the Gananoque police station in Gananoque, Ontario. It is 11:30 a.m. on Thursday, July 8, 2014. With me is Sergeant Bob Kaminski. Corporal Julian Carter is part of the team but is not present at the moment. He will be joining us later. Also present is an unidentified female who was rescued from the St. Lawrence River eight miles from here at 3 a.m. this morning. She was picked up in the water after having apparently abandoned a larger boat that had come under coastguard surveillance. The dingy she was in was apparently defective and had sunk."

Brown looked up from his notes and stared at Katya like a headmaster wondering where to start with a troublesome student. Katya looked over to Vanier. He gave a shrug and a closed-mouth smile.

"What is your name?" said Brown.

"My name? Katya Babyak."

"Date and place of birth?"

Katya was twenty-six. Born in Poltava, in Ukraine. She had come to Canada in January or February, she wasn't sure of the exact date.

Brown led her through her odyssey from Kiev to Montreal, sucking facts out of her in a way that made her sound like she was reading from a ship's log: places, dates, times, and modes of transport. Vanier listened as closely to Brown as to the girl. Brown was stripping Katya's narrative of meaning, turning it into something that had as much human content as a railway timetable.

The door opened, and Carter walked in, balancing four coffees in a tray in one hand and clutching a fifth and a brown paper bag in the other. Brown held up his hand. "It is now 12:15 p.m., and we are pausing for a break." Then he switched off the recorder as though he were conducting some kind of ceremony.

Carter handed out the coffees and tipped the bag to spill a pile of small plastic creamers and sachets of sugar onto the table.

"For our guests," Brown said, "there will be no talking during the break. Inspector Vanier, do you understand?"

"Thanks for the coffee."

"Yes. Many thanks," Katya said.

Brown rolled his eyes. "I said no talking. I do not want to undermine this interview."

Brown and his two helpers huddled while Brown brought Carter up to date on the timeline of Katya's journey to Canada. When he had finished, he took the lid off his coffee and hunted through the creamers scattered on the table. They were all empty. He looked at Carter. "You didn't get enough creamers."

He raised his arm again. "Ready?"

Nobody responded.

"We're going back to the transcript. Three, two, one." He switched on the recorder.

Vanier resisted the temptation to applaud the switch-flicking ceremony.

"We are resuming at 12:30 p.m. Constable Carter has joined us, and I have briefed him on the earlier part of the interview. Ms. Babyak, for the next part of the interview, Sergeant Kaminski will ask you questions in Russian, and I want you to respond in Russian."

"Da."

"What?"

"Yes," said Kaminski.

"So you understand. Constable Kaminski will ask questions in Russian, and you will respond in Russian. Okay?"

"Yes. Okay."

Kaminski started hesitatingly, but in seconds he and Katya were talking back and forth like old friends, as if Katya had been waiting for the opportunity to tell her story in her own language, and was in a hurry to get everything out. Brown made an effort to look like he was following the conversation but his expression quickly faded to blank.

Vanier could barely pick up even the normal pattern

of sentences, but he could see the change. Katya became animated, sitting forward in the chair and gesturing wildly with her hands. Her confidence had increased a couple of notches, and she seemed to be explaining rather than just answering questions, talking in paragraphs instead of stunted phrases. Her rising anger was unmistakable.

Brown was having trouble letting go. He kept interrupting, halting the flow to have hushed conversations with Kaminski.

Half an hour into Kaminski's questioning, the sun hit the window and the temperature in the room began to rise. Vanier took off his jacket and rolled his sleeves up. Katya had long since taken off her sweater and sat in a T-shirt and jeans. Vanier realized the bra he'd bought was too big. She was constantly adjusting it, trying to make it fit. It wasn't the first time he'd overestimated the size of a woman's underwear. Women could be forgiving with bras that were too big, but not panties, Vanier mused. Go large on panties and you'd hear about it forever.

The three RCMP officers had their backs to the window, but they did nothing to acknowledge the heat, except sweat. Vanier watched a single drop hanging on the edge of Brown's eye. It swelled and succumbed to gravity, slipping down the side of his face. If Brown felt it, he didn't let on.

Every now and then Kaminski would place a pack of photographs in front of Katya, a mixture of mug shots with serial numbers, and surveillance photos. The first batch seemed to be from Ukraine, then Vanier heard Rotterdam mentioned, then came a set for Montreal. Katya recognized some of the people; for others she gave a shrug or shook her head. In the Montreal pack she punched five with her finger. Vanier recognized the Kedrovs, mother and son, and pumpkin-head, but not the others. Kaminski placed the last pack on the table. Vanier assumed they involved the boat trip. Katya focused on one photograph. She became agitated and her voice started rising until she was shouting, tapping her finger up and down on one photograph, a headshot of an ordinary-looking guy smiling into the camera.

Brown stopped the recording and had another whispered conversation with Kaminski, while Katya sat back in the chair, folded her arms and waited. Vanier had seen the same victim's pose hundreds of times: *You have what you want from me, that's him. Now, please, go and do your job.*

When they resumed, the rhythm of the questioning had changed, and Vanier sensed the interview was winding down. Kaminski looked up from his notes and turned to Brown. "Unless there's something else, sir, this part is done."

Brown reviewed his notes and thought for a few moments. He leaned towards the microphone. "Ms. Babyak, we thank you for your cooperation. We think that is all for today. It is now 2:15 p.m., and we are concluding the interview."

Before he could turn off the recorder, Katya interrupted. "What is to happen to me? I am valuable witness, no? They tried to kill me. Four people died last night.

You know who is responsible. You have photos. I am witness."

Brown looked agitated. He leaned forward to the microphone again. "We are studying all of the possibilities, Ms. Babyak. We may or may not lay charges against you. We haven't decided yet. When we do we will let you know."

"Charges? I do not understand. I am witness."

"By your own admission, you have entered Canada illegally, engaged in prostitution and attempted to enter the US illegally. For the moment, you will remain in custody until we have made some decisions."

"Fucking Christ," Vanier said.

Brown swivelled in his chair, furious. "Didn't I say to remain silent? So, please, shut the fuck up or you're leaving."

Vanier sat at the edge of his seat and glared impotently at Brown. Brown held up his hand again, though no one was looking. He switched off the recorder. "I am now going to start again and see if we can get a clean transcript." He glared at Vanier. "Inspector Vanier's intervention will be erased."

Vanier stood up. Before the door closed behind him, he heard Brown give his final instructions.

"Get someone to take her back," Brown told Carter. "Get her delivered to CBSA at the airport today. I want her on a flight out of here tonight."

"No. Please," Katya was begging. But nobody was listening.

Vanier waited until he saw Katya being escorted back to the cells by the constable before he went back into the interview room. Brown was helping pack up the equipment. He looked up. "Come back to apologize?"

"I want to know what's going on."

"None of your business. I shouldn't have let you sit in on the interview in the first place. Why don't you just go back to Quebec."

"You're holding somebody who is a witness to crimes that occurred in my jurisdiction. I want to know what you intend to do with her."

Brown was still sweating in the suit and tie, but the rivulets of sweat had been cleaned up.

"You really don't get it do you, Vanier?"

Vanier refused to answer.

"I'm running a task force to combat human trafficking in Canada. Big-picture stuff. When we're ready we'll do real damage to these organizations. That whore is just a small piece in a very big puzzle. She's given us all she's got. Some of it is useful. Not much, but it confirms some theories. That's all. I'm putting her on a plane and she's going back to whatever hellhole she came from. She'll be on a plane out of Toronto tonight and that's the last I want to see of her."

"Tonight? I told you, she's a witness. An important witness. I need her in Montreal." Vanier knew she wasn't a witness to any investigation he was carrying on, but that didn't matter. She had been forced into prostitution and had seen four people killed. He didn't like seeing any of that go unpunished. He also didn't mind butting heads with Brown.

"You can't have her in Montreal. I know you, Vanier. You have a reputation. But you're a big fish in a very small pond. I'm not fucking up our investigation just because you want to look flash back home. If I have any other questions for her, which I doubt, we'll fly to Shitville, Ukraine, and ask her there. She's not staying in Canada."

Vanier had no leverage. Katya was the RCMP's prisoner, and Brown was going to decide what happened to her.

"You have family, Brown?"

"None of your business, Vanier."

"This girl. This kid. She didn't choose this life. She was forced. She's the victim here. She almost died with the others."

"Save it, Vanier. If we don't get her on a plane tonight she'll wake up and make a refugee claim, and then she's here for three years while her claim is assessed. And we both know that in the end she'll still be sent back. You think Canada needs another whore? Like we don't have enough. I'm doing her a favour."

"Don't put yourself out."

"I won't, don't worry."

Everything was packed, and Kaminski and Carter were waiting by the door. Brown picked up his own bag.

"I've arranged transport." Carter told Brown. "Someone from the station is going to deliver her to the immigration people at Toronto airport. She's booked on a ten o'clock flight to Frankfurt and then a connection to Kiev."

"And we're even paying her ticket." Brown said. "It's been nice meeting you, Vanier."

"I'm sure."

Vanier walked over to the window and waited until they emerged into the parking lot. Kaminski was driving. Brown opened the back door and stood outside the car, letting the heat escape. Then he removed his jacket and folded it, leaning into the car to place it carefully on the back seat. Once they had pulled out of the parking lot, Vanier turned for the door.

On the ground floor, a constable pointed him to the shift sergeant, a big guy who dwarfed the small desk where he was poring over paperwork, holding a pen like he was ready to crush it in his ham of a hand. He looked up as Vanier approached, beaming at him like he was looking at an old friend. Vanier had never seen him before.

"Vanier, *comment ça va, mon ami?*"

His name badge said Jean Godin.

"*Vous êtes Québécois?*"

"No. I'm Franco-Ontarian."

Vanier smiled. "Me too. I was born just up the road from here, at the military base."

"Yeah, but you got back to the mother ship. I'm still stuck here on Planet Anglo. Planet fucking weirdo, if you ask me. I heard you had a long morning with the Mounties."

Vanier was about to answer, but Godin held up his

hand. He shouted over Vanier's shoulder. "Sheehan. I thought I told you, take car fifteen to the garage. The back seat is knee-deep in vomit. Christ, it's been there since last night."

Sheehan grumbled, but Godin wasn't having it. "It's been sitting in the sun all day. If it doesn't get cleaned out, the smell's going to be permanent. And I'll make sure you're driving it next winter. You'll like that. Windows up tight and the heaters going full blast. It'll smell to kill your nose hairs."

He turned back to Vanier. "Where was I?"

"RCMP."

"Oh yeah. Can you believe that guy? What was his name, Brown? They all think we're a bunch of country assholes. The ones in uniform, they're ordinary cops like you and me. But the guys up there in Ottawa are a bunch of pussies. Look what they did with the Air India investigation. Ever see such a farce? And Airbus. And the disappearing Native women? The list goes on and on. A bunch of fart-catchers for politicians, that's what they are. And now this," he was waving a sheet of paper. "They want me to take someone off shift to take a prisoner to Toronto. Does it say fucking airport taxi service on the cars outside?"

"I'm going to Toronto tonight. My girl lives there. Figured I was halfway there, so I should stop by for a visit. I can take your prisoner, if you want."

"Seriously?"

"The airport, right?"

"Year. Canada Border Services Agency at the airport. Apparently she's on a flight out tonight."

"Not a problem."

"That would help me. My guys get nervous when they drive out of town. They go to Toronto, they get tickets for speeding. When they go to Montreal, they get tickets for going too slow! Every time they leave town, they get tickets." Godin exploded in a belly laugh. "When are you leaving?"

"Soon as I can."

"Okay." Godin fished a sheet of paper from somewhere in the pile. "Here, sign this. A receipt for the prisoner."

Vanier wrote his name on the form and signed. He handed it back to Godin. "Can you print out another one of these for when I deliver her to CBSA? I guess I need to get them to sign off."

"Sure. Listen, I really appreciate this." Godin punched the keyboard with his thick fingers, then got up and grabbed a sheet off the printer. He handed it to Vanier. "Why don't you bring your car around the front, and I'll have someone bring her out."

Vanier pulled out his card and wrote his cell number on it. "Jean, if you ever want to visit the mothership, give me a call. Okay?"

"Sure thing, man. Thanks." Godin grinned.

Ten minutes later, Godin came out the front door leading Katya by the arm and carrying two Walmart bags. Katya's hands were handcuffed in front of her. Vanier opened the passenger side door, and Godin put his hand on the top of Katya's head as she stooped to get into the car. She gave Vanier a smile.

Godin threw the Walmart bags into the back seat and went around to the driver's side. "Here's the keys, and my card. When you've delivered her, give me a call."

"You want the cuffs back?"

"Keep them. A souvenir. She needs to be at the airport for eight-thirty at the latest. And don't forget to charge those bastards in Ottawa for the mileage. Charge them for your time, too."

Vanier leaned across Katya to secure her seat belt. He raised his hand to Godin and took off.

"Where do we go?" Katya asked.

It was coming up to five o'clock in the afternoon. If he pushed it, he could be at the airport in two hours. "Walmart. It's on the way to the highway."

Katya settled back into her seat. "Okay. Walmart." She said it slowly, as though learning a new word.

The parking lot was big enough for an airport. In one corner he counted fifteen large RVs, a caravan of Bedouin seniors looking for a safe place to camp in the wilderness.

He parked the car and released Katya from the handcuffs. "Don't run away."

Then he got out and marched across the expanse of empty tarmac to the main entrance, Katya trotting to keep up with him.

Inside the door an ancient man was holding on to a shopping cart to stay upright. He smiled at both of them.

"Welcome to Walmart."

"Thank you," Katya said.

"Women's clothes?" Vanier asked.

The old guy shuffled his feet back and forth to turn himself around and raised an arm to point vaguely to the centre of the store. "Up there, son. Up there, on the right."

Katya took off slowly in the direction he was pointing, taking everything in like a tourist in a cathedral. Vanier caught up with her. "First time?"

"I saw in movies. But first time, yes." She spun around. "All this?"

"Yeah, all this."

When they got to the women's section he led her around, picking things up. "You like?"

She liked everything; it was easy shopping. "The sizes are good?" Vanier asked.

Katya pulled at the waist of the jeans he had bought earlier. There was room to fit a small child in with her.

"Sorry"

"Is okay. Can I look?"

"Sure. You look. You choose. I need to get a cart. Stay here and choose some stuff. I'll be back in two minutes."

"Okay."

Vanier went back to the main entrance and grabbed a shopping cart. When he got back to the women's section, Katya was nowhere to be seen. He abandoned the cart and started the kid-lost-in-a-department store dance every parents knows by heart, half shuffling, half running in ever larger circles, chasing flashes of images, a colour he thought he recognized, blonde hair, the right body type. He rushed through the fishing section, electronics, menswear, food aisles and housewares. Back in women's, an assistant was folding clothes.

"I've lost somebody."

She looked up at him, concerned. "A child?"

"No. Adult. Twenty-six. Blond. So high," he gestured with his hand.

The concern disappeared from her face and she shifted back to boredom. "You tried the changing rooms?" She nodded to a sign.

He pushed the swinging doors and called her name. Katya stepped out in a plain blue dress. She was barefooted. "Good?"

"Very good."

She smiled. "I am ready." She disappeared back into the cubicle and emerged carrying an armful of clothes.

"Is too much, no?"

"No. Just right. Let's go."

Vanier pointed to the pile he had selected earlier. "These too?"

"No. They are nice," she said, pointing to the clothes in the shopping cart. "But these are right size."

As they were walking towards the cash, Katya abandoned the cart and disappeared into the pharmacy section, searching up and down the shelves. She reached down and grabbed a box of large Band-Aids, examined it closely and then lobbed it underhand up the aisle and into the cart.

"Good shot." He picked up the box. "You're hurt?"

"No."

Before they had pulled out of the parking lot, Katya was already elbow deep in the bags. She grabbed the box of Band-Aids and ripped it open. She carefully applied a square patch to her arm, covering the eagle tattoo. She held it up to examine it, and showed Vanier. "I am free."

Vanier said nothing.

The highway was two miles from Walmart. The sign pointed right for Montreal, and straight across the overpass for Toronto.

He turned right.

Katya continued to rummage through the bags, pulling out bits of clothing one by one to examine them, holding them up in the air for the full effect, and then holding them up for Vanier to see. "You like?"

"Nice, very nice," Vanier responded. "Lovely, oh yes, very smart."

And Katya echoed. "Nice, very nice, lovely, oh yes, very smart."

Vanier drove for an hour. Katya was fast asleep. He fished Godin's card from his pocket and punched the numbers into his phone.

"Jean?"

"Yeah. Who's this?"

"Vanier."

"Vanier, you there already? *Ostie*, you guys drive fast."

"There's a problem. The girl. She's gone."

"No, don't tell me this. Don't tell me. She was hand-cuffed, for Chrissake."

"I know. I had to stop for gas and to take a leak. I came back and she's gone. I looked everywhere. I think she must've gotten a lift on a truck."

"There's a thousand trucks on that goddamn highway. So she's long gone."

"Looks like. I've looked everywhere."

"How special was she?"

"What do you mean?"

"The RCMP sends three guys to interview her, and she doesn't even get to go to the hospital for a checkup. But when they finished, they didn't seem think she was so important."

"She was a victim, Jean. No more than that. Brown sucked her dry of information and was sending her home. He said if he needed to speak to her again, he could fly to the shithouse she calls home. That's what he said."

"So it's no big loss for him?"

"But it makes us look bad."

"Luc, don't worry. I can take care of that. I'll have to write a report. You too. I'm going to say that I insisted that they take their prisoner to Toronto themselves, but those lazy bastards refused. I'll say I told them I could only spare one man and it wasn't secure. They'll look like assholes. Don't worry, my friend. Us francos have to stick together. You go and visit your daughter, have a good time. The girl will show up one day."

"So no hard feelings?"

"If I had to choose between a cop and an Ottawa pencil pusher, there's no choice. I'll send you a copy of my report in the morning. Okay? And you write yours, back me up, okay? This is Brown's problem, not ours."

"If you put it that way, I'll take the rest of the day off."

"You do that."

Vanier's next call was to David Reynolds. "I need your help."

"Inspector Vanier?"

"The same. I have someone who needs your services. Somewhere to stay for a few days. I'll pay the rent."

Reynolds hesitated. "That's a problem."

Too many people were looking for space, and nobody was leaving. Always more people arrived than left. When you were illegal, your options were limited. Reynolds promised to see what he could do. "In a few days, maybe we can find a spot for her."

Vanier had no choice but to accept.

"Call me in two days about your friend."

While Katya slept, Vanier pondered his options. There weren't many. The first thing Brown would do would be to send someone to check Vanier's place. Then there was Kedrov to think about. She would want her girl back, and it wouldn't take much to figure out that Vanier had been the last person to see her. He thought about asking Anjili if she could put Katya up for a few days, toyed with the idea of testing her, of seeing how she'd react. Instead he called Alex.

"Yo!"

"Yo yourself. Alex, I have a favour to ask."

Alex had been a basket case when he had returned from Afghanistan. He had spent the first year living with his dad, trying to pull himself together. Then he got a job at the Botanical Gardens. A simple job, he liked to say, low-stress, outdoors, manual labour in a setting that calmed his spirit. He spent his days digging, weeding, clearing brush, clipping trees, deadheading flowers. He spent his days watching things grow. Every night he got home exhausted, and most nights he slept as peacefully as a ditch digger; the dreams that had haunted him couldn't seem to break through the exhaustion of a day of hard physical work. Six months earlier, he had said it was time to find his own place, and within two weeks he had moved out of his father's apartment. Vanier worried, but it had been time.

Alex's place was in Verdun. The rent was cheap because the building was old and hadn't been renovated in fifty years. The landlord was waiting for the first reasonable offer from a developer, and figured there was no point in throwing money at a building that was going to be knocked down for condos. Each of the three floors was divided into two apartments. Alex was on the third. He kept a spare room with a mattress on the floor for when his sister visited from Toronto.

Vanier made the introductions at the door and Alex and Katya exchanged a tentative handshake and even more tentative smiles. It was late at night but the apartment was still steaming hot after baking all day under the flat tar roof. All the windows were open, but the air was thick and sticky.

"It's just for a few days, Alex."

"Sure, Dad. Not a problem." He turned to Katya. "Consider this Hotel Vanier."

"I can cook and I can clean," she said.

"Me too," Alex said, smiling.

"Katya's a witness. I need to keep her off the streets for a few days. She's had a hard time, Alex. She needs to rest."

Then he turned to Katya. "This is very important. You need to stay inside. If you want anything, ask Alex and he can call me. I'll come by every day."

She nodded. Alex grabbed the Walmart bags and led her down the corridor. "This is Elise's room. She's my sister. She's in Toronto."

Katya looked inside and started. The room was bare except for a small dresser and the mattress. There were signs of the previous occupant: a woman's toiletry bag, small hair elastics, and a hairbrush.

"What's the matter?" Vanier said.

"Nothing." She paused. "Yes, something. It reminds me of the place before, small room. Nothing but to wait for next man."

"It's not that." Vanier said. "You're safe here. And it's only a few days."

"Yes."

"I'll get some sheets." Alex turned and walked down

the hallway.

"Alex is a good man. You can trust him."

"Yes. Alex is a good son, no?"

Katya walked into the room, dropped her Walmart bags on the floor against the wall. Alex came back with sheets and a towel. "It cools down at night," he said, acknowledging the oppressive heat as he dropped the sheets on the mattress. "Back in a second."

Katya leaned against the wall. Looked up at Vanier. "It is nice. Thank you."

Alex came back in with a large fan, plugged it in and showed Katya how to operate it. He pointed it at the bed and pushed some buttons. It oscillated side to side, pushing hot air up and back along the top of the mattress.

Vanier followed as Alex gave Katya a tour of the apartment. They ended up in the kitchen, and Katya accepted Alex's offer of tea. "It's decided, Dad. We're ordering pizza for supper."

"I wish. But no, I have to go. I'll be back tomorrow."

Alex walked him to the door. "She's fragile, Alex, like you were," Vanier told his son. "She's been through a lot."

"Don't worry, Dad. I'll look after her."

TWENTY-SEVEN

"When does an accident become a disaster?"

"What?"

Vanier was reading the documents Saint Jacques had gotten from Google, the one entitled *Memorandum of Understanding: Compensation Fund – Chajul*. He spread the four pages on the table in front of him. The other document was a schedule.

He had read through the contract three times. It was simple. There were five preambles giving the background and identifying three parties—Essence and the governments of Guatemala and Canada. The rest was about what each party was to do. Essence was to pay fifty million in the compensation fund, but only if the Canadian government pitched in another fifty. The Guatemalans were to distribute the funds in accordance with the agreed-upon schedule, and they also had to pass a law prohibiting any of the victims from filing lawsuits against Essence or any of its employees. At the end, there was a clause whereby

Essence insisted that there was nothing in the agreement to be taken as an admission of liability. The last page had lines for three signatures. Richard Susskind was to sign for Essence. The names of those signing for Guatemala and Canada hadn't been filled in.

"How many people died?" Vanier asked.

Saint Jacques didn't have to consult her notes. "One hundred and twelve. Thirty were children. Over two hundred families lost their homes."

"That's a disaster in my books, not an accident."

"'Accident' has better optics," said Saint Jacques.

"And this is how they're going to make it right? Canada pays fifty million, Essence pays another fifty million. And that's it. Everything is okay?"

"There's no admission of liability."

"Essence cuts corners to save money, and a lake of polluted water from the mine causes a mudslide that destroys a village. They pay fifty million and get to start up the mine again. Looks like a good deal for Essence. How much were they making from the mine?"

"Thirty-five million a year."

"I can see why they wanted to keep the deal quiet. There's more. Only half of the money is actually going to the compensation fund. Section 4 says the money is to be distributed in accordance with the schedule." Vanier pointed to the schedule. "The compensation fund only gets fifty and five individuals divide up the other fifty. Who are these people?"

The names meant nothing to Vanier. There were four

Spanish names, and one English, Lindon Hastings. "See what you can dig up. Then we go back to Susskind. The bastard told us he knew nothing, and he's the one signing for Essence."

Two hours later, Vanier and Saint Jacques were on the way to Essence. They had decided that Saint Jacques would ask the questions, and Vanier would sit back and watch. He had a theory on nonverbal communication: there were no rules. You could tell a lot from how people acted and reacted, but everyone was different. You just had to watch carefully to see if you picked up anything.

Every couple of years, the department would pay for the latest expert to teach detectives how to read physical cues to tell when people were lying. The only problem was, the latest expert always contradicted the previous expert. The only thing all the experts agreed on was that police interrogators didn't have a clue. The courses always started with a bunch of studies of what cops believed and what the empirical research showed, and the two were always worlds apart.

Vanier preferred to observe carefully, and to think about what he was seeing and hearing. Too many people had lost the ability to do either, looking without seeing and only listening for gaps in conversation so they could start talking themselves.

This time, Vanier and Saint Jacques were put in a boardroom, designed to impress, with tasteful, expensive furniture, and a view over the golf-course-green lawn with its pond and large fountain. The walls were lined with black and white aerial photographs of Essence's mines, roads, and bridges.

Susskind was five minutes late. The same two acolytes were with him, Sylvie Nadeau and Adriana Menendez. The two women sat down directly across from Vanier and Saint Jacques. Susskind remained standing, resting his hands on an empty chair to support his bulky frame.

"Don't mind if I stand for a while? I do my best thinking when I stand up." He looked at his watch. "I've got a meeting in twenty-five minutes, so I hope this won't take too long."

"We're trying to get some clarification, sir," Saint Jacques said. "You know, to make things clear."

"Sure. Whatever. I mean whatever I can do to help." He leaned forward, and started doing calf stretches, like he was getting ready for a jog.

"The kidnapping inquiry has turned into a murder inquiry."

"I heard. And you still haven't found the guy?"

"We're following a number of leads, sir."

"I don't know where we come in." He was low to the table, stretching the muscles in his calf. Menendez was scribbling everything down. Nadeau, the lawyer, was listening intently.

"You remember, we had asked about some translation work Sophia Luna was doing for Essence?"

"I seem to remember she was not doing work for us. I recall you asked about a particular contract but we had no record of it."

"That's right. Just to clarify, did you find out anything more about the contract?"

Susskind looked to Nadeau. She looked Saint Jacques in the eye. "We promised to see if we could find any record of a document sent to ALT for translation around the time you mentioned. We couldn't."

"And I can't think of what it might have been. Must have been a mistake," Susskind said.

"Again, just to be clear, you do not know what, if any, document was sent to ALT for translation into Spanish? Job number 14-0629?"

"Like Sylvie said, we came up negative," Susskind replied, "and I know nothing about it. So, no." Susskind was having trouble working his quadriceps, pulling his left foot up behind him. It would have looked odd if Susskind had been anywhere near in shape, but with Susskind's weight, it looked like a circus performance, by a clown, not an acrobat.

"Thank you," said Saint Jacques. "Now I am going to read you a list of names and I would like you to tell me if you recognize them."

"Sure."

Saint Jacques pulled out the draft schedule to the contract and started reading.

"Juan Arbenz?"

The name caught Susskind balancing on his left leg, his right foot clutched in his hand. Putting on the warm-up display had become a high-wire act, and the smallest misstep was amplified. He was tottering on one leg, his knuckles turning white on the chair back. He made a show of thinking. "It kind of rings a bell. But I'm not sure. You know how it is, I meet people all the time."

He dropped his foot to the floor and shifted his weight from one leg to the other, like a boxer waiting for the bell. "If you have other names, why don't you give them to Adriana and she'll get back to you."

"Why don't I just continue?" Saint Jacques picked up the schedule, pushed her chair back from the table and crossed her legs. "You tell me if you recognize the names. If you don't, you can check your address book and get back to us."

Susskind looked like he was going to sit down. He reconsidered. "Okay, go on."

Nadeau wasn't looking at Saint Jacques anymore. She had turned to look up at Susskind.

"Héctor Sandarti?"

"Nope. Maybe. Put that down as the same as the first. I'll have to check."

"How do you spell that?" Menendez asked. Saint Jacques spelled the name and the assistant wrote it down carefully.

"Otto Rosales?"

"Same thing."

"For the record, you don't recognize the name."

"That's not what I said." He was beginning to sweat, small beads appearing on his forehead. "Maybe they are familiar. Maybe. Look. I do know someone called Otto

Rosales. He's in the Guatemalan government."

"So, you do know him?"

"If it's the same person."

"Would you provide me with his coordinates?"

"Well, wait a second," Nadeau intervened. "I think you need more than a name. Mr. Susskind can't simply give you someone's personal contact information from his address book just because you've asked for it. Next name?"

Saint Jacques looked back to Susskind. He had stopped rocking on his feet. "Mr. Susskind, are we talking about the same person?"

"I don't know. I told you. The Otto Rosales I know is a minister in the government in Guatemala." Susskind pulled out a chair and sat down. There was a damp sheen on his face.

"Minister of what?" Saint Jacques asked.

"Justice."

"Do you know him?"

"Of course I do. He's leading the file from Guatemala on the incident. He was their point man on the negotiations for compensation."

Saint Jacques had been making a point of writing out her answers, like she was ticking boxes on a checklist. She took it slow. She looked up. "The incident?"

"Yes, the Chajul incident. There was an accident there."

She waited for more. There was only silence.

"Okay. Last name. Lindon Hastings. Do you know a

Lindon Hastings?"

Susskind looked worn out. "The only Lindon Hastings I know is the Canadian Minister of International Development."

"Is he involved in the Chajul negotiations?"

"Was. The negotiations are finished. Essence and Canada contributed to the compensation fund. Minister Hastings was involved with the Canadian side of the negotiations. He's the one who approved the payment."

"Any idea what these names might have in common?"

Susskind opened his mouth to speak. Nadeau beat him to it. "You're asking him to speculate on something he knows nothing about and for which has no context. I don't think he should do that."

Susskind was looking at his watch. "I have another meeting starting now."

"We won't be much longer, sir."

Vanier pushed an envelope along the table to Saint Jacques. She pulled the memorandum out and slipped it across the table to Susskind. "Do you recognize this document?"

Susskind did a perfunctory flip through the pages, thought for a few seconds and said, in a low voice, "I've never seen it before."

Saint Jacques waited.

Susskind couldn't help himself. A salesman hates silence. "It's probably… No, I'm not going to speculate. I don't recognize this document. I've never seen it before."

"Even though you're the one who's supposed to be

signing it?"

"I didn't sign it, if that's your question. It could be anything. It's only a draft. A thing like this means nothing until it's signed. Listen. I've got to go." He got to his feet again.

"We're finished here," Saint Jacques said.

Susskind was walking to the door before she'd finished talking.

Vanier stood up and spoke to Susskind's back. "Oh, Mr. Susskind."

Susskind stopped and looked back.

"You know when you said you'd never seen the draft memorandum before?"

"I haven't. I don't see every document."

"I don't believe a word of it. And you know what that means?"

Now he turned around to face Vanier. "That you're calling me a liar?"

"That now is a good time for you to start worrying. Sleep on it. You want to talk, you call me."

Susskind left without saying a word.

TWENTY-EIGHT

There are good crime scenes and bad ones. The best kind is where the victim is dead at home, and the simple questions can usually be answered just by looking around. When the body is lying on the living room carpet, most of the important questions are straightforward. Who was he? Did he know the perpetrator? Was there a struggle? Was it a robbery?

The worst crime scenes are the body drops, where the body has been transported somewhere else and dumped. Garbage dumps are the worst of all.

All there was to connect Camara to where he had been killed was the body, the carpet, and the route taken by the dump truck. They still needed to find where he had been killed.

Vanier and Saint Jacques drove along the route the dump truck had taken. It was clear that guesswork wasn't going to do it. The truck had started out on Jean-Talon and followed Côte-des-Neiges on its long slow ascent up the western flank of the mountain. Côte-des-Neiges was a densely packed immigrant neighbourhood divided by a wide street lined with stores, banks, and restaurants. The side streets were lined with aging apartment buildings that made public housing projects look appealing—homes for immigrants, where landlords did nothing but collect the rent for rodent-infested apartments with broken toilets. The area was a magnet for newly arrived immigrants, and for those who had been in Canada for years but couldn't make the dream work. Anyone who needed a cheap place to live.

The truck's first stop was behind the Plaza Côte-des-Neiges shopping centre. After that it stopped at every block up the hill and every block on the way back down. The dump truck had made sixty pickups on the way up and thirty more on the way down, ending at a large supermarket.

Vanier and Saint Jacques were drinking iced coffees on a terrace at the top end of the street.

"We can't do a door-to-door," Vanier said. "It would take years. And we'd need twenty translators."

"But we could do a public appeal. Look at how many people go by. Look at the bus."

Vanier looked. It was three o'clock in the afternoon, but the bus was packed.

"If we got two posts," Saint Jacques continued. "One near the bottom, one up here, with a blow-up picture of Camara and a poster: *Do You Know This Man?* It would take manpower, but it's our best shot at finding out where he was living."

Vanier was watching the street. "Or," Saint Jacques continued, "we could just wait until the landlord reports it."

"Around here? The place will be rented out in a heartbeat if he's not around to pay the rent. We need to get to it before anyone else does. Let's go with the public appeal."

Saint Jacques pulled out her cellphone and started making the calls.

It took two days to set up the command posts. The uniforms started at eight o'clock, and by nine-thirty they had a positive identification. At ten-thirty, Vanier and Saint Jacques were standing outside a building on Berkeley.

Vanier leaned on the buzzer marked Janitor, and a small South-Asian man in slippers and a dressing gown came shuffling out of the darkened hallway. He opened the glass door cautiously.

"Yes? Can I help you?"

Vanier held up a photograph of Camara. "Police. Do you recognize this man?"

The janitor pulled a pair of glasses from his pocket and put his foot against the door to stop it from closing. He squinted at the photograph.

"Yes. Yes. Mr. Condé, he lives in 103, at the back." He gestured down the hallway behind him.. "But I don't think he's home. I haven't seen him for a few days. Very quiet fellow."

Vanier pushed open the door and walked in. Saint

Jacques followed.

"You have the keys?"

"I don't think …"

"It's urgent. A murder inquiry." The janitor looked at Saint Jacques for confirmation and then back to Vanier.

"I'll get the keys." He came back in two minutes with a large bunch of keys. He held a toasted sandwich in the other hand. "I was just going to have breakfast when you rang the buzzer."

Vanier stood behind him while he played with a key in the lock. It clicked into place and he pushed the door. Vanier took him by the shoulders and moved him aside. "Stay here."

The apartment was one room with a small bathroom. A tiny alcove housed a sink and hot plate. A thick length of steel was lying by the side of the door, a security doorstop that would have been propped under the door handle. The door wouldn't open with the bar in place. There was only one window in the place, a double-hung that gave onto the alley in the back. The bottom frame was pushed all the way up.

The room had been searched. What little Camara owned had been strewn over the floor. Vanier moved around the apartment slowly.

"Reminds me of Luna's place and Bélair's office," Saint Jacques said. "They're still looking for something."

"Maybe they found it this time." Vanier pointed to the bed. The mattress was still on the bed. "They had sliced the mattress open when they searched Luna's place."

Vanier went over to the window. There was a single bullet hole through the glass in each frame, but the holes didn't match. He turned to look back at the door, and took a pair of latex gloves from his pocket before turning back to the window. He pulled on the lower frame. When it was about six inches from the windowsill, the bullet holes matched, at a height that was level with Vanier's shoulder, and that would have been level with Camara's head.

He turned back to Saint Jacques. "Someone comes to the door and Camara decides to leave in a hurry. He goes to the window, opens it, and he's shot, falls back onto the carpet."

He pointed to a faint line of accumulated dirt outlining a rectangle.

"After he shoots Camara, the shooter pulls the window up, climbs in and opens the door."

"So there were two of them?"

"Camara was always ready to run. If there had only been one, it would've taken him time to realize the door wasn't going to open. With the security bar, Camara would have had plenty of time to disappear out the window. Call the SOC guys and get them here. We've got our crime scene."

While Saint Jacques was on the phone, Vanier wandered around looking for anything out of the ordinary. There was hardly anything personal in the place. Camara travelled light, and he didn't seem to have accumulated much since he had found his own place. Vanier pulled the mattress up off the bed, but there was nothing underneath, and no rips or tears. He got down on his hands and knees to look under the bed. Nothing. He walked around the edges of the fitted carpet, bending to pull at it every few feet but it was tight as a drum. Then he moved into the kitchen alcove and pulled out a drawer, bending look under it. He straightened up and removed the plastic cutlery tray. Then he pulled the drawer all the way out and held it up for Saint Jacques to see. She gave him the thumbs up while she continued talking. A brown envelope was taped under the drawer. Peeling away the tape that was holding the envelope to the drawer, Vanier released it. The brown envelope wasn't sealed, and there was a smaller white envelope inside it. He pulled it out. The printing said it was from the Office of the Minister of Citizenship and Immigration, and it was addressed simply to Mr. Sékou Camara. Vanier pulled out the letter. The letter was signed by the Minister himself. Saint Jacques was still on the phone, trying to read the letter over Vanier's shoulder. Vanier started reading out loud:

> "Pursuant to section 25 of the *Canadian Citizenship Immigration and Refugee Protection Act*, I hereby grant permanent resident status to you, Sékou Camara, on humanitarian and compassionate grounds."

It was signed by Michael Showers, Minister of Citizenship and Immigration. Signed four days before Camara's body had shown up at the dump.

"The Minister makes him a legal resident and then he's killed. What's going on, boss?"

"I wish I knew."

Saint Jacques went to the car for the yellow tape. By the time she got back, a patrol car had arrived, and they let the uniforms seal up the place.

On the way back to the office, Vanier and Saint Jacques decided to visit Henri Cabana, hoping that he could explain Camara's letter. The immigration lawyer read it carefully, thought for a second, polished his glasses, and read it again. He looked up at the detectives. "It looks genuine. It's signed by the Minister. But that's amazing."

"Why amazing?"

"This guy doesn't do humanitarian and compassionate."

"Showers?"

"Michael Showers. Canada's Minister for Citizenship and Immigration." Cabana leaned back in his chair. "He has the authority to grant permanent resident status to anyone on humanitarian and compassionate grounds. That power was used in the past. Rarely, but it was used. Mostly for the really tragic cases that get into the newspapers. You know, some family failed in the refugee claim, but there is something special that pulls at the heartstrings. I had a client years ago where the father had saved some kid in a swimming pool. He was a hero, and Canada was going to deport him and his family. No politician likes that kind of bad publicity. So the Minister at the time issued a permit on humanitarian and compassionate grounds. But not Showers. He doesn't do that."

"Could Sophia Luna have applied for one of those?" said Vanier.

"We discussed it. I told her it was as likely as getting a pardon for a pedophile axe murderer."

"She didn't qualify?"

"Under Showers, nobody qualifies. This guy doesn't even approve of immigration. At best, it's a necessary evil. His philosophy is, if Canada needs more people, women should make more babies."

"So Sophia Luna would not have received a Minister's permit?" said Vanier.

"A leftist, lesbian journalist? Not a chance in hell. Among immigration lawyers, the word was that the Minister hadn't issued a single permit. I guess we were wrong. He issued this one." Cabana tapped the plastic sleeve with his finger. "Who is the lucky recipient?"

"A failed refugee claimant. A guy from Guinea."

"He must've had a great story."

"You mean his claim?" Vanier asked.

"Not his claim. The humanitarian and compassionate grounds. His claim must have been rejected. Otherwise, he wouldn't need a permit. No, the Minister would only grant a permit if there were compelling humanitarian grounds."

"You mean like family reasons, heartstrings kinds of stuff?" said Saint Jacques.

"Exactly. But it would need to be a damn good story.

So what was it? A Muslim extremist who became a born-again Christian?"

"He was a thirty-five-year-old African with bad eye-sight. No family in Canada that we know of. Nice guy, but that's all."

"Then I don't understand," said Cabana.

"I'm beginning to." Vanier was on his feet, picking up the letter. "You've been a great help."

"Can I have a copy of the letter?"

"Afraid not. Maybe when this is over."

"It's a head scratcher," said Cabana.

"It is that," said Vanier.

TWENTY-NINE

The squad room was hushed, and the atmosphere was tense. Saint Jacques was bounding back and forth on her crutches as though to sit down would be to give up. Vanier had his feet up on the desk and hadn't said a word in half an hour. Everyone was trying to put the pieces together in their heads.

"As theories go, it's a good one. It holds together. But it just doesn't make sense," said Laurent.

"We have a draft, unsigned contract that seems to show several people, including a Canadian minister, skimming millions off the compensation fund. We know that Luna saw the draft and would have been familiar with the Guatemalan players. But that was two months ago."

Saint Jacques spoke up. "We know that someone at Essence went to great pains to get the document back. Luna was looking for someone to help her with some transaction, and she was kidnapped and killed. So maybe she had a copy and was blackmailing them?"

"Why kidnap her?" said Laurent. "Why not just kill her?"

"Because she had put the copies in a safe place and had a backup plan to release the documents if they didn't co-operate," said Vanier.

"Camara?"

"Exactly.

"So they kidnapped her to force her to give up her copy," said Saint Jacques.

"But the contract was circulated for translation months ago. Why did they wait to grab her?" Laurent asked.

"Maybe they didn't wait." Vanier said. "Maybe she waited. The deal was only done a few weeks ago. So she waited, and then she contacted them. There's no way anyone would sign the contract in draft form, with the names. Maybe the names were just placeholders."

"The draft showed who would be getting the money, but the final contract would have covered all that up," Saint Jacques said. "They would have dressed it up to look legitimate. So Luna waited until the money had been paid. Maybe she had proof of who was getting paid."

"With that information, she could try to get a Minister's permit," Vanier continued. "Camara got one."

"But how do you tie in the Immigration Minister? He's the one who signed the permit," said Saint Jacques.

"True, but these are politicians. They trade favours. You don't get to be a Cabinet Minister without help. Maybe he owed Hastings a favour," Vanier said.

"So Lindon Hastings was getting squeezed by Luna.

He tells Essence what's happening, and they pick her up," Saint Jacques concluded.

"The security firm GSC does. They do the dirty work for Essence," said Laurent.

"Camara told me he made a copy of whatever was in the safety deposit box. He figured it out for himself. After they killed Luna, he tried to make the same deal. Give up the papers in return for permanent residency. But he was more successful," said Vanier.

"He knew what he was up against. He was a careful guy, Maybe he had a better plan," said Saint Jacques.

"So this time they actually issued the permit. Then, once they get the documents back, Camara's the only one outside the circle who knows what went down. So they kill him," said Vanier.

"What about us? We have the draft, and we're outside the circle," said Saint Jacques.

"We're still a problem for them, but what have we got? We've got an undated draft. Their lawyers will be all over that. It's nothing. Essence probably assumes we can't go anywhere with that," Vanier said.

"So we've got a theory. But there's no good evidence, nothing concrete. You can't get a search warrant on speculation," said Laurent.

"So what do we do?" said Saint Jacques.

The squad room fell silent again. Vanier pulled his feet off the desk and leaned forward. "Let's shake the cage."

He pulled the keyboard of the computer into place and looked up the Minister of Immigration. The first result was the Minister's Ottawa office. Vanier used an internal phone, the kind that blocks caller ID. He dialled the number and put the phone on speaker. In seconds, someone answered.

"Minister Showers's office." A woman's voice.

"I'd like to speak to the Minister."

"Hold on. I'll put you through to a member of his staff."

He was put on hold and then reconnected. "Minister's office." A man's voice this time.

"The Minister, please."

"Could you tell me what it's about?"

"It's personal."

"Then you should call him on his personal phone."

"I'm not a friend. I don't have the number."

"Then you need to tell me what it's about and I can direct you to the right person."

"Okay. Got a pen?"

"Yes. Go ahead."

"Tell the minister to call me back. Tell him it's urgent. I want to talk to him about Essence, the Chajul compensation fund, and his good friend Minister Hastings. Got that?"

"I think so, yes. You want to talk to Minister Showers about Essence, the Chajul compensation fund and Minister Hastings."

"His good friend, Minister Hastings. Write that down."

"Yes. Right, his good friend Minister Hastings."

Vanier left his cell number.

"And your name, sir."

"No name," said Vanier, and clicked disconnect. He looked up. "If he calls back, there's a connection and we're not crazy."

Vanier pulled open his desk drawer and began searching through the clutter. Things went into the drawers, but rarely left, an accumulation of junk that might come in useful someday: staples, paper clips, pens, batteries, notepads, loose sachets of Alka-Seltzer, Tylenol, over-the-counter remedies for intemperance. Finally, he pulled out a small cube with a cable connector and attached it to his cellphone.

"A cell-phone speaker. Alex gave it to me."

"Impressive," said Saint Jacques.

The call came in fifteen minutes later, from an Ottawa number. Vanier hit connect. "Mr. Minister. Thanks for calling back."

"What the hell is this about?"

"My name is Detective Inspector Vanier, I'm with the Major Crimes Squad in Montreal. I wanted to ..."

"A policeman?" He was yelling. "You want to speak to a Minister of the Crown, you go through normal protocol. You understand me? Who the hell do you think you are?"

"Minister ..."

The line had already disconnected. Vanier looked across to Saint Jacques. "He knows. Jesus. We're not crazy," Vanier said.

"Yes, and now he knows that we know," Saint Jacques said. "Things could start getting rough."

The bar at the Queen Elizabeth Hotel was as close to a businessman's club as you could get without investing your retirement fund in a membership fee. All dark wood and muted fabrics, it was the kind of place where even changing the carpets would get the historical society picketing the front door. Even the waiters were old. They wore black and never spoke louder than a church whisper. The doors of the coolers behind the bar closed with the sound of velvet on velvet. It was an oasis where the only background noise was ice clinking on crystal, and where murmured conversations were not meant to be overheard.

Susskind was on his second martini, and he felt like he was drinking water. Despite the air conditioning, he could feel the sweat soaking his shirt under his suit jacket. He resisted the urge to loosen his tie. Appearances count, and he needed to look in control.

Joe Merchant was already half an hour late. Susskind's phone was sitting in his breast pocket. He'd switched it to vibrate, as the sign at the entrance instructed. Now, the stream of incoming emails vibrated over his heart every few seconds. He took another slug of the martini and examined the backs of his hands. They were covered in an ugly red rash, the skin brittle and peeling.

When Merchant finally arrived, forty-five minutes late, he didn't apologize, just sat down heavily in the chair, and looked at Susskind. "Traffic."

Susskind was about to say something, but the waiter beat him to it.

"What can I get you, sir?"

Merchant looked at Susskind's glass. "Martini looks good."

"Gin or vodka, sir?"

"Who the fuck puts vodka in a martini?"

"People like it, sir. It's very popular."

"Not me."

The waiter turned to leave. Susskind said, "I'll have another." He wasn't sure if the waiter heard him.

Susskind leaned towards Merchant. "We're almost there."

"That's what you said last time."

"We had to do what's necessary. You know that."

"This is turning into a cluster fuck, and you're getting me worried. Seriously worried."

Susskind tried to look calm. He hated delivering bad news. "The cop, Vanier. He called Minister Showers. All hell has broken loose."

"God almighty. What did he say?"

"Who, the Minister? Vanier?"

"Let's start with Vanier."

"Nothing. That's the thing. He left a message for the Minister. He mentioned Essence, the compensation deal and Minister Hastings. He left a number, and Showers called him back."

"Asshole. I hope he didn't say anything."

"He says no. But Vanier's not stupid. He knows that

Ministers of the Crown don't return strange phone calls. Just calling back gave Vanier too much information. Vanier has become very dangerous."

Susskind looked up at Merchant, hoping he would get the message without his having to say it directly.

"Don't even go there," Merchant said. "Don't even think about it."

"Think about what?"

"There's no way we're going after a cop. A detective, no less. That's just not going to happen."

"Do you have any idea what's at stake here?"

"Yeah. Maybe fifty million in payoffs. And if you ask me, we're wasting a lot of effort paying off a bunch of crooked politicians."

The waiter came back with the drinks, and they waited in silence until he left.

"Fifty million is nothing. Essence has a market cap of four billion dollars. If any of this leaks, the company goes down the toilet faster than you can flush. I don't even want to contemplate that. Essence depends on public contracts, and we can lose them in a heartbeat with a corruption scandal. Even the rumour of an investigation would send the shares crashing. That's real money coming straight out of our shareholders' pockets. If we start losing contracts, we're finished."

"The cop's fishing. He needs evidence and he doesn't have any. Suspicions aren't enough. If he knew anything, you'd be dealing with search warrants, not prank phone calls."

"Maybe you're right." Susskind wasn't convinced.

"Of course I'm fucking right."

"A situation like this, you've got to control it. Minister Hastings was on the phone to me screaming that he'd have my skin. He could call anybody on our board, and I would be out of a job in the morning. But this is not about me. It's about all of us."

Merchant listened, waiting for the threat.

"You know how politicians are. If Showers thinks he's in trouble, he'll grab a lawyer and make a deal with the cops. Everyone knows the first guy to go to the cops will get an immunity deal. That's what we have to avoid. We need to convince them, Hastings and Showers, that there is no problem."

"That's your job."

"And I'm doing it. But I need help. I need to get Vanier to back off."

"Killing him is off the table. It's a stupid idea." Merchant looked at Susskind for emphasis. Both knew it was Susskind's best idea. His only idea.

"Joe, this is your jurisdiction. We need to get him out of the picture. I don't know how to do these things. Give him money? You need to give me something. We'll find the money. We need to stop him. Soon."

"Let me think about it."

"Overnight. Okay. Think overnight. I need to know first thing in the morning."

Merchant finished his drink and stood up. "Yeah. First thing."

THIRTY

Alex was feeling good. He was tired, and his muscles hurt, but in the satisfying way that manual labour in the sun makes you feel.

His alert level was down to civilian—he was comfortable, almost blind to most of what was going on around him. It had taken time to get there, time and medication. He had been on red alert when he got back from Afghanistan, and couldn't figure out how to switch down. Walking the streets of Montreal had been no different to him than Kandahar, every doorway, every window or rooftop concealing a threat; the slightest movement could mean a sniper preparing to pull off a shot. He had been primed, scanning people for bulges, checking where their hands were, checking their faces, their eyes, whether they were walking too slowly, or too fast. And there were always noises: trucks speeding up or slowing down, footsteps running towards him or away to escape an explosion. He would listen for the silences as carefully as he would for the noises, for the silence that preceded everything bad, because the world is never as quiet as when it's holding its breath.

Being on red alert had kept him alive in Kandahar, and he had gotten used to it. His life depended on it. But it was crippling when he got home and found the switch was broken. For months, he had lived as though every moment was filled with the potential to be his last. But he was unarmed and defenceless, a civilian in a war zone.

It had taken months for him to dial down, and he could only do it slowly; five minutes of peace every now and then became fifteen, then the occasional hour. Now he could work in the garden without needing to process the meaning of footsteps on gravel, or a man emerging from the trees. Now he functioned for days as a near-civilian, ignoring the daily noise, like everyone else.

The day had cooled into evening, and he was looking forward to preparing supper. He had a bag in each hand, filled with fresh vegetables, cold cuts, and cheese. Katya's appetite had surprised him, even inspiring him to cook—a rare event. He half expected Domino's pizza to send someone over to see if he was okay. He was enjoying having someone to look after.

He was thinking of nothing except supper as he climbed the staircase. He pulled his keys from his pocket and reached for the door. It was open. In a second, Alex was back on red alert, and time slowed down. He put the bags on the floor and walked slowly into the apartment. The first thing he saw was the scrawled message on the wall:

DON'T PLAY WITH MORE LIVES!

Two chairs were lying on the floor, but nothing else seemed out of place. From the bathroom he heard the sound of running water. He walked down the hallway, sweat beading on his forehead. He wiped his eyes with his sleeve, pushed the door, and walked in. The shower was going full blast, but there was no steam. Katya was lying still and white on the floor of the tub, naked under the cold spray. A bead of blood ran from her nose and was washed down her face by the pounding water. A thin, faint line of blood followed the water between her legs to the drain.

Alex bent forward to feel for a pulse, but everything went black. He fell to his knees and pitched forward, ending up half in the shower with his legs splayed on the floor, his arm inches from Katya's neck, his shirt soaking up the spray. Katya stirred, lifted her hand and reached out to cradle his head. Alex didn't open his eyes. Five minutes passed, and Katya moved again. She stood shakily and stepped out of the tub. She lifted Alex's arm and placed it behind her neck, then grabbed his waist and half pulled him, half convinced him, to his feet. She led him down the hallway to his bedroom and let him drop onto the bed. She lay beside him, and pulled the blanket over both of them.

Vanier was stroking his son's forehead, watching him sleep. The sedatives had finally taken hold, and Alex looked like he would sleep for hours in the hospital bed.

Anjili Segal occasionally reached out a finger to touch Vanier's free hand, as if to remind him that she was there.

Katya had eventually called Vanier, who had driven them both to the hospital. David Reynolds had met them there and had taken charge of Katya while she went through the trauma of the tests at the sexual assault centre. He said he would look after her when it was all finished.

"We are all in danger, Luc. That's what this means, doesn't it?" Anjili asked.

The question went unanswered for a few seconds. She moved towards Vanier and held onto his arm.

"The people who did this were sending me a message," Vanier replied. "They'll wait to see if I get it."

"And are you going to do what they want? Are you going to walk away?"

Vanier didn't say anything.

"A girl was beaten and raped in your son's apartment, Luc. That's too close to home."

Vanier looked at her.

"You're not, are you?"

Vanier fished his phone from his pocket and started punching numbers. "I have to call the Chief."

It was eleven o'clock at night. Bédard sounded like he was already in bed. "Luc?"

"Chief. Sorry to wake you."

"You didn't wake me." Bédard was defensive. "I wasn't in bed. It's only eleven o'clock."

Vanier had a vision of Bédard sleeping like a baby every night. "Something's come up. I need to take a few days' leave. Starting now."

"Personal?"

"Personal."

"Of course, Luc. Is there anything I can do?"

"No. Thanks, but no. It's something I need to do."

"The murder case, Luna. It's going nowhere, right? A couple of days won't matter, I suppose."

"We've hit a wall. We've got theories, but no evidence. You're right, it's going nowhere."

"So we can put it on hold till you get back?"

"Maybe it's best. Unless we get something new, we're stuck."

"Okay, Luc. Do what you need to do. I'll get someone to cover for you. Nobody will even notice you're not there."

"No. Make sure everyone knows. It's important. If there are calls for me, tell them I've taken leave, you don't know for how long."

"If that's what you want." There was a pause. "Luc, what's this about? Is there something I should know?"

"Like I said. It's personal."

There was silence for a moment at the other end of the phone. "Okay, Luc. Keep in touch."

Vanier disconnected and looked down at his son.

"We could go away for a few days. The three of us," Anjili said. "Tomorrow if you want. We could go to Maine." She tried to force a smile, and only half succeeded.

"I've always liked Maine," he said. "I like the sea."

"I know. So why not? I can call in to the office, make an excuse. We could leave in the morning."

Vanier put his phone back in his pocket. "Twenty-four hours. I need twenty-four hours."

She knew there was no point in arguing. She followed him to the door.

"Alex will sleep for at least six hours. I'll take him back to my place. Be careful."

"Take care of Alex. And yourself. I'll call you." Vanier leaned down and kissed her. He straightened up, looked her in the eyes and leaned in again. This time he hugged her closely, breathed in her scent. He wondered why he couldn't stay like that forever.

"I'll be okay."

THIRTY-ONE

The first thing Richard Susskind did every morning was check his email. He wanted everyone to know that he was up and working when most people were still in bed. If he could respond to an email at five a.m. it was a good thing. Four-thirty, even better. That was how reputations were made. After a flurry of electronic activity, he would shower, have breakfast, and get dressed. Always the BlackBerry was within reach.

At six-thirty, he took the elevator down to the parking garage where he kept his Mercedes. Closed-circuit cameras tracked every movement; in the hallway, inside the elevator, as he walked to the parking level, as he pointed at the car and clicked the door open, as he sank into the rich leather. There was even a camera at the exit ramp as he drove out.

He turned right out of the garage and pointed the car downtown. The street was deserted, and he pushed on the gas, feeling the quiet power of acceleration. He made a Montreal stop at the corner, briefly taking his foot off the gas before turning right. It was a fifty zone and he was cruising at eighty. At first, he didn't react when Vanier stepped out from between two parked cars into the path of the Mercedes. His foot stayed on the gas until he saw Vanier raise both his arms and point a gun. Susskind slammed on the brakes, and the Mercedes screeched to a halt in front of Vanier, with inches to spare. Susskind reached for the gear shift and swivelled in his seat to reverse. He heard a loud crack of metal on glass, and turned back to see Vanier at the driver's window aiming the gun directly at Susskind's head. Susskind brought both his hands up in the air.

"Open the door," Vanier said.

Susskind lowered the window and Vanier reached in and pushed the gun barrel to the side of Susskind's skull.

"Keys. Now."

Susskind pushed the gear stick into park, removed the keys and handed them to Vanier.

"Open the passenger side."

Vanier went around the front of the car without taking his eyes off Susskind, and got in. He handed the keys back to Susskind. "Drive. Slowly."

"You're crazy, Vanier. You'll never get away with this."

"Shut up and drive." At the end of the street, Vanier said, "Turn right here."

Vanier gave directions, and Susskind followed them, occasionally stealing glances at the detective. Vanier was wearing a pair of latex gloves and held the gun loosely in his lap. After ten minutes, Vanier had him turn onto a deserted industrial street.

"Pull up behind the Volvo," he said, pointing.

Susskind pulled the Mercedes up to the curb as he was told, and Vanier reached over, shut the engine off and pulled out the keys.

"You're finished, Vanier. You'll be sweeping floors after this."

The street was deserted, a bleak park on one side and a windowless factory wall on the other.

"Out."

Susskind got out of the car, and Vanier followed. He leaned Susskind against the Mercedes and searched him, taking two cellphones. He left everything else. Vanier led Susskind to the Volvo and popped the trunk. Inside was a spare tire, some spanners, a hammer, and a pile of greasy rags. It looked like it hadn't been cleaned since leaving the showroom fifteen years ago. Vanier pointed the gun at Susskind. "Inside."

Susskind turned, a panicked look on his face. "It's not necessary. We can work this out. Whatever it takes. Just tell me."

Vanier holstered his gun. "Okay."

Then he wheeled toward Susskind and punched him in the stomach, feeling his fist go deep into the fat. Susskind's legs buckled and Vanier tipped him into the trunk with a blow to his back. He lifted Susskind's legs after him and closed the trunk.

It wasn't a long drive. Within minutes, Vanier parked the car outside a small auto-repair shop. He got out, unlocked the roll-up door, and drove inside. He got out of the car and went back to pull the door down and lock it. They were in a long, narrow space, with a single car lift at one end. Tools and spare parts hung above the wooden workbenches that ran along the wall. Vanier went to the Volvo and opened the trunk. "Get out."

For a fat guy, Susskind got out of the trunk fast, huffing and sweating from the effort. He bent down, resting his hands on his knees, trying to catch his breath. Then he exploded up, launched his full weight at Vanier. Vanier stepped aside and stuck his foot out, tripping Susskind as he passed. Susskind fell to his knees, but was back up in seconds. Vanier stepped back and pointed the gun. Susskind froze. Vanier motioned to the space in front of the car lift. "Go over there and put on the overalls. Then sit down on the chair. We need to talk."

Susskind looked to where Vanier was pointing. A table and two chairs were arranged on a large blue tarpaulin. A folded pair of yellow, one-piece coveralls, the kind you would use for the dirtiest jobs, was lying on the table. Susskind was rattled, still trying to talk his way out. "All right. Money. One million. That's more money than you'll ever see, Vanier. Just let me go and it's yours."

"Put the suit on and sit on the chair."

Susskind straightened up, stood with his feet apart. "No. I refuse. You're not a killer, Vanier. You don't scare me." He moved towards Vanier. "Go ahead, shoot me."

312

They both knew Vanier wasn't going to shoot him. Vanier holstered the pistol. He walked over to the blue tarpaulin and sat on one of the chairs. Susskind walked to the door.

"Tell me. Who killed Sophia Luna?"

"None of your fucking business, asshole." Susskind was at the door, trying to find a way to open it.

"And who killed Sékou Camara, Mr. Susskind?"

"Wouldn't you like to know?" He reached down, grabbed the handle and pulled. It didn't move.

"It's locked," said Vanier.

"Then open it. Right now."

"Can't do that, Mr. Susskind. Who went to my son's apartment yesterday and raped the girl who was there? Is that the kind of shit you're involved with, Mr. Susskind?"

Susskind wheeled around to face Vanier. "You're crazy, Vanier. I'm a businessman. I don't get mixed up in that sort of thing."

"Tell me about the Chajul mine disaster."

"I've got nothing to say." Susskind was still trying to figure out a way to get the door to open, pushing at it so it made a loud crashing noise. "Open the door, Vanier. Look, let's forget any of this happened. I swear. Why don't you just take a holiday, and get on with your life."

Vanier didn't answer right away. He let the suggestion hang there. Susskind was kicking at the door, getting frustrated.

"Who wrote 'Don't play with more lives' on my son's wall? Was that a message that I should take a holiday, or else?"

"How should I know?"

"Is that what you want me to do, Mr. Susskind? To back off? The people who raped Katya yesterday were threatening my family. Do you know anything about that?"

"I have no idea what you're talking about. In your business, I'm sure there are lots of people threatening you. Now, please, open the damn door."

"We need to sit down and talk, Mr. Susskind. You and me. Come over here. There are things I need to know."

Susskind turned from the door and slowly approached. When he was about six feet from the table, he grabbed a large wrench from the workbench and spun towards Vanier, wielding the wrench like a baseball bat. His speed was surprising. Vanier ducked, but the wrench caught him a glancing blow on the side of his head, knocking him forward off the chair. Susskind stood over him and raised the wrench a second time, aiming again for Vanier's head. As the blow came down, Vanier raised his arm to block it and rolled into Susskind's legs, pushing him off balance. Susskind fell forward, pulled by the momentum of the wrench in his hand, and landed on top of Vanier. Still, he wouldn't stop. He grabbed Vanier's throat and squeezed. With Susskind's weight holding him down, and the fat hands cutting off his air, Vanier was struggling. Susskind leaned into the task, closing off Vanier's windpipe. They were face to face, and Vanier was losing strength. Susskind leaned in close. "Like I said, Vanier. You're finished."

Susskind kept his face close to Vanier's, staring into his eyes as he squeezed.

Vanier was trapped beneath Susskind, his head on the concrete floor, like he was waiting to die. Susskind never saw the head-butt coming. Vanier whipped his head off the floor and his forehead connected with Susskind's nose. They both heard the crunch of bone and cartilage. Susskind let out a scream of pain. He didn't loosen his grip on Vanier's throat, but he was forced to shift his weight to keep his face away from Vanier's head. Vanier twisted around, managed to release an arm from underneath Susskind, and smashed his fist into Susskind's bleeding nose. Susskind grunted. This time his grip loosened, and Vanier was able to twist himself out from under the fat man. Susskind seemed to know it was over, and Vanier had handcuffs on him in seconds.

Vanier pulled at Susskind's collar until he got to his knees. Blood was pouring from his nose, staining his white shirt. His chest looked like he had been shot. Vanier kept pulling until Susskind stood up. He led him over to the chair, and Susskind sat down heavily. Vanier picked up the yellow coveralls from the table and got down on his knees. He took Susskind's shoes off and guided his feet into the coveralls, pushing the ends of the pants into Susskind's socks. He used duct tape to make sure the pants stayed enclosed in the socks. Then he made Susskind stand, and pulled the coveralls up above his waist.

He sat Susskind back down and duct-taped his legs to the chair. Then he undid the handcuffs and made

Susskind stand again while he pulled the rest of the coveralls up over Susskind's body, guiding his arms into the sleeves and zipping up the suit. Susskind sat back on the chair.

"I got 6X Large. I hope it fits."

Susskind said nothing.

"You're probably wondering what the tarp is for. I thought there might be blood. The tarp makes it easier to clean up. Sometime in the next twelve hours, you may want to shit, and I don't want to have to clean that up. That's why you're wearing the coveralls."

Vanier slowly wound the duct tape around Susskind's upper body, fixing him to the chair. His left arm was taped along with his body, but Vanier left Susskind's right arm swinging free. He grabbed a grease-stained towel and wiped it across Susskind's face. The man looked a mess, blood, sweat, and grease mixing together.

"The bleeding will stop in a while."

Vanier pulled a chair up and sat down opposite Susskind, leaned in and said, "Here's my problem. I need answers, and I have no time to waste. So I want you to tell me everything. Now. Start to finish."

"You want to beat a confession out of me? You're crazy. You'll never be able to use it in court."

"Not for court. For me, that's all. I want to know."

"I've nothing to say."

Vanier picked up the wrench in his right hand and walked behind Susskind. Then he reached down and took Susskind's hand in his left hand. He placed Susskind's hand on the table. "Last chance, Mr. Susskind. I want to know everything."

Susskind tried to pull back but Vanier had his arm stretched behind him. He couldn't move it.

"Goddamn you, Vanier."

Vanier held Susskind's hand tightly on the table, raised the wrench and brought it down hard on Susskind's thumb, smashing the bone. Susskind screamed and shifted violently in the chair before settling into low sobs that seemed to come from deep within him. Vanier put the wrench down on the table, out of Susskind's reach, and sat back down.

"I'm not stupid, Mr. Susskind. I know I won't be able to go to court with any confession. But you threatened my family, and I need to protect them. So here's the deal. You tell me everything, I get it on tape, and then I take a leave of absence. The case goes nowhere and I know you won't hurt anyone close to me. If you move against me, I release the tape to the press and you're finished."

Susskind was lost in pain, sobbing to himself. He didn't seem to know what to do with his hand. Every few seconds he would change its position, moving it off the table to let it hang, resting it back on the table. Vanier figured it hurt like hell either way.

He pulled his chair forward and took Susskind's hand in his own. He had Susskind's attention.

"Did you hear what I said?"

"I told you. Go to hell." He spat in Vanier's face.

Vanier took Susskind's broken thumb between his own thumbs and squeezed, rolling the broken pieces of bone. Susskind's chair seemed to lift off the ground as he screamed. "Please. Stop. Whatever you want. Just no more. Please."

"I want the whole story. Start to finish. No holding back. You understand? I'm going to record it and it will be my protection. You can go back to doing what you do, but you stay away from me and my family. Clear?" Vanier squeezed, and Susskind screamed again.

"You're getting off easy compared to Sophia Luna and Sékou Camara. Compared to Katya. Oh, and let's not forget Maître Bélair. You're getting off easy, Mr. Susskind."

Susskind was sobbing again. Vanier checked his pulse. "Your heart rate's up, but that's to be expected."

Vanier pulled a digital recorder from his pocket and put it on the table. "When I turn this on, you're going to start talking, and the sooner you get through it, the sooner you can go home."

Susskind nodded.

"You start with your name, title and who you work for. Then go on from there. Your story, start to finish. I want everything to be on the tape. You start lying and we go back to the beginning. Leave anything out and we go back and start over. And every time we have to go back to the beginning it will hurt. Like this." Vanier reached for Susskind's hand and pushed on the thumb. Susskind screamed.

Vanier switched on the recorder and looked at Susskind. He was slow to start, with coughs and deep breaths. When he spoke, it was almost in a whisper. "My name is Richard Susskind. I am the Vice President of Latin America for Essence Incorporated." Vanier picked up the recorder and played it back. The sound was good, crystal clear.

"Okay. Start again, a little louder."

"My name is Richard Susskind. I'm the Vice President of Latin America for Essence Incorporated."

He started slowly, hesitating about naming the deeds, but once he got over the first murder, there didn't seem to be any point in holding back. Vanier had him go back to the beginning.

"Where do I start? I suppose the logical place is the landslide, that's where it all started. The landslide was our fault. No doubt about it. It destroyed half of Chajul. Our engineers had built the tailings pond on the cheap. The assholes built it on a hill just outside the village. In the best of circumstances, it was dangerous. It was a dumb-assed place to build it, but anywhere else would have cost more. So the mine goes operational and we're making money. But over time, the tailings pond was filled to three times its designed capacity. Our own experts had been telling us it was a catastrophe in the making. Six months before the thing collapsed, I got a memo from the mine manager begging that something be done. You know what I did? I fired him. It was too expensive to fix."

Susskind's gaze drifted off Vanier's face. He seemed to withdraw into himself as he spoke, confirming what had happened in the hope of making sense of it. Vanier had seen it before, when confession becomes therapy, a search for meaning.

"We went into crisis management. We knew we'd have to pay damages, but the goal was to limit the cost. I was the point man for all the negotiations. We made a deal with the Guatemalans so that all claims would be dealt with by a compensation fund that we would set up. We promised fifty million. I was able to convince Minister Hastings to have the Canadian government pitch in another fifty. It doesn't sound like much but it was a fortune for the people who lost their homes and their relatives. A fortune. You know how much these people earn a year?"

He looked at Vanier. Vanier waved for him to continue.

"In return for the compensation, the Guatemalans were going to pass a law prohibiting anyone from suing us. It was a beautiful deal. We'd be off the hook without paying a cent. Our fifty-million contribution was being paid by our insurance. The only problem was, you don't get deals like that without spreading the wealth.

"The Guatemalans wanted kickbacks for agreeing to the deal, so we agreed. Four of them were supposed to get ten million each. When Minister Hastings got wind of what the Guatemalans were doing, he got greedy. He wanted his share before he'd sign off on the Canadian government's contribution."

Susskind started coughing, wincing with each cough.

"Up to now, this was all pretty normal stuff. Nothing we couldn't handle. It's the way business is done. But someone fucked up and sent a draft of the contract outside the organization, to a translator. Worse, some idiot put real names into the schedule. Those names weren't supposed to be in the contract. They were still setting up the companies that would be getting paid, all offshore, untraceable companies. You would never know who was behind them. So, instead of waiting for the names, or just putting fake names, someone wrote the real names in the draft. But we got the draft back, and everything looked good. The deal went through and everyone got paid."

Vanier pushed stop on the recorder and picked up a towel from the workbench. He wiped some of the blood from Susskind's face. Susskind coughed again, deeply, and spat a ball of red mucus onto the floor.

"Where was I?"

Vanier sat back down. "The deal went through. The payments were made."

"Oh, yeah. At that point, we think everything has worked out perfectly. Except one morning, Hastings gets an email from Sophia Luna. She says she knows everything, and she wants a Minister's permit in exchange for keeping quiet. She must have known what was going on when she saw the draft. Then she waited until the deal was done and probably used her contacts in Guatemala to follow the money when it was paid out. So she had proof that Hastings was on the take.

"Hastings blew a fuse. He refuses to make a deal. Tells me to deal with it, to get the documents back and there's no question of giving her anything.

"I figured it was just a question of picking her up and

scaring her a bit and we'd have the documents. But it was a total screw-up from day one. Those guys in GSC are great at security in some Third-World hellhole, but absolutely shit here. All they had to do was to pick her up, scare the shit out of her, and get the documents. Then the plan was to send her back to Guatemala on the corporate jet and let the Guatemalans deal with her. But things started to go off the rails from the start, and they kept getting worse."

Susskind nodded towards the recorder, and Vanier turned it off.

"Water. I need water."

Vanier looked around. The only tap was in a tiny toilet at the back. He found a coffee mug and filled it, brought it back to Susskind.

Vanier sat down. "You were saying how things started to go off the rails."

"Yeah. Okay. Switch it back on."

Vanier turned the recorder on and sat back to listen.

"First, there was the lawyer. The guys from GSC had been watching her, waiting to pick her up. The assholes should have grabbed her earlier, but no. They let her go meet the lawyer. So when she doesn't have anything on her, they figure she'd given him the documents, or access to them, who the hell knows. So we sent that lunatic Santos to check out his office. He finds nothing there and he goes off to the hospital. Brilliant piece of work: Santos is going through the lawyer's bag in the hospital and the lawyer wakes up. Santos puts his hand over his mouth to stop him screaming. Couldn't think of anything better than to kill him. He said he was afraid the cop was coming back.

"Meanwhile, the bitch, Luna, is scaring Merchant and his crew. She never stops talking. First she's trying to make deals, and then she starts threatening them. I heard her myself. She was crazy. Anyway, we arrange with the African guy to swap her for the documents. Another screw-up. The African is lying on the floor in the bank like he's sick and refuses to move. He probably figured we weren't going to let Luna go. And while all this is going on, Hastings, the Minister, is calling me, like, six times a day, screaming at me to fix the problem. This is someone who could ruin my career in a heartbeat.

"Anyway, the African puts together this insane scenario where we have to deliver Luna before he gives us the document. But guess what? After we've held Luna for a few days, she knows more than ever. I mean, she had even seen me and Merchant. So there was no way we could let her go. And sure as hell the African was finished too. So the plan was to park Luna in Place Ville-Marie and wait until the African got the call to say she was safe. Then they were going to whack her. She was half dead already with the amount of drugs she'd been given. Crazy as the plan was, it almost worked. We got the documents, Luna was dead. The only problem was the African. He took off. Escaped on a bike, for Chrissake! That was where everything was supposed to end. Luna and the African would be dead, and we would have the documents. But Merchant screwed up again. He let the African get away.

"So the African was still out there, and, guess what. Two days later he calls to say—surprise, surprise—he's made a copy, he knows everything and he's going to talk to you if we don't give him a permit. So we're back to square one."

Vanier reached forward and stopped the recorder. "You? You said 'He's going to talk to you,' There is no you. You're talking into a recorder and you're by yourself. Do you understand? I'm not here. Nobody's here. So we're going back.to where you said, 'So the African's still out there', and start again."

Vanier rewound the recorder, pushed record and nodded at Susskind. Susskind looked resigned, took a deep breath and started again.

"The African was still out there. So we're back to square fucking one. I'm reporting everything to Hastings. When he hears that the African's after a Minister's permit he does an about-face. Maybe he can get the Minister of Immigration, the Showers guy. He says maybe he can convince Showers to issue one. Hastings must have been getting scared. Two days later, he told me he gave Showers fifty thousand dollars in cash to issue a permit for the African. The bastard said that's how much I owed him. Like ten million wasn't enough. But he got the permit signed. I saw it. I couldn't believe it. Are they all crooks in Ottawa?

"The African gave us everything, photocopies of bank transfers, the works. But Merchant decides on his own that the African has to die. This is after the fact. Every-

324

thing is finished. But Merchant doesn't want any witnesses. Again, they screw up. The police find the body. But I figured they still have no proof. So we tried to shut the investigation down. We tried to scare Vanier off the case."

Susskind looked to his captor as if for approval. Vanier nodded, and Susskind continued.

"So, yes, I admit I told Merchant to make sure Vanier went off the case. He was supposed to scare Vanier. I know nothing about any rape."

Vanier clicked stop on the recorder. He pulled a sheet of paper from his pocket and held it up in front of Susskind's face. "Now read this."

Susskind was breathing heavily through his mouth. His nose had stopped bleeding, but it was swollen and blocked with dried blood. He bowed his head to read the note. He was almost crying. "No. Please. Don't do this, Vanier. I'm begging you."

"Read it."

Susskind opened his legs and the paper fell to the floor. Vanier reached out and grabbed Susskind's free hand. The thumb was now double its normal size. Vanier put his own thumb on the top of Susskind's and moved it back and forth. Susskind screamed, and started crying again.

Vanier picked up the paper and put it back in Susskind's lap. "Read it."

He leaned back in the chair and clicked play.

"I can't go on," Susskind read. "It has to end. For once in my life I'm going to do the right thing. Goodbye."

Vanier left for Ottawa at 10:30. He was on the highway in minutes and settled in for one of Canada's most mind-numbing drives. The first thirty minutes through identical suburbs you could only tell apart from the exit signs. At the edge of the urban blight, there was a stretch of identical factory homes in a treeless expanse, more parking lot than neighbourhood, a factory farm for humans, bought with twenty-five-year mortgages and two-hour commutes.

Eventually, the highway reached what passed for countryside, each field boasting seed-company placards announcing the variety being grown, so a motorist speeding by could judge the relative merits of P7213 versus 39V07. In the age of industrial agriculture, seeds are no longer named to appeal to the imagination. No more Caramel Crisp, Honey and Cream and Golden Bantam—they have all been ditched for names fit for chemicals.

Vanier was trying to watch the road while scrolling through the list of old calls on his phone. When he found what he was looking for, he clicked connect. Someone answered immediately.

"Minister Showers's office."

"Message for the Minister. Tell him that Vanier wants to speak to him. Tell him it's important. And tell him if he doesn't call me back, it will be the biggest mistake of his short career. Got that?"

"What?"

"Minister Showers needs to call Vanier as soon as possible. It's urgent and it would be a grave mistake for him not to call me back."

"Can I have the number?"

Vanier gave her the number. "Tell him I'm waiting for his call."

The Minister called back ten minutes later.

"You must really be interested in early retirement."

"I'm on leave of absence already. Didn't you hear? I've decided to take a day trip to the nation's capital. I'll be there in an hour and a half. We need to meet."

"Impossible. I'm fully booked all day."

"Susskind is dead. He left a note."

There was silence at the other end. "Call me back on my BlackBerry." He gave Vanier the number. Vanier hung up and redialled.

"What does Susskind's death have to do with me?"

"It has everything to do with you. You're involved. Maybe not as deeply as the others, but you're involved."

Showers didn't respond to the accusations. "You mentioned a note."

"It's a recording, actually. Where do you want to meet?"

Two hours later, Vanier was riding the elevator up to the Rideau Club, the private sanctuary of Ottawa's elite. The club was on the fifteenth floor of a high-rise on Bank Street, and the only way in was a single, dedicated elevator with a discreet sign. Inside the elevator there were only two buttons, one for the lobby, the other for the club. The elite don't like having to mingle with the working-class inhabitants of the building.

Vanier stepped out of the elevator. It looked like he'd stepped back in time, by a century at least. Up the hall to his right there was a greeting room with a black and white tiled floor and dark red wallpaper. A uniformed man sat at a desk reading the paper. He looked up as Vanier approached, his face going from *Welcome* to *Are you sure you're in the right place*? Vanier looked like he should have been begging for coins in the street below. His shirt was speckled with blood, and he hadn't shaved or slept in thirty hours.

"Can I help you?" There was a long pause before he added, "Sir?"

"Vanier."

The doorman's face showed a flash of recognition, and his demeanour softened.

"Oh yes. We're expecting you. The Minister hasn't arrived yet, but he asked that you be seated." The doorman rose, leaning heavily on his arms. "If you'll follow me, sir."

Vanier followed him along the carpeted hallway into a small, windowless room. An antique sofa was against one wall, two straight-backed chairs against the opposite wall and a dark wooden coffee table cutting the room in two. It wasn't the kind of conference room where people took notes; it was a place for eye-to-eye contact, where note-taking would be frowned upon. Just what Vanier was looking for.

"Somebody will be along with refreshments in a few moments, sir." The doorman was backing towards the door.

"Could you bring me a sandwich? I'm starving."

"Certainly, sir. I will send someone along. I will need a credit card to open an account."

"The minister's paying."

The doorman hesitated a second. "Yes, sir. I will send someone along with a menu."

Vanier was halfway through a roast beef sandwich when the minister arrived. Showers walked over to the sofa and sat down without a word, glaring at Vanier. A brush-cut kid in a suit closed the door and sat down next to his boss.

It was the first time Vanier had been this close to a cabinet minister, and he had to admit he looked good, like someone who was used to getting his photo taken, who was always ready. Everything about him was immaculate; there was nothing out of place. Not even the look of contempt in his eyes.

Vanier returned the minister's glare, nodded at the kid. "Staff?"

"Yes. This is Vincent Katz, my chief of staff."

The kid opened his notebook and started writing.

"Doesn't matter to me, but you may not want him here. I have some bad news. You might want to digest it in private first."

Showers turned to his chief of staff. "Vincent. Perhaps if you could wait outside. This shouldn't take long."

Vincent looked offended, but he was used to taking orders. "Yes, Minister. Call me when you need me."

They both waited until he had closed the door behind him.

"What's this about Susskind? I tried to reach him."

"I told you. He's dead. Suicide. He left a recorded message. It seems his conscience was finally beginning to trouble him. How is your conscience, Minister?"

"Absolutely fine. I don't know what any of this has to do with me."

"You will. I brought Susskind's recording." He held up the small recorder. "Want to hear it?"

"If that's the only way to put an end to this nonsense, then I suppose I have to."

Vanier took another bite of his sandwich. When he had finished chewing, he put the recorder on the small table and pushed play.

"My name is Richard Susskind."

Vanier finished his sandwich and poured a coffee while the minister sat and listened. As Susskind went through his story, the colour drained from Showers's face. At one point Vanier stopped the recording, reversed it for a few seconds and played it again.

"I'm reporting everything to Hastings. When he hears that the African's after a Minister's permit he does an about-face. Says maybe he can get the Minister of Immigration, the Showers guy. He says maybe he can convince Showers to issue one. Hastings must have been getting scared. Two days later he told me he gave Showers fifty thousand dollars in cash to issue a permit for the African. The bastard said that's how much I owed him. Like ten million wasn't enough. But he got the permit signed. I saw it. I couldn't believe it. Are they all crooks in Ottawa?"

Showers looked up at Vanier. "Okay, I've heard enough. What are you looking for?"

Vanier switched the recorder off and leaned forward. "First, I want you to hear everything. There's more. I want you to know who you were taking money from and what they were doing."

Vanier made him listen to Susskind explaining why Camara was killed, and how he was responsible for Katya's rape.

The Minister was looking at the carpet. "Play it again. Start to finish."

Vanier played it through once more, but it was clear Showers wasn't listening. He was thinking. Vanier sat back and gave him time to work through the options. There weren't many.

Finally, Showers raised his head and looked at Vanier. The contempt in his eyes had disappeared. "What are you looking for?"

"I have a major problem. Susskind's dead, so he's not going to jail. But I've got at least three murders, a rape, and massive corruption. I would like to make sure you and scum like you are punished. But I also need something. So I'm ready to make a deal."

Showers said nothing. He was still listening.

Vanier continued. "This is the only copy of the tape. I'll give it to you. But I want two things in return. First,

I want a Minister's permit for the girl who was raped. You wrote one for Camara and he was killed, so that one was wasted. Call this one a replacement. I've written her details on Camara's letter. Maybe you can ask your boy to get working on that now." Vanier pulled the passport from his pocket. "Here's her passport. I want it stamped to show she's a landed immigrant as of today."

"Those are the two things you want? The Minister's permit and the stamp?"

"No. That's two parts of the same thing."

"What else?"

"Your resignation. Effective late this afternoon. Right after Katya Babyak becomes an official landed immigrant, after you've signed her permit."

"That's a non-starter." Showers was looking at the door, like he was ready to bolt.

Vanier leaned over and handed him a note. "Here's the text of what you will say to the press. Verbatim. You don't say the words, you don't get the tape."

"I'm not doing it. I only had a minor role in all of this. My colleague asked me to intervene in the case of a failed refugee claim, and I thought there was merit in doing that." It was as though he was rehearsing the excuse, wondering how it sounded out loud.

"You exercised your ministerial power for fifty thousand dollars. You were bought."

"There's no proof. All you have is the word of a dead man."

"Maybe. But I have the recording. The press would

love to get hold of this. The RCMP too."

"You wouldn't."

Vanier didn't answer. He didn't have to. They sat for several moments in silence.

"Sign the permit and resign," Vanier said. "You betrayed the government, your party, the people. Shit, you probably betrayed yourself for all I know. You can save your skin by doing the right thing. You resign and go get yourself a lawyer and a public-relations guru. Your lawyer will probably get you a deal if you cooperate and tell them what you know. If you do nothing, I will be executing search warrants in the morning and this tape will be playing on the news. Your choice."

Showers sat motionless with his head down. He was still doing the calculations. Finally, he picked his phone off the table, punched a number on speed-dial. "Vincent, you can come in now."

Showers looked over at Vanier, then reached for the passport.

The chief of staff came in. "Minister."

"Vincent, two things. Both urgent. Take this—" Showers handed Katz the passport. "Draft a permit letter for me to sign this afternoon, and get this stamped so the holder is a landed immigrant as of today. And book a room here for a press conference at four o'clock."

"It's a bit late for a press conference, Minister. Not sure how many people I can get."

"Make sure you get at least two," said Vanier.

"Is everything all right, Minister?" Katz was used to

seeing a minister who was in charge. He looked like he would gladly attack Vanier, if only his boss would ask.

"Everything is fine, Vincent," the minister said. "Let's get this done."

"The press conference, is there a subject? Can I draft a statement?" Vincent asked.

"Important announcement, that's all. I'll look after the text."

At three o'clock, the minister's chief of staff was back in the Rideau Club. He handed a brown envelope to his boss. Showers barely looked at it, passed it to Vanier. "This what you're looking for? What is she, your girl-friend? Your whore?"

Vanier took the envelope. "And you would know whores. Don't push your luck."

Vanier opened the passport and checked the stamp; Katya Babyak was now a permanent resident of Canada. The letter was folded in an unsealed ministerial envelope. He pulled it out and read it. "Here," he said, sliding the letter across the table. "Sign."

Showers took out a fat Montblanc fountain pen and scribbled his signature. He waited a moment for the ink to dry, and put the letter back in the official envelope. "Vincent? Are we set to go with the press conference?"

Vincent looked deflated. He sat down on the couch. "Yes, Minister. Four o'clock. But we've only got four people confirmed so far. It's the middle of summer."

"Four is plenty," Showers said.

Katz left to finish the arrangements for the press conference.

Showers leaned over the table and started revising the text that Vanier had prepared. If he was going to make a statement, it was going to be his statement, one that showed him in a good a light as possible. After fifteen minutes he passed it across to Vanier. "This is what I'm going to say."

Vanier read the text. "It'll do. But don't go off script. Word for word, nothing more."

Showers took the paper back, folded it and put it in his inside jacket pocket. Then he picked up his cellphone. It didn't take him long to set up a meeting with his lawyer. He wasn't even going to have to leave the building, just ride the express elevator down to the ground floor and back up to the twelfth floor, with the ordinary people.

At four o'clock, they moved into the bar. A table had been cleared away at the far end of the room and a podium set up in its place. Five reporters had decided to show up and had pushed two tables together so they could sit as a group. They had convinced someone to open the bar early. The minister arrived and acknowledged their presence with a curt nod. Vanier held back, leaning against the wall next to the door.

Showers stepped up to the podium and started talking. He didn't bother with the microphone, and the journalists had to scramble to clip their own microphones to the podium.

"Good afternoon, ladies and gentlemen. In recent

days, I have learned that I have been taken advantage of by people I trusted. I accepted the word of a Cabinet colleague and acted upon that word to make a decision that ought not to have been made. It has now become clear that Minister Hastings and officials of the Montreal-based company Essence have been engaged in criminal activities."

Vanier moved forward, staring at Showers. He had already gone off script. Showers focused his attention on the press table, ignoring Vanier. The journalists were sitting up and taking notice. Vanier walked over to the bar.

"Mr. Susskind, the Vice President for Latin America of Essence, has confirmed that he has been involved in criminal activities, including kidnapping and murder, and I am sorry to say, the corruption of a member of the current government, Minister Hastings."

"More particularly," Showers reached into his pocket and pulled out the speaking notes. He cleared his throat and started reading out loud.

"I have information that leads me to believe that all of the contribution made by the government of Canada to the Chajul disaster compensation fund has been diverted. It appears the money that was supposed to provide compensation to the victims of that disaster was used instead to pay bribes to certain Guatemalan officials and, I regret to say, to my Cabinet colleague, Minister Hastings. Mr. Susskind was the principal architect of that bribery scheme. In order to cover up this crime, Mr. Susskind, and perhaps others at Essence, orchestrated a kidnapping and several murders in Montreal, and I call upon the Montreal police to investigate Mr. Susskind's activities, and those of Essence Incorporated as quickly as possible."

Katz was sitting with his head in his hands. Vanier went over and whispered to him. He got up and followed Vanier to the doorway.

"I would not make these allegations without being convinced of their truth," Showers went on. "And it saddens me deeply to have to bring this to the public's attention. However, I am faced with no choice. As a result of the criminal activity undertaken by Essence, I was asked to exercise my ministerial authority in a particular way, and I did so, unaware of the underlying criminality that led to that request. I should have known better, and I regret my actions. While I have not engaged in any criminal activity myself, I am compelled to tender my resignation effective immediately as Minister of Citizenship and Immigration. It has been my distinct honour to serve the Prime Minister, this government, and the Canadian people. I have made a grave mistake and I accept the consequences of that mistake.

"I will not be taking questions. Thank you, ladies and gentlemen."

Showers grabbed his notes, stepped down from the podium and made straight for the door. As he passed, Vanier slipped the recorder into his hand. Then Vanier and the chief of staff followed him through the doorway. Vanier pulled the door closed and gestured to the newly unemployed Katz to hold the door against the journalists.

"Don't let them out until we're both in the elevator. Your last official duty."

Vanier caught up with the minister at the elevator and they both got in.

Showers stared at the numbers counting down without acknowledging Vanier's presence. As the elevator slowed at the bottom of the shaft, Showers spun around to face Vanier.

"Pray that you're never tested."

"Fifty-thousand isn't much of a test." Vanier said.

"It wasn't the money. He was a friend. We go all the way back to university. I don't have many friends, Inspector, but Lindon was my friend, and he was desperate. So I helped him. The money is still in my office. I haven't touched it."

The doors opened and Vanier watched him leave.

On the way back to Montreal, Vanier called Saint Jacques.

She answered on the first ring. "Boss, where have you been?"

"I took the day off. Listen, the Minister of Immigration, Showers, has just resigned, and his statement, and what we already have, gives us more than enough to get a search warrant on Essence. With a bit of imagination, we can tie in GSC as well. I want you to get working on the search warrants so we can go in as soon as possible. You'll get the minister's statement off the wire service, but here are the highlights. This is verbatim."

Vanier pulled a sheet of paper from his pocket, a copy

of the statement he had given Showers, and read the part the minister hadn't changed.

Saint Jacques was scribbling furiously. "He said that? And you heard him? What's going on, boss? I don't understand."

"Sylvie, we had a lucky break."

Next he phoned Anjili Segal.

"Luc, you said you'd call. I've been worried."

"I'm sorry. Things got out of control. But I'm on my way home. I should be in Montreal by 6:30, but I have some stops to make before I go home."

"I'm taking Alex out for supper. Why don't you call us when you're ready and you can join us. I have something special planned. Let's say it's a new direction."

Vanier hesitated a second. "New directions are always good. And Anjili? Yes, I want to come home."

"I love you, Luc."

Vanier's first stop was to David Reynolds's group home, where he got the same frosty reception from the ladies on the balcony. He didn't bother ringing the bell, just opened the door and walked in. Reynolds was in his office.

"How's Katya? I have news for her."

"She is in the kitchen." Reynolds said. "She's been through a lot, but she's strong. She's going to be okay." Before leaving the desk, he reached for the black book.

"Can I see the book?" Vanier stretched his hand out. "I've been wondering what it is. I figured it's too small for a bible."

Reynolds hesitated. Then he handed the book to Vanier. Inside the cover, someone had written *To David, on your First Holy Communion*. Vanier flipped through the gossamer-thin pages, remembering his own First Communion prayer book, wishing he still had it. "Everyone needs prayers."

Reynolds nodded. "I hope it's not more bad news."

"Sometimes prayers are answered. Come and see."

Vanier led the way into the kitchen. Katya was sitting at the table with a large glass of iced tea. She looked up and smiled as the came in.

"Katya, I have something for you."

"More clothes from Walmart?"

Vanier laughed "No. Read this."

He passed the envelope across the table. Katya opened it tentatively and tipped the letter and passport onto the table. They both followed Katya's eyes scrolling slowly over the text of Minister Showers's letter. They could tell when she got to the end, studied the signature and started back at the top. After she had read it twice she looked up at Vanier.

"This means …?"

"Look at the passport."

She did as he said, and stopped at the page stamped Permanent Resident.

"It means you can stay. It means that you can work towards citizenship. It means that you can bring your brother to Canada. Katya, it means you're safe."

"What?" Reynolds reached across the table, and Katya

handed it to him. She walked around the table and threw her arms around Vanier in a hug.

"How in God's good name did you manage this?" Reynolds was still reading the letter.

Vanier smiled, shrugged. He turned to Katya. "Listen I have to go, but I'll come back and see you tomorrow. I just wanted you to have this. You're safe." Katya was laughing and crying at the same time, bouncing up and down.

Vanier's next stop was the garage. Susskind was still in the chair. He looked like he had been sleeping. His face was bruised and crusted with blood. His hand was swollen to twice its normal size, the skin stretched and red.

"You should get to the hospital and have that looked at."

Susskind said nothing.

Vanier bent down to undo the duct tape and his stomach heaved. Susskind smelled foul. Vanier had to make an effort not to retch.

"Vanier. I've been thinking about this. I really thought I was going to die. But when I didn't, I spent hours going through all that's happened. I want to make a statement."

"No dice. No statement. Maybe if you go get yourself a lawyer and come back, we might take a statement from you. I don't want any case against you getting thrown out on some harebrained allegation of police brutality. What we had here today didn't happen. And if you say it did, I'll come back for you."

Susskind could hardly stand, and Vanier had to help him walk to the car. Susskind grabbed the passenger-side handle, and leaned on it for support, waiting for Vanier to open it.

"No. In the trunk," said Vanier.

"Please. You're not serious? I mean it's finished. It's over."

"The trunk. Look at the coveralls." Susskind looked down. The coveralls were wet and soiled below the waist, sticking to his legs.

"I don't want that on my upholstery. You're lucky I'm giving you a lift in the trunk."

Susskind shuffled along the car to the end and climbed into the open trunk.

Vanier dropped Susskind at his Mercedes. When Susskind was inside, Vanier leaned in the window. "By the way. If you do want to make an allegation about police brutality—"

"I don't. Let's forget it."

"You know the guy who owns the garage?"

"No, I don't."

"Well, he was working there all day. He's a good friend from way back. He even promised to clean up for me."

Vanier stepped back from the window. Susskind put the key in the ignition and gunned his engine. Vanier's phone gave a short beep—a text from Anjili, with the address of where she and Alex were heading to dinner. Vanier didn't recognize the restaurant.

A normal person would have gone to the hospital, but Susskind went home. He had things to do. First, he spent an hour in the shower, under scalding water. Now he was standing in his living room with a thick white towel around his waist. He had a plan, and Vanier was going to pay for what he had done. Susskind liked to think of himself a survivor. He was resilient, and it would take more than a crazy detective to shut him down.

His lawyer had promised to be there in an hour or so. The lawyer would negotiate the best deal he could get in exchange for Susskind's testimony. There might be some jail time, but nothing serious, a couple of months, with time off for good behaviour. The best thing was that Susskind would see Vanier charged with kidnapping and assault, maybe even attempted murder. Vanier was finished.

Susskind had also booked himself into a private medical clinic on Sherbrooke Street to get his nose and his hand fixed up. He poured himself a half-tumbler of gin and a dash of tonic, and threw open his wardrobe, wall-to-wall dark suits and crisp blue shirts.

Everything was going to turn out just fine. Of course, he would have to quit Essence, but he had enough money hidden away; he wouldn't have to work. In a year or so, after all the legal proceedings were finished, he would be living like a king in a tropical paradise.

The intercom buzzer rang. He looked at his watch. The lawyer was early. He went into the living room to check the closed-circuit image of the lobby on the television screen, and froze. Joe Merchant was outside the front door, pulling at the handle, waiting to be let in.

Susskind had no time to get dressed and leave. He watched helplessly as Merchant pulled something from his pocket and began working on the lock. Seconds later, Merchant pulled the door open. Susskind grabbed the television remote, changed the view to the lobby camera. He watched Merchant push the elevator button and step inside. Susskind clicked the remote to change the view again, and brought up a four-screen shot, one for each of the elevators. Merchant was in one, staring up at the camera. The elevator doors slid open and Merchant disappeared from the screen.

Susskind grabbed his phone. He didn't have the lawyer on speed-dial yet, and had to scroll one-handed through the call log. He found the number and pressed. While he was waiting for the lawyer to pick up, he heard a rasping metallic sound from his front door. The phone went to voice mail. Susskind babbled, "Susskind here. Please come as quickly as possible. Merchant is here. I'm in grave danger. Please hurry."

"Mr. Susskind." The voice boomed across the room. Merchant was standing by the door with his hands in his pockets. "You need to get better locks. A place like this, I would have thought they'd have better locks."

"What do you want? It's all over. It's finished."

"No. You're finished, Mr. Susskind. Me? I'm on my way to the airport. I thought I'd stop by to say goodbye."

Susskind reached down to put his cellphone on the table and reached for a baseball-sized Inuit sculpture, small but heavy. Merchant approached. When he was close enough, Susskind launched himself, aiming the sculpture at Merchant's head. Merchant easily stepped out of the way. Susskind recovered, turned to face Merchant, and saw the gun.

"Sit down. And drop the toy."

Susskind collapsed into the armchair.

"Just so you know," Merchant said, looking at his watch. "I will be on a flight in about ninety minutes. You, however, are a loose end."

Merchant pulled a silencer out of his pocket and attached it to the pistol.

Susskind watched in horror. Merchant approached the armchair and leaned forward, touched the barrel to the side of Susskind's head, and gently squeezed the trigger. Blood spurted onto Merchant's hand. He pulled back, watched as it continued to gush for a few seconds then slow to a steady flow. He grabbed a towel from the kitchen counter and wiped his hand. Then he wiped the pistol, and unscrewed the silencer. He pocketed the silencer and put the pistol back in his underarm holster. He was walking to the door when he heard someone pounding.

"Police. Mr. Susskind, this is the police. We have a warrant to search the premises. Open the door."

Merchant froze. "Two seconds. Let me put my pants on."

He ran over to the balcony and looked down. It was too high for jumping. He climbed over the railing and lowered himself down. Hanging from the bottom of the railing, he was about ten feet above the balcony on the floor below. He swung his legs and propelled himself inwards, landing with a thud on the balcony below. The sliding doors were locked shut, and there was no outside lock to pick. He kicked the glass a few times but it didn't break. So he pulled out the gun and shot, the tempered glass exploded out of the frame and he walked through into the apartment.

The sound of gunshot was unmistakable, even to Flood and Descartes in the hallway upstairs. Flood backed up and launched a kick at Susskind's door. It gave easily. The first thing they saw was Susskind's body in the armchair, a bloody hole right above his ear. Everything around him was splattered with blood. Flood checked for a pulse. "Shit. He killed himself."

Descartes scanned the room. "Where's the gun?"

In seconds Flood realized his mistake. "The balcony?"

The balcony door was open. From the balcony, they could see the broken glass strewn on the balcony below. Flood grabbed his phone and speed-dialled Saint Jacques. "Susskind's dead. Shot. It just happened. The shooter may be headed in your direction. Call for backup. We're coming down."

Saint Jacques was sitting in an unmarked police car in the parking lot below, a precaution, given that she was still limping. When Merchant emerged from the front door, she slid down in her seat. He crossed the driveway and made for a white car that was backed in, against the wall. Saint Jacques turned the ignition and gunned her car

across the lot, slamming it to a halt in front of the white
car just as Merchant closed his door.

Merchant leaned on the horn. A second later, he recognized Saint Jacques, and noticed the gun she was pointing at him. He put both hands in the air.

Vanier was parked outside a single-family home on Tonty
Street just behind the Botanical Gardens. He checked the
address Anjili had texted. He called her. "Anjili, the address is wrong."

"Where are you?"

"I'm parked outside the address you gave me. It's a
home. There isn't a restaurant in sight."

"No mistake. We're around the back. Come in."

Then he noticed the For Sale sign planted in the lawn.
He leaned forward and rested his head on the steering
wheel. Of all the things he wanted to do, house hunting
was not one of them. His grip tightened on the wheel.
With his head still resting on the steering wheel, he
reached for the key and turned it. The engine burst to life.

"Luc."

He didn't move.

"Luc," she repeated. She was at the open car window.

He raised his head and looked up. She started. He
must have looked like someone pulled from a car wreck,
splattered with blood and smelling faintly of fecal matter.

"Luc. I'm so sorry. I wasn't thinking straight. The
agent gave me the key and suggested we order chicken,
wait for you in the garden. She told me to lock up when

we were finished. I wasn't thinking, Luc. Give me a few minutes, and we'll go home."

Vanier reached up. Touched her hand. "Chicken?"

"And wine. I bought a bottle."

"Anything stronger?"

"I noticed some whiskey in the bar. I'm sure they wouldn't mind."

He looked up at her. "I could do with a whiskey."

Vanier turned the engine off, and followed Anjili up the paved stone path and around to the garden. The garden looked peaceful. It was enclosed by six-foot hedges on all sides, and a small path wound through shrubs, flowers, and large moss-covered rocks.

Alex was sitting at the table on the patio, staring out into the garden. He turned to look up at his father and almost managed a smile. He pushed a take-out box across the table. "Chicken, Dad."

"Hey, Alex."

Anjili pointed to a room off the patio. "In the bar. Inside. I'm sure they wouldn't mind if you helped yourself."

Vanier stepped inside. He found a bottle of Chivas in the bar and poured himself a stiff one, then went looking for ice. He took a sip and felt the glow. He began to wander.

He had been inside hundreds of homes. He knew this one had been cleaned up and uncluttered for sale. Even so, it felt like it was built for comfort, not to impress. And it had room, lots of it. After his first walk-through, he refilled his glass, and did another walkabout. This time he paid attention, looking for problems, searching for the deal breaker. He didn't find one. He began to imagine the two of them negotiating the spaces, finding a way to occupy the same house without killing each other. There was room to be alone as well as space to live together. There was even a small room with a bathroom in the basement if Alex ever decided to stay over, or Elise came to visit.

He made one last trip to the bar and carried his drink out onto the patio. The garden had changed in the twilight with the fading sun reflecting bright green off the mossy rocks. He heard bees. Vanier had never imagined himself a gardener, but the garden soothed him.

"I hadn't thought about a garden. Must be a lot of work," he said. The words fell like stones.

Alex pulled himself up in his chair and leaned forward. "I could help with the garden, Dad. If you want. I could help."

Vanier took a sip of the whiskey. Smiled. He turned to Anjili. "I feel good here."

The three of them sat in silence watching the shadows change as the light faded.